Gerald and Elizabeth

Books by D. E. Stevenson

Gerald and Elizabeth
Sarah's Cottage
Sarah Morris Remembers
The House on the Cliff
The Marriage of Katherine
Katherine Wentworth
The Blue Sapphire
Fletchers End
Bel Lamington
The Musgraves
Still Glides the Stream
Anna and Her Daughters
The Tall Stranger
Summerhills
Amberwell
Blow the Wind Southerly
Five Windows
Mrs. Tim Flies Home
Shoulder the Sky
Music in the Hills
Vittoria Cottage
Young Mrs. Savage
Kate Hardy
Mrs. Tim Gets a Job
The Four Graces

Listening Valley
The Two Mrs. Abbotts
Celia's House
Crooked Adam
Spring Magic
Mrs. Tim Carries On
Rochester's Wife
Alister & Co.
The English Air
The Green Money
A World in Spell
The Story of
   Rosabelle Shaw
The Baker's Daughter
Smouldering Fire
Miss Dean's Dilemma

Omnibus Volumes

Mrs. Tim of the Regiment
   and Golden Days
Miss Buncle *containing*
   Miss Buncle's Book *and*
   Miss Buncle Married

Gerald
and
Elizabeth

by
D. E. Stevenson

HOLT, RINEHART AND WINSTON
New York · Chicago · San Francisco

Designer: Berry Eitel

SBN: 03–066555–8
Printed in the United States of America

CONTENTS

Gerald and Elizabeth

1. The Harriman Family

The S.S. *Ariadne* was on her way from Bombay to Southampton via the Cape. She was not one of the larger passenger ships nor very up-to-date but she was comfortable and well-found. Mr. and Mrs. Harriman had engaged the best suite which consisted of a stateroom, two double cabins and a bathroom with a shower. It suited them admirably, for they were travelling with their daughter, Penelope, and their niece, Marion. At first they had found the accommodation somewhat cramped (they were used to larger ships), but they had settled down now and, as Mrs. Harriman observed, there were compensations. The Captain was much more approachable; he was cheerful and amusing; their fellow passengers were friendly; there was a pleasant atmosphere on the *Ariadne*.

The Harrimans were Americans. Mr. Harriman had made his pile and had partially retired from business; his partners were capable and trustworthy, so he was free to travel and see the world with his family. They had travelled widely in the last few years; they had done Europe and had cruised in the Mediterranean; the elder Harrimans had been round the world on a conducted tour.

This trip was different, for Mr. Harriman had said firmly that he was tired of being hustled and bustled and forcibly fed with a whole lot of indigestible information, so they had made no plans but had gone when and where they pleased. If they

1

liked a place, they stayed; if not, they moved on somewhere else. It was much more enjoyable. They intended to stay in London on their way home. Mr. Harriman was pretty sure he had cousins somewhere in Buckinghamshire—distant cousins, of course, but all the same he meant to find them. Mrs. Harriman, not to be outdone, had vague recollections of her grandmother talking about a farm on the Yorkshire moors and a white pony.

"I wish I had listened properly," she added with a sigh.

"We all wish we had listened to the old folk talking," declared Mr. Harriman.

"Why didn't you?" asked Penelope.

"Well, it wasn't the fashion," replied her mother. "When I was young, we just weren't interested in having English relatives."

"Yorkshire!" exclaimed Marion. "Why, we might be related to the Brontës! Just think how interesting that would be!"

Mr. Harriman smiled and held his peace. He had a feeling that the Brontë family, though talented, was not a family with which he would care to be related. (And anyhow they had all died young, hadn't they?)

Mr. Harriman was much more anxious to establish a link with his mother's family. She had been Charlotte Audley before she married. Her father (whom he vaguely remembered) had been Charles Audley, the elder son of James Audley, who was said to have come from Buckinghamshire in England.

Mr. Harriman had tried to find out more about the family but without success. (If only he had listened to the old folk talking!) However, Audley was not a common name, so he was hopeful. The discovery that Buckinghamshire was a large county with a sizeable population did not daunt him. Most obstacles could be overcome with perseverance—so he had found. In fact the only ambition which had eluded him was the acquisition of a son to perpetuate his name and succeed him in his business. He had intended to call his son Audley—Audley Harriman sounded good—but Audley had not materialised. Audley was a dream son.

As a matter of fact Mr. Harriman thought of Audley

quite often and sometimes dreamt of him: Audley as a kid (with fair hair like Penelope) getting into mischief; Audley at college, winning prizes; Audley growing up, making dates with girls, playing baseball and beginning to take an interest in business. Mr. Harriman would sooner have died than have mentioned Audley to his nearest and dearest (he prided himself on being a hard-headed businessman), but at the back of his mind there was a vague sort of hope that in Buckinghamshire he might find a young Audley cousin who would fill the bill . . . and, if so, thought Mr. Harriman (if the young Audley cousin were all that could be desired), he might marry Penelope and become a son-in-law—which would be almost as good. Mr. Harriman had begun to plan what branch of his business would suit the young Audley cousin (not sales, thought Mr. Harriman; Englishmen hadn't enough push) when his day-dream was interrupted.

"What are you thinking about, Elmer?" enquired Mrs. Harriman.

"He's thinking about Table Mountain," suggested Penelope. "The Captain says we shall see it tomorrow morning."

"I'll be sorry," Marion declared.

"You'll be sorry?" exclaimed Mrs. Harriman in surprise. "Why, Marion, I thought you wanted to see Table Mountain!"

"George is disembarking at Capetown," murmured Penelope. She added kindly, "Never mind, Marion. There will be other nice young Britishers. The Captain said so."

"George is amusing," admitted Marion without embarrassment.

"What about Clem?" asked Penelope.

"He wouldn't mind," replied Marion. "He likes me to enjoy myself."

Penelope was not so sure. Marion was engaged to Clement Hogan; the two families had been friends for years. Mr. Hogan had a large and flourishing business with branches all over the States and Clem was doing well. Sometimes Marion wore Clem's ring on her engagement finger but more often on a ribbon round her neck. Marion loved Clem and was looking forward to marrying him in the spring, when he was due for a partner-

3

ship; but, as she had explained to Penelope, she found it "easier to talk to people" when Clem's ring was invisible.

"I wear it all the time," added Marion, sensing her cousin's disapproval.

Penelope said no more.

The girls were very attractive and were used to receiving a great deal of attention. All the unattached males on board the S.S. *Ariadne* had fallen victims to their charms. Penelope was fairy-like with ash-blonde wavy hair and sea-blue eyes; Marion's eyes were brown, her smooth hair was cut to fit her well-shaped head like a dark brown cap. They were very fond of each other, and had good fun together, and they enhanced each other's charms.

When the ship called at Capetown, the two girls leaned on the rail and waved goodbye to their friends.

"It's a little sad," said Penelope. "We've met so many people—but perhaps it's just as well."

Marion understood what she meant of course. She had been sorry to say goodbye to George, but it was "just as well." He had said he would write to her, but she knew he wouldn't—they never did. After a short silence she said, "You can make friends on a ship quite easily because you know you'll never see them again."

"Do you want to see George again?" asked Penelope with some anxiety.

"Not really," Marion admitted.

They looked at each other and smiled.

After lunch the girls returned to their post and watched the new passengers arriving. There were one or two couples (oldish people who looked rather dull), and a harassed mother with a family of children. They all straggled up the gangway, turning to wave to friends who were seeing them off. Next came a group of young men (Marion decided that they were "Britishers" going home to England); they paused when they saw Penelope and Marion and gazed at them hopefully . . . but the girls were talking to each other and did not seem to notice.

4

"Nothing doing, Jack!" exclaimed one of the young men, giving his friend a hearty buffet on the shoulder.

They laughed and passed on.

One man behaved differently. He was alone and obviously he had no friends to see him off, for he strode up the gangway without looking to left or right. He glanced at the girls in passing, but without the slightest interest and, pushing through the crowd on deck, disappeared into the bowels of the ship presumably to find his cabin.

"Did you see him?" whispered Penelope in her cousin's ear.

"Not really," Marion replied. "He was going too fast."

Penelope agreed that he was going much too fast—she had not seen him either—but they decided that he was of medium height and had a thin brown face and blue eyes. "Grey-blue eyes," said Penelope.

"What colour was his hair?" Marion wondered.

Penelope thought his hair was brown, but she could not be certain because his green felt hat had an unusually wide brim. Marion had noticed that his grey flannel suit was a little the worse for wear and that he had lost a button off his jacket. Penelope had noticed that he had green socks and highly-polished brown shoes.

They had not really seen him, he had been going too fast, but obviously they would know him again when they saw him and quite soon they would be able to get into contact with him.

"You could offer to sew on his button," suggested Penelope.

"Clem wouldn't like it," Marion replied primly.

They both laughed—it was the sort of joke they enjoyed.

All this time other people were arriving, singly or in groups. Two young men paused and looked at the girls with pleasure and appreciation. One of them hesitated as if he were going to venture a remark . . . and then thought better of it. The other young man removed his hat and smiled and said,

5

"Lovely weather, isn't it?" The girls smiled back quite kindly and agreed. He was tall and well-set-up with copper-coloured hair and very white teeth (which his smile showed to advantage), but all the same the girls were not interested in him.

By dinner-time the girls had discovered that the man with the green socks and highly-polished brown shoes was Mr. Gerald Brown. It was a dull name and they were rather disappointed. They expected to see him at dinner of course and every time the door opened they looked up eagerly, but he did not appear. The ship had left Capetown by this time and Table Mountain was disappearing in the evening mist, but the sea was so calm that they could not believe Mr. Brown was suffering from sea-sickness. They discussed the matter while they drank their soup and ate their fish.

Mr. and Mrs. Harriman listened to the discussion in silence, but when *filet de boeuf à la jardinière* appeared, Mrs. Harriman could contain her curiosity no longer and enquired why they were so enthusiastic about the man.

Marion replied, "He looked at us as if we were a couple of steamer chairs."

"He didn't see you," suggested Mrs. Harriman.

"He saw us, but he didn't see us," explained Penelope.

"I don't know what you mean," declared Mrs. Harriman.

"It's quite easy," said Penelope kindly. "When you board a ship and see a couple of dirty old steamer chairs lying around, you see them with your eyes—but you don't really see them. That's how he saw us."

Mrs. Harriman frowned. It seemed strange. Afterwards she spoke to her husband about it but found him unhelpful. Elmer Harriman had given up the attempt to understand his female relations. He loved them dearly and was extremely proud of them, but he just accepted them as they were. Sometimes they amused him immensely, but he had a poker-face and kept his amusement to himself. (Audley would have understood and enjoyed the joke.)

Marion and Penelope were looking forward to establishing friendly relations with the mystery man. It was easy to make friends on shipboard—in fact it was difficult not to—but Mr. Brown eluded them and, apart from a chance meeting in the corridor when he hurried past with a muttered "Good morning" in answer to their smiles, no contact had been made. He was never visible except at meals when he sat at a small table in the corner of the dining-room, eating and reading a book. He was never to be seen on deck. He took no part in games nor swam in the swimming-pool. There was a dance one night, but apparently Mr. Brown was not a dancer. Mr. Harriman assured them that he did not spend his time in the bar.

"Why bother about him?" asked Mrs. Harriman. "There are plenty of nice boys for you to be friends with. That good-looking boy with the red hair has lovely manners and his father is a baronet. . . ."

"Oh, we're friendly with him, Aunt Ada," said Marion.

"We've plenty of friends, but we're *interested* in Mr. Brown," explained Penelope.

One evening Mr. Harriman met the man face to face in the passageway outside his cabin and invited him into the private stateroom for a chat.

"Oh, thank you! It's very kind of you, but I'm rather busy," replied Gerald Brown. "Thank you *very* much, sir."

It was a polite refusal—almost too polite, thought Mr. Harriman, as he watched Brown scurrying down the passageway and disappearing into his cabin like a bolting rabbit.

Mr. Harriman had hoped to please his daughter and his niece but had failed in the attempt.

Meanwhile the girls had obtained some interesting information from one of the stewardesses. In exchange for a lavish tip they learned that Mr. Brown got up early, ran round the deck and swam in the swimming-pool long before his fellow-passengers were awake. He had given the stewardess his jacket to have a button sewn on. Whilst engaged in this task, she had discovered that the lining of his jacket had come loose and had been mended with black cotton thread, so she had unpicked it and repaired it with grey silk which she happened to have in her sewing-basket. Luckily it matched exactly, so she was able to make a neat job of it. Mr. Brown spent most of his time in his cabin, reading books which he obtained from the ship's library. He had read *Diamonds Are Forever* and was now reading a big fat book with pictures in it, called *The Adventures of Robinson Crusoe*. As far as she knew, he had received no letters nor postcards nor cablegrams. He was a nice polite gentleman and gave no trouble except that he was always in his cabin when she wanted to clean it and make his bed. In answer to further questioning the stewardess said that she thought he went out for a walk on deck late in the evening—but she could not be sure.

When they had pumped the stewardess dry, Marion and Penelope talked it over. Marion was of the opinion that he was a criminal flying from justice and was travelling under an assumed name. Penelope did not agree. "He has lovely eyes," she said with a sigh.

Penelope had heard of *Robinson Crusoe*; she had been under the impression that it was a story for children—but perhaps she was wrong? She decided to have a look at it when Mr. Brown returned it to the library.

2. Gerald Brown's Secret

Gerald Brown was unaware of the trouble he was causing; he was too wrapped up in himself and his own affairs. He had chosen *Robinson Crusoe* from the library because he remembered that the man had been wrecked upon a desert island. Gerald envied him.

Gerald thought there were too many people in the world —the ship was full of people who would not let him alone. They said "Good morning" to him or "Good evening" as the case might be and he was obliged to reply in the same meaningless words. It was impossible to escape from people except by shutting himself up in his cabin.

The Adventures of Robinson Crusoe interested Gerald profoundly; he read it for hours on end, forgetting his own troubles in following the troubles of Crusoe . . . but, whereas Crusoe had found much to be thankful for in his plight, Gerald was unable to find anything at all to be thankful for in his.

He was wrong, of course. Everyone has something to be thankful for and Gerald had quite a lot. Hundreds of thousands of people, lying sick in hospitals, would have considered themselves fortunate in having a strong fit body free from pain. Gerald never thought of that. He took care of his body, of course. He ran round the deck every morning and at night when nobody was about; he swam daily and did strenuous exercises in his cabin for, although he did not count fitness a blessing, he had no intention of allowing his muscles to go soft.

It was a friendly ship and for the first few days Gerald was pursued by his fellow-passengers and invited to play games —or swim—or dance. He refused everything and eventually they gave him up in despair . . . all except the American family. Mr. Harriman asked him to come in for a drink—and he refused.

That would end the matter, thought Gerald. But it did not end the matter. In spite of his bearish behaviour Mrs. Harriman continued to nod to him when she happened to catch his eye in the dining-room and the two girls continued to smile at him when he met them in the passage-way outside his cabin. He had a vague sort of feeling that they were interested in him.

The stewardess who looked after his cabin (and who was the only person on board to whom he spoke) confirmed this suspicion. One morning when she came in, she smiled and said that the young American ladies had asked her what he was reading.

"Asked what I was reading?" enquired Gerald in astonishment.

"I told them it was *Robinson Crusoe* and they seemed surprised. I hope you don't mind, Mr. Brown," she added a little anxiously.

"Oh, no, it doesn't matter at all," replied Gerald. He had finished the book by this time. The second part was less interesting (it was the first part about the island which had appealed to him), so he returned it to the library and took a thriller by Helen MacInnes in its place. The following day he went in to see if *Robinson Crusoe* was still there, but it had vanished.

"It was the young American lady who took it," explained the librarian. "Miss Penelope—the fair one that is."

"Oh, really?"

"The dark one, Miss Marion, has more style," suggested the librarian. He hesitated, wondering if he should venture to say that some gentlemen preferred blondes, but decided not to. Mr. Brown did not look as if he could take a joke.

Mr. Brown returned to his cabin and lay on his bed reading *The Venetian Affair* until it was time to dress for dinner. It was a good story, but all the same it did not hold his attention completely. He could not help wondering what Miss Penelope Harriman was making of *Robinson Crusoe*. She wouldn't get very far with it, thought Gerald with a rueful smile.

As the ship forged northwards, the weather became colder. The awnings which had sheltered the passengers from the blazing sunshine were taken down and put away. The deck-chairs were grouped together in corners sheltered from the wind. Girls who had strolled about in summer frocks were now to be seen in brightly-coloured pullovers. Later they appeared in tweed coats with scarves tied over their heads and knotted beneath their chins.

It was September and the sea breezes were bracing. Gerald had begun to feel a good deal better, but he continued to avoid his fellow-passengers as if they had the plague. He was looking forward to London; nobody bothered about you in London. He would take a room in a small hotel or a lodging-house and look for a job. Once he had found a job—any sort of job—he would be less miserable.

The voyage was nearly over; the *Ariadne* was steaming up the channel with a following wind. The passengers had been given an especially good dinner and were now dancing in the lounge. Gerald Brown was the only passenger who was not taking part in the fun. He was leaning on the rail looking at the distant lights which were strung along the English coast like a necklace of gems. The sound of talk and laughter and music came faintly to his ears.

It was a moonlight night and rather cold, but Gerald was wearing an overcoat and a thick blue muffler, so he found the chill in the air rather pleasant. He had been leaning on the rail for some time, and had just decided to walk briskly round

11

the deck before going to bed when he realised that he was not alone.

"We shall be in London tomorrow night," said Miss Penelope Harriman. She added, "I just love London, Mr. Brown."

Gerald's first thought was to reply briefly and fly for his life, but second thoughts were bolder. He decided that as this was the last night of the voyage he might as well talk to the girl. After tomorrow he would never see her again, so there was no danger of getting involved. Besides he had been feeling a little sad.

"Do you know London well, Miss Harriman?" he enquired.

"Oh, yes! I was at a school near Ascot for a whole year and we often went to concerts in London."

"Did you like the school?"

"Well, not at first," she admitted. "It was so different from home—and the girls were different too—but after a bit I just loved it. I didn't want to come away."

Gerald nodded. The fact that she had been at school in England "for a whole year" explained something which had puzzled him: Miss Penelope Harriman spoke almost—but not quite—like an English girl.

"We've been in England often," she continued. "We've travelled a lot. Last time we were over Marion and I saw the Tower and Westminster Abbey and Hampton Court. It's history come alive. Do you live in London, Mr. Brown?"

"No," replied Gerald. He sighed and added, "I don't live anywhere. My parents died when I was in Africa, so I have no home."

"But I expect you have relatives in England?"

Gerald hesitated and then replied reluctantly, "Yes, I've a sister—at least she's a half-sister—but I don't intend to be a bother to her. I shall take a room in London and look for a job."

"It sounds kind of lonely," said Penelope.

He looked down at her. She was wearing a mink coat and her lovely little face was framed in the fur collar, which she had pulled up to her ears. The blue eyes which were

12

raised to his were sincerely sympathetic. It was so long since Gerald Brown had been given the sympathy of a fellow-creature that his heart was touched and, somewhat to his surprise, he found himself admitting that he did feel a bit lonely now and then . . . but it was better to depend upon oneself rather than be "let down" by people whom one had believed to be one's friends.

The statement was muddled and not very well reasoned, but Miss Harriman seemed to understand.

"Oh, dear!" she said sadly. "That's why you're so 'stand-offish,' Mr. Brown! But people aren't all like that. The person who let you down couldn't have been a true friend, so she isn't worth thinking about any more."

"It was a man. I thought he was my friend—but he didn't believe what I said. I can't tell you about it," added Gerald hopelessly.

There was a short silence. "I'm reading about Robinson," said Penelope at last. "It was dreadful for him being all alone on that island with nobody to talk to . . . but he's got Friday now. I'm glad he's got Friday. Is it true, Mr. Brown? It sounds true."

"Partly true," replied Gerald, trying to remember. "I think something of the kind happened to a man called Alexander Selkirk—but I expect Defoe cooked it up a bit to make a better story."

"It's still pretty raw," declared Penelope with a little chortle of laughter. "Marion wants to read it when I've finished, but I guess she won't like it much."

Gerald agreed that it was "pretty raw." He had not wanted to talk to Penelope Harriman—or anyone—but he was finding it rather pleasant . . . and there was no fear of getting involved with her. After tomorrow he would never see her again.

"Listen," said Penelope, laying a little white hand on his arm and speaking very earnestly indeed. "I've been very, very interfering and it would serve me right if you told me to mind my own business—but you aren't playing fair."

"Playing fair?"

13

"Just because one man disappointed you."

"Oh, I see what you mean!"

"You've got a grouch," Penelope told him. "You've got a grouch against the world. You said you had a sister in England, but you aren't going to see her—you aren't going to give her a chance. It's not playing fair, Mr. Brown. There, I've said it! I guess you're annoyed."

"Wait!" exclaimed Gerald. "Wait a moment! You've got it wrong. I haven't a 'grouch' against the world."

"What is it, then?"

"It's difficult to explain," he replied thoughtfully. "I want to—to stand on my own feet. I want to make good before I get in touch with—with anyone. I don't want to go to Bess as a down-and-out asking for help—see?"

"She might be glad to help you."

"That isn't the point."

"I wish I had a brother," said Penelope wistfully. "If I had a brother, I'd want him to tell me his troubles. I'd want to help him all I could."

"But I've told you I must make good. I must do it for my own sake. I must get a job and settle down——"

"She might be able to help you," Penelope interrupted.

"Bess is much too busy to find me a job."

"Is she married?"

"No, she's on the stage."

"On the stage?"

"Yes, she has just been given the leading part in a new musical play, so she'll be very busy. I'm not going to bother her with my troubles."

"A new musical?" enquired Penelope, pricking up her ears.

"It's called *The Girl from Venus*."

Penelope gave a squeak of excitement. "*The Girl from Venus*? But that's Elizabeth Burleigh! Oh, Mr. Brown, how thrilling! We saw her in *Monday's Child*—she was wunnerful! And you're her brother! If only we had known before! Tell me about her. What is she really like? Is it true that she lives a quiet life and won't go to parties? Is it true that she hates being photographed? Please, please tell me about her."

Gerald groaned inwardly. Too late he saw his mistake. He should never have talked to this girl—it had been madness!

"Tell me about her," repeated Penelope. "What is she like in real life? She's lovely on the stage—just lovely. We went to *Monday's Child* three times and we're going to *The Girl from Venus* on Thursday night—we wired to the theatre and reserved a box. Why is she called Elizabeth Burleigh?"

"It's her name," replied Gerald reluctantly. "Elizabeth Burleigh-Brown. She dropped the 'Brown' when she went on the stage because she thought it sounded better."

"So you're really Mr. Burleigh-Brown?"

"Yes."

"Oh, dear, how exciting!" cried Penelope. "Marion will be thrilled to bits when I tell her."

"Please don't!" exclaimed Gerald in alarm. "Please don't tell anyone."

"Why not?"

"Because it's a secret. I didn't mean to tell you. I don't want anyone to know that Bess is my sister; it would be dreadfully embarrassing for me—really it would. You've been kind and—and understanding, so I'm sure you'll understand."

"A secret?"

"Yes, a secret," repeated Gerald in desperation. "You'll keep my secret, won't you, Miss Harriman? Please say you will."

"Elizabeth Burleigh! But she's marvellous! Why are you ashamed of her?"

"I'm not!" he cried. "I'm proud of Bess. She has made a success of her life—and all by her own efforts. It's the other way about."

"I don't understand!"

"She's a success in her chosen career. I'm a failure. I had a good post and I've lost it. I was sacked without a reference."

Penelope was silent.

The ship steamed on. Thick clouds, billowing up from the southwest, had swallowed the moon and it had become quite

15

dark, too dark for Gerald to see the girl's face. He wondered what she was thinking. He hadn't intended to say it, of course; the words had burst out of his mouth involuntarily, but now that he had said it he saw that he would have to explain further.

He said quietly, "Well, Miss Harriman, now you know my secret. You know why I'm unsociable. If I told you my story, you wouldn't want to speak to me again. I'm a failure—a man under a cloud."

"But look!" she cried. "The clouds are blowing away!"

It was true. The moon had come out from behind the swiftly moving clouds and was shining brightly.

"My cloud isn't so easily scattered," said Gerald bitterly.

"I'm sorry," said Penelope sadly. She added, "Don't worry, Mr. Brown, I'll keep your secret. There's just one thing I want to tell you—to show you that I understand. Long ago something happened to me—something horrid. I was under a cloud too. I was miserable because I thought it would go on forever—I didn't see any chance of it being put right. When . . . well, then something very unexpected happened—something I had never thought of— and the trouble was all cleared up in ten minutes."

"My trouble can never be cleared up," declared Gerald.

"That's what I thought about mine," Penelope told him . . . and with that she drifted away like a little grey ghost and left him alone.

For a long while Gerald stood there, leaning on the rail. He had watched the girl from a distance; he had seen her surrounded by a crowd of admirers, laughing gaily and chattering nineteen to the dozen, and had assumed that she was a beautiful little butterfly with no thought in her head except to have a good time . . . but the assumption had been entirely wrong. Penelope Harriman was intelligent (a bit too intelligent thought Gerald ruefully). He reviewed the conversation and tried to remember how he had given her the clue to his secret. The last thing he had intended was to claim relationship with Bess. The fact was he had lived so long in the wilds that he had not realized how famous his adored sister had become. I ought to have known, thought Gerald. There was always something wonderful about Bess!

Gerald's father had been married twice. Bess was the child of his first marriage, Gerald of his second, so Bess was already a beautiful little girl when Gerald was a baby. They had been brought up in an old farm-house in Scotland and had run wild together over the moors. The land was poor—much of it was boggy—so the crops were scanty. The only plant which flourished was the white bog-cotton, or "cannoch," which was useless of course. It was strange that anything as beautiful as cannoch could be a menace to a farmer, but such was the case at Cannochbrae.

Goodness! thought Gerald. I haven't thought of Cannochbrae for years. It was that girl made me think of the past . . . but it's no good thinking about the past. I must think about the future and make plans. Above all I must avoid talking to people. I was a perfect fool to talk to that girl. It was because she was kind.

Yes, Penelope Harriman had been kind and to tell the truth her kindness had comforted Gerald. He had liked her so much that it would have been pleasant to have her as a friend; she was so nice that he would have liked to tell her his troubles. The idea of pouring out the whole wretched story had actually crossed his mind—but fortunately he had realised in time that the story was much too long and complicated. Worse still, it was incredible! Who would believe it? Certainly not a chance acquaintance. His best friend hadn't believed it.

All the same Miss Harriman's words had given him food for thought. He hadn't a "grouch against the world," but he saw that he must wash out the past and start life afresh. He must get a job which would restore his self-respect—that was the first thing to do. Then, when he was settled in a worthwhile job, he would get in touch with Bess.

3. The Girl from Venus

Gerald had decided to get a job before seeing Bess, but after a week in London, living in a comfortless lodging-house and jostled by unheeding multitudes, he was feeling so lonely and miserable that he changed his mind. He could see Bess without being seen—and just to see her would be a comfort.

Under the blazing African sun he had longed for London; he had yearned for crowds and lights and drizzling rain, but now that he had come to London and had got what he wanted, he felt more lonely than he had ever felt in all his life. Already he had discovered that without a reference he would never be able to get a reasonably good post in a respectable firm. His experience in electrical engineering was useless without credentials. He could wait, of course, for during his years of work in the diamond mine he had saved up a substantial sum of money—there was no temptation to spend money in that desolate place—but his few thousands in the bank would not last for ever. Oh, well, if the worst came to the worst, he could dig or carry coal, so there was no need to panic!

Gerald's first purchases in London were warm clothes, a waterproof coat and an umbrella. Thus armed against the cold drizzle he set out for Shaftesbury Avenue. He was too early; the doors were not open, so he sheltered in an archway on the other side of the street and stared at his sister's name in neon lights over the portico of the theatre:

THE GIRL FROM VENUS
ELIZABETH BURLEIGH AND
ARNOLD KNIGHT

Although it was still early, the queue for the cheaper seats stretched all the way down the street and round the corner: people in mackintosh coats, people with umbrellas, all waiting patiently in the rain to see the show!

A young policeman in a shiny black cape stopped for a moment and looked at Gerald enquiringly.

"It's a wet evening," said Gerald. He nodded at the queue and added, "Would there be any chance of my getting a seat?"

"Not a hope *there*," replied the constable. "It's been a full house ever since it started—but you might get a returned seat in the stalls. That's your only chance. People will stand for hours in the rain to see Elizabeth Burleigh."

Gerald nodded.

"Perhaps you saw her in *Monday's Child*?"

"No, I've been abroad for three years."

"She's better in this," declared the young policeman, adding in a burst of confidence, "I've been twice and I'm going again tomorrow night and taking my mother." He walked across the road, took a look at the patiently-waiting crowd and came back to the archway. "It's a good story," he said, continuing the conversation. "She's the girl from Venus of course. She arrives in a space-ship. The door opens and out she comes. She doesn't know where she is—it's all quite different from Venus—but it seems a lovely place to her, specially the flowers. There aren't any flowers on Venus. Then, while she's singing, the space-ship suddenly shuts itself up and flies away."

"Go on," said Gerald. "What happens after that?"

"Well, I don't want to spoil it for you, sir. You ought to see it for yourself," replied the young policeman. He chuckled and added, "There are funny bits, you know. The girl has queer ideas—she's a fish out of water. She's so beautiful that all the chaps fall in love with her and their wives and sweethearts

19

don't like it. Why don't you have a try at the box office and see if there's a seat?"

"Yes, I'll have a try," replied Gerald.

Cars and taxis had begun to arrive and to deposit their passengers at the lighted portico, so Gerald dodged across the street, pushed his way through the crowd and asked at the box office.

"You're lucky," said the girl. "There's a returned ticket just been handed in. It's a single in the stalls."

It was not until he was actually in the theatre, seated in the stalls, that he realised he was in the front row. A seat in a less conspicuous position would have suited him better, but he was too shy to make a fuss. Three years in the wilds of Africa had not prepared him for the noise of chatter and the hustle and bustle of a crowded theatre. He felt a bit dazed. Like the girl from Venus he was a fish out of water.

Gerald had come to see Bess—just to look at her. He had always loved Bess, he had always thought her the most wonderful person in the world.

His first "picture" of Bess came to mind as he sat in his plush seat in the crowded theatre, waiting for the curtain to go up. He was playing under the big table in the sitting-room (it was a favourite place to play, for the red cloth came down all round making it into a private tent). When he drew aside the cloth and peeped out, he saw Bess sitting on the hearth-rug reading a book with the firelight shining on her copper-coloured hair. She had looked up and said, "Want to see pictures, darling?"—and he had crawled out of his tent and sat himself down beside her.

He must have been four years old—which meant that Bess was seven—but he remembered it quite clearly. (He had known Bess always, of course. She had been part of his life ever since he was an infant, but that was the first time he was conscious of seeing her.)

Gerald's next childhood "picture" was Bess again. He was older now and it was summer-time. They were playing in the hay loft at Cannochbrae. He was sitting on a pile of hay—he remembered the sweet smell and the tickly feeling of the clean dry hay on his bare legs—and Bess was telling him a story. Bess was a wonderful story-teller; she acted the stories as she went along, which made them real. Gerald could "see" her drifting about the hay-loft in a faded blue overall and acting the parts of the characters. First she was the little boy, straying from his home and getting lost in the woods; then she was the fairy, who found him asleep and took him to her home in the round green hill. (Bess and Gerald both believed in fairies—not "silly fairies," but "little people" who lived in round green hills.) Another time Bess was a beautiful lady imprisoned in a tower. She was feeling very sad when a handsome prince on a milk-white charger came to rescue her. Then away they went together, galloping, galloping, galloping round the loft . . . and the dust flew up in clouds, hiding them from their pursuers. This story was so exciting that Gerald asked for it over and over again in spite of the fact that the dust tickled his nose and made him sneeze.

There had been lots of people at Cannochbrae Farm: Father and Mother and Uncle Gregor and Aunt Maggie and Cousin Matt—and the farm-hands and their families, who lived in the cottages. Gerald knew them all, but Bess was by far the most important person in his life. They did everything together: They paddled in the burn and caught little fish—as long as your finger! They fed the pigs; they climbed the trees in the woods; they found a cave amongst the rocks on the hill above the farm. It was a tiny cave, just big enough to shelter them from a passing shower if they sat very close together. Bess was the leader in all their games; it was Bess who thought of all the interesting things to do! "C'm on, Flick!" she would cry, spreading out her arms and rushing down the hill, her feet scarcely touching the ground, and Gerald would follow as fast as his short fat legs could take him.

Why had she called him "Flick"? He didn't know. There must have been some reason, he supposed, but it was lost in the hazy memories of his childhood.

The footlights went on; the lights in the auditorium went off . . . and Gerald awoke from his trance to see the curtain rising. At first the stage was almost dark (it was early morning), but gradually the dawn came and the scene took shape. There were cottages with summer flowers in their gardens; there were trees and bushes; the only sound was the dawn chorus of birds.

Then, in the distance, a humming noise became audible and in the sky behind one of the cottages a curious object appeared. It was a shining steel space-ship, which hovered for a few moments and then settled down gently in the middle of the stage. A door in the side of the ship opened and a girl stepped out.

Gerald had expected this—the policeman had told him—but despite his preparedness his heart gave a wild leap . . . for it wasn't "Aurelia" (as it had said in his programme), it was just Bess. It was Bess herself, looking as beautiful as ever. It was his own dear Bess. She was wearing a pale-green filmy garment, which floated round her as she moved; her feet were bare and her lovely copper-coloured hair fell in soft waves to her shoulders.

There was no sound now; the bird-chorus was stilled. Bess looked about her, wonderingly. She had come to a strange new world. Presently she began to sing softly to herself and to drift across the stage in a graceful dance, picking the flowers in the cottage gardens and crooning over them in delight. She was so entranced that she never noticed that the door in the space-ship had closed, never noticed that the ship was rising from the ground. It was not until it had risen high above her head and was disappearing rapidly in the early morning sky that she realised her plight; she had been abandoned! She was alone in the strange new world!

She ran about, calling to her friends to come back; she was in despair . . . then she realised that it was hopeless! The flowers fell from her hands, her shoulders drooped and she wandered away slowly and disappeared into the woods.

The sun had risen; the stage scene brightened and the village awoke. It was market-day. Peasants arrived with hand-carts and proceeded to erect their stalls and to lay out their produce. An old woman in a donkey-cart with a crate of live hens drove onto the stage. There was talk and laughter and a good deal of squabbling; the stall-holders fought for convenient positions. A lad was discovered stealing a punnet of straw-berries, set upon by the owner and soundly thrashed. Two pretty girls strolled on and were surrounded by admiring swains.

The scene was gay, it was colourful and amusing; the audience was ready to laugh—and rocked with mirth at the somewhat ribald jokes—even Gerald, who was in no mood for laughter was obliged to smile.

Gerald decided that the man who had written this play was a clever psychologist; like Shakespeare he was giving his laughter, was obliged to smile.

The merriment was at its height when there was a sudden hush and every head was turned, every eye was fixed in aston-ishment upon the graceful figure of the girl from Venus which had emerged from the woods and was standing upon a little grassy knoll. There was something so strange about the un-earthly visitant that some of the villagers fled in alarm, while others, attracted by her beauty, surged forward to greet her. The curtain fell upon a scene of confusion.

Gerald saw from his programme that there was to be an interval of ten minutes. The lights went up and many people in the audience went out talking and laughing, but Gerald remained seated, lost in dreams. The play was a fairy-tale—a modern fairy-tale—but it suited Bess. It gave her plenty of scope for her own particular form of acting. There was a fairy-tale quality in Bess.

He was awakened from his trance by a touch on his arm and looked up to find a girl in a white overall standing beside him.

"Mr. Gerald Burleigh-Brown?" she enquired.

"Yes."

"Miss Burleigh wants to see you."

"What?" he asked incredulously.

"She wants to see you. I'll fetch you after the show." She smiled and gave him a sealed envelope and hurried away.

It had never occurred to Gerald that a member of the audience could be seen from the stage. How had Bess seen him? He opened the envelope. It contained a pencilled scribble:

> Flick, darling! Why are you in town? What has happened. Why haven't you been to see me? I've been worried to death about you. Come round after the show. I must see you. It's *assential*. Bess.

He had not intended this, of course, but he would have to obey the summons. Perhaps he might have refused if it had not been for their own private signal, which was underlined so fiercely that the pencil had torn the paper. If something was *assential* it was vitally important; it was an S.O.S. which could not be ignored.

When Bess was twelve years old, she had been invited to go and stay with her mother's sister, Aunt Anna, and had gone away quite happily, but after three days Gerald had received a letter from her saying that she wanted to come home. Father must fetch her immediately: "Please make him do it. It is *assential*." Father had been unwilling to offend his first wife's sister, but Gerald gave him no peace and eventually showed him the letter.

"Oh, well, I suppose I had better go and fetch her," said Father.

"You must, it's *assential*," Gerald declared.

"That isn't the way to spell it," said Father.

"It's the way to get it done," said Gerald earnestly.

He was right. Bess was fetched home the following day.

On the way home in the car Mr. Burleigh-Brown informed his daughter that the word was wrongly spelt and added that a big girl of twelve years old should know better. She was told the exact meaning of the word "essential" and given its Latin root. Bess listened meekly and promised to remember. Mr. Burleigh-Brown was so anxious to instruct his daughter that he forgot to ask why it had been essential for her to come home. Gerald was told in confidence.

"Aunt Anna was queer," explained Bess. She sat and cried all the time. I asked her if she had a pain—but she hadn't. She just felt miserable. I was dreadfully sorry for her, but I couldn't bear it."

"It must have been awful!"

"I thought of writing to Father, but I was so afraid he wouldn't do it."

"I made him do it, Bess. You said it was *assential*, so I made him," said Gerald proudly.

Gerald had been wafted far away into the past so the second act of *The Girl from Venus* did not make much impression upon him. He woke up a bit for the third act, but he had lost the thread. However, it didn't matter much; he had come to see Bess—and Bess was on the stage nearly all the time. (Her name in the play was Aurelia—but she was just Bess.) She was so beautiful that all the young men fell in love with her; he didn't blame them. The other girls were jealous of her; he didn't blame them either. The manners and customs of Earth were entirely different from Venus, so there were all sorts of things that Aurelia didn't understand. She didn't understand "marriage." Why did two people shut themselves up in a house together instead of going about with anyone who took their fancy? Apparently there were no animals on Venus, so when she saw a cow, she could scarcely believe her eyes. As the policeman had said, some of it was very funny indeed.

Gradually Aurelia learnt about Earth. She was happy in "The World of Flowers" and especially happy with Giles, the farmer's son. They sang a duet: "Teach me about Love."

It was a good tune and their voices harmonised delightfully . . . and Aurelia learnt about Love very quickly. She

25

promised to marry Giles and agreed that it would be blissful to live alone with him in a little cottage in the woods. They had a cow and a pig and hens. Aurelia had discarded her filmy draperies and appeared looking like a Dresden shepherdess to scatter corn for the chickens.

Gerald was quite prepared for the play to end with Aurelia and Giles living happily ever after—he had a feeling that "musicals" always ended happily—but this one was an exception to the rule and he was forced to admit that the unhappy ending was the more artistic.

Two emissaries arrived from Venus with the tidings that the old King was dead. (The wicked old King was Aurelia's uncle and it was he who had banished her to Earth.) Now that he was dead, Aurelia was the rightful queen of Venus and she must return and take up the reins of government.

Aurelia refused to go! She would stay forever in The World of Flowers with Giles, her beloved husband. There was a fierce argument and a dramatic song—a quartet in which the two emissaries and Giles and Aurelia took part! It ended in a fight. The men from Venus were victorious. While Giles lay unconscious on the ground, the men seized Aurelia and told her plainly that unless she changed her mind and came quietly, Venus would despatch a secret missile to destroy her World of Flowers and everyone in it. So to save Giles and all her friends Aurelia was forced to agree.

The last scene was the same as the first—but it was late afternoon and the space-ship was to be seen in the background standing upon the grassy knoll . . .

Aurelia and Giles took a fond farewell of each other and Aurelia sang her song: "Goodbye to the World of Summer Flowers."

The Villagers sang the chorus: "Farewell, lovely Venus maid!"

Aurelia walked up the hill slowly and sadly; she was taken into the space-ship and flown away. The villagers left the stage and only Giles remained, the heart-broken Giles, and a single red rose which had fallen from Aurelia's bouquet.

When the curtain fell, there was a moment's silence before the audience recovered sufficiently to show its approval. The noise of clapping was deafening; the curtain rose and fell again and again. First there was the whole cast; then the principal actors; then Bess and Giles and the Venus men. Bouquets were handed onto the stage and distributed. Then Aurelia came forward with the conductor of the orchestra; then Aurelia alone, a tall graceful figure . . . she was smiling happily. She came forward and held out her arms and at once there was silence.

"Thank you, dear people," said Elizabeth Burleigh. "Thank you for being such a wonderful audience. Goodnight, everyone!"

There was more clapping, and more bouquets.

Then it was over.

What an ovation! Gerald had never seen anything like it—and all the excitement was for Bess! It was for his own dear Bess whom he had always loved better than anyone else in the world! His eyes were dim with unshed tears as he groped under the seat for the green hat with the unfashionably wide brim, which had sheltered him from the South African sun.

When he stood up, the girl who had brought him the note was waiting for him and signed to him to come. He followed her through a door and up some stone steps and along a draughty passage.

"This is her dressing-room," said the girl. "She isn't seeing anyone else tonight. It'll be a whole-time job keeping them away."

Then she pushed Gerald into the room and shut the door behind him.

Immediately he was enveloped in a close embrace. Bess's arms were round his neck, her face was hidden against his shoulder. She had changed the diaphanous garments which she had worn on the stage for a thin white silk kimono and as Gerald put his arms round her, he discovered that there was nothing much beneath it. It was an amazing thing to have her in his arms like this: her soft warm body, the scent of violets, her copper hair tickling his nose.

27

"Flick!" she murmured. "Oh, Flick, darling! Oh, naughty wicked boy! Why did you frighten me?"

"What do you mean?"

"You didn't write . . . you disappeared . . . I thought you were ill! I thought something dreadful had happened . . . I thought you were dead! Oh, Flick! I cabled to Koolbokie and they said you had gone away. I cabled again, but they didn't know your address. Oh, naughty wicked Flick! Why did you frighten me like that?"

"I'm sorry, darling, I didn't mean to frighten you. I was—I was ill for a time. I was a bit—upset."

"You could have cabled!"

"I never thought," said Gerald remorsefully. "I was—upset —and—and miserable. I never thought!"

"And why—oh, why didn't you come to me the moment you arrived?"

He kissed her.

"How long have you been in London?" she demanded.

"Just a few days."

She sighed. "Oh, well, you're here. That's all that matters. You must come and stay with me, of course. You can come home with me, can't you?"

"Not tonight, Bess."

"Why not? There's plenty of room in my flat."

"Not tonight," repeated Gerald, disengaging himself gently.

"Is it a girl, Flick?"

"A girl?"

"You're different," she explained. "Something has happened to you, darling. You're in some sort of trouble. Is it a girl?"

"No, it isn't a girl," he replied, smiling a little at the idea.

"Well, what is it?" she asked anxiously.

"I'll come and tell you about it."

"Tomorrow morning," agreed Bess. "Promise, Flick! Promise faithfully that you'll come tomorrow morning. You can get a taxi and bring your luggage."

He promised faithfully to go and see her tomorrow

morning; she wasn't satisfied until he had written down her address in his notebook. Then he kissed her and came away.

They let him out at the stage-door where there was a group of people waiting in the rain. They were waiting in the pouring rain for a glimpse of Elizabeth Burleigh as she crossed the pavement and got into her car.

4. Gerald's Story

Bess had said, "Come tomorrow morning. You can get a taxi and bring your luggage." Gerald had not replied to that. He had very little luggage, just a suitcase and the garments he had bought in London . . . and he didn't intend to stay with Bess. Perhaps when she had heard his story she wouldn't want him to stay; besides it was better to be free. He couldn't stay with Bess and be out all day searching for a job and he had a feeling that if he were staying with Bess she would drag him out to parties. Bess was popular, so naturally she would lead a gay life! There would be luncheons, cocktails, dinners . . . no, not dinners, of course, because of *Venus*. It would be supper-parties and dances which would continue late into the night. Gerald certainly didn't want that kind of life; it would be intolerable.

The morning was fine and dry with a pleasant nip in the air, so Gerald decided to walk. A helpful policeman told him the way to Molyneux Mansions. It was a large block of modern flats near Regent's Park with a strip of garden in front; an imposing dwelling-place, Gerald decided.

The hall-porter also was imposing (he was a watch-dog to keep out strangers in shabby clothes), but he thawed and became quite human when Gerald gave his name.

"Miss Burleigh is expecting you, sir," he said. "Your luggage will be coming later, I suppose. I'll take you up in the lift. Miss Burleigh won't be up yet, but Miss Meredith will look after you. I'm Bold," he added.

"You're bold?" asked Gerald in surprise.

"Bold is my name," explained the man. He was tired of jokes about his name.

The lift moved noiselessly to the third floor where there was a wide corridor carpeted in crimson. Bold led the way to a cream-coloured door and pressed the electric bell. The door opened immediately.

"This is Mr. Burleigh," said Bold. "His luggage is coming later. I'll bring it up when it comes, Miss Meredith."

"Thank you, Bold," said Miss Meredith.

Gerald was astonished at the beauty of Miss Meredith's face. He had seen pictures of saints which were just like that, with pale, calm faces marked by suffering patiently borne, with wide dark eyes and smooth hair drawn back and knotted at the nape of the neck. It was not until she turned to open the door of the sitting-room that he saw she was a cripple, a hunchback.

"I'm so glad you came early," she told him. "Miss Burleigh hoped you would. She usually gets up about eleven and has a cup of coffee before she takes her dog for a walk in the Park. Perhaps you would like to sit down and look at the papers? She won't be long."

"Thank you," said Gerald. "Please tell her not to hurry."

Miss Meredith put a log on the fire, gave him the daily paper and went away. He sat down and looked about. It was one of the most beautiful rooms he had ever seen—certainly the most peaceful. The fitted carpet was a soft dark green, with a white fur rug in front of the fire. There was a large sofa, several comfortable chairs and wide window-seats with cushions on them. There was a grand piano, several bookcases, and cupboards full of exquisite china. The big windows which looked out onto the Park were of double glass, so the room was quiet. It was quiet and restful and spacious.

Gerald rested peacefully and listened to the gentle tick of the clock which stood upon the chimney-piece. He had had no peace for months; no real peace, no silence. There was real peace here in this lovely room.

It was surprising that there were no flowers. Last night Elizabeth Burleigh had been showered with magnificent bouquets.

The thought had scarcely crossed his mind when Miss Meredith came in with a china vase full of pink roses; they were still in bud with long stems and dark-green shiny leaves.

"This is a lovely room," said Gerald. "It's very quiet. You might be miles from London's busy streets."

Miss Meredith nodded. "Yes, I love this room. It's so restful. The whole flat is restful; I never want to go out."

"Those are lovely roses."

"Yes. Miss Burleigh doesn't like a lot of flowers. She gets too many—we send them to the hospital. She just likes a few roses. Sir Walter sends her roses twice a week."

Miss Meredith put the vase on a low bookcase and re-arranged the flowers. Then she turned and added, "You aren't reading the paper."

"I'm enjoying the peacefulness. The paper is sure to be full of horrors."

She nodded. "But it's good for us to know what's happening in the world."

"Is it good for us?" asked Gerald. "Does it do us any good to read about people being robbed or drowned or murdered —or to look at pictures of miserable refugees?"

"I'm not sure," replied Miss Meredith doubtfully. She hesitated and then added, "Perhaps you'd like to see your room, Mr. Burleigh?"

"I don't think I shall be staying here," he replied.

"I expect you will," declared Miss Meredith smiling. "Miss Burleigh usually gets what she wants."

Then she went away and soon after Bess came in. She greeted Gerald warmly and sat down beside him on the sofa.

"Now, Flick," she said. "Now you're going to tell me all about it. Then we'll have our coffee and take Gubby for a walk."

"Gubby?"

"He's a black and tan dachshund," explained Bess. "A friend gave him to me when he was a puppy, and he was so greedy that we called him 'Mr. Gubbins.' Then he began to put on weight, so Matilda and I decided to harden our hearts. We enjoyed giving him titbits—but it wasn't fair. So we made a hard and fast rule, like the Medes and Persians, that no matter how sweetly Gubby begged he was to get nothing—absolutely nothing—except his proper food. Two meals a day," said Bess sternly. "Gubby knows now and doesn't bother, so it's better for everyone—and he has an extremely elegant figure."

"You're very wise," declared Gerald. "It certainly isn't fair to overfeed dogs. I shall look forward to meeting the elegant Mr. Gubbins."

"And you can help to exercise him, can't you? Take him out for a walk when I'm busy."

"But I'm not going to stay with you."

"Not going to stay with me?"

"No," replied Gerald. "I'll come and see you whenever you want me and I'll willingly take Gubby for a walk, but I'm not going to stay with you, Bess."

"Why not?"

"Because I've lost my job and I've got to find another."

"You've lost your job?" she asked incredulously.

"It's true," he declared. "I was caught red-handed. The stones were sewn into the lining of my jacket."

"Who put them there?"

"I don't know," said Gerald miserably. "All I can tell you is they were found sewn into the lining of my jacket, so of course I was sacked without a reference."

"You were sacked?"

"Yes, then and there. It was decent of Proudfoot not to prosecute me and have me sent to prison. I'd have got five years at least—probably more."

Bess took his hand and held it. She said, "For goodness' sake stop talking nonsense and tell me in plain words what happened."

33

For a few minutes Gerald was silent. Then he said, "It's a long story and—and I don't know where to begin. Angus Proudfoot is the manager of Koolbokie—you know that, don't you? Pat Felstead was my assistant."

"You got him the job."

"Yes, he was with me at the technical college. We both took the course in electrical engineering, so it was natural for me to recommend him when I heard he was out of a job. Besides he was my best friend, so I knew we should get on well together. You remember him, don't you, Bess?"

She nodded. "Yes, you brought him home sometimes to lunch or supper. You used to tell us how clever he was."

"He is clever—he was an excellent assistant—and good company as well. We shared a bungalow for eighteen months and never had a disagreeable word."

"Go on, Flick. Come clean," said Bess encouragingly.

Gerald saw that he would have to "come clean." He knew Bess of old and was aware that nothing would satisfy her but the whole story. It was all the more difficult because there were so many things that must be explained, and because life at Koolbokie was so utterly different from the life Bess was leading in London. He felt hopeless of making her understand.

The diamond mine was in an isolated spot, miles from Johannesburg. It was like a little village in itself with huts for the miners and bungalows for the manager and his staff. Gerald and Pat Felstead rarely had a weekend off duty at the same time—it was better that one or other of them should be on the spot—but occasionally they managed it and went to Jo'burg in Gerald's car for a spree.

One Friday morning, when the two were starting off together, they saw a group of native workers waiting at the gate. It was essential that they should be examined before they left the mine in case they had stones in their possession. They were examined in the X-ray department. (It was the only way to make certain that they had no diamonds hidden in their mouths or in their hair or, that they had not swallowed a couple!) Neither Pat nor Gerald was subjected to the indignity of an

34

examination; they were above suspicion and were free to come and go as they pleased. Some of the other members of the staff had the same freedom; others had not.

Pat was always cheery, but on this particular morning he was in the wildest spirits, for he was going to meet a girl in Jo'burg—a certain Miss Lily Oxton—who had taken his fancy. Gerald had heard a great deal about Lily and knew his friend's plans, so he wasn't surprised when Pat stopped to have jokes with the native miners. Pat was throwing his hat into the air and catching it on his head or on his foot. The men were grinning at his antics. Gerald was annoyed with Pat for behaving like a mountebank. He stood and waited impatiently. He was even more annoyed when he heard Pat saying that he was going to be X-rayed.

It was just Pat's fun, of course, but it was a mistake, Gerald thought. The men respected you if you behaved in a dignified manner . . . and it was easier to maintain your position of authority if they respected you. By allowing himself to be examined Pat was putting himself on a level with the natives.

"Come on, Gerry!" shouted Pat. "You must be examined too. Everybody should be examined. Everybody—or nobody! Your turn now!"

"We haven't time," replied Gerald, adding under his breath, "Don't be a fool, Pat. You know I don't like this sort of thing."

"Oh, come on! It won't hurt you—just for once!" cried Pat, laughing and taking his arm. "The chaps enjoy a little fun."

The men were watching eagerly to see what was going to happen and Gerald realised that it would be less undignified to agree than to make a fuss so he allowed his friend to lead him into the X-ray department.

Having got thus far in his story Gerald stopped short and hid his face in his hands.

"Go on, Flick," said Bess encouragingly.

"I've told you," muttered Gerald.

"You haven't told me!"

"Yes, I have. They found five stones sewn into the lining of my jacket."

"How did they get there? Who put them there?"

"I don't know."

"But, Flick darling, you must have some idea. . . ."

"No, I haven't the slightest idea how they got there. I was never so surprised in my life."

"You're shielding someone?"

"No."

Bess hesitated and then said, "What happened after that?"

"Oh, there was frightful consternation. They sent for the manager, Angus Proudfoot. He was furious with me. He raged and stormed and said the most dreadful things. It's like a nightmare, Bess. I can't bear to think of it."

"But, Flick, didn't you tell them——"

"Of course I told them! I told them over and over again that I had no idea how the stones had got into the lining of my jacket. They didn't believe me. Angus said he would send for the police and charge me with theft. That scared me properly; I knew it meant prison. Pat was almost in tears, he said, 'Angus you can't! It will mean five years—or more! You know that as well as I do. Please listen to me! Please listen!' At first Angus wouldn't listen, he was too angry, but Pat went on trying to persuade him to let me go and say no more about it. They argued and argued—it seemed like hours to me—but at last Pat wore him down and made him listen. Pat pointed out that if Angus charged me with stealing diamonds, the case would be tried in court and cause the most awful scandal; everyone would be talking about it. 'Let him go,' repeated Pat. 'We can hush it up. You don't want everybody talking about it, do you, Angus? Please consider the matter seriously! You don't want headlines in all the newspapers.' Angus saw the point. He hesitated and then said 'All right, have it your own way. He can go now—this minute—and I hope I shall never see him again.'

"I was so dazed that I was helpless. Pat hurried me out to the car and helped me to get in. He kept telling me to get a move on and drive, hell for leather. He said I had better make for Capetown, where nobody knew me. He said, 'For heaven's sake hurry before Angus changes his mind.' I had a last try. I said, 'Pat, listen! There's some mistake. I swear I didn't do it.' He turned his back and walked away.

"So that was that," said Gerald bitterly. "My best friend believed I was a thief. I started the engine and made for Capetown. I had to stop at several places on the way, of course. I don't know where I stopped. I had my suitcase with me (we had intended to go to Jo'burg for the weekend). There had been no time to go back to the bungalow for more clothes—and anyhow I had never thought of it. When I got to Capetown, I felt terribly ill. I collapsed in the street and they took me to a hospital. The doctor said it was pneumonia."

"Oh, poor Flick!" murmured Bess compassionately.

"I was there for weeks," continued Gerald. "They were good to me, so perhaps it was the best thing that could have happened. When I came out of hospital, I sold the car and managed to get a cabin in a ship bound for Southampton. I put my name down as Gerald Brown. Now you know why I'm not going to stay with you, Bess."

"Of course you're coming to stay with me!"

Gerald looked at her. She was smiling. He said in surprise, "Do you believe my story?"

"Believe it? Of course I believe it! Did you think I wouldn't believe it? Oh, Flick, what a donkey you are!"

"I thought you might not want to have me," he muttered. "I'm a down-and-out. I've lost my job and there's no hope of getting another."

"Nonsense!" Bess exclaimed. "You've let it get you down. It was a frightful shock to you—I see that—but it's over now, so you must put it behind you and start afresh. You must put it out of your mind."

"I can't," he told her. "I can't put it out of my mind because I shall never be able to get a decent job. I've tried,

37

so I know. When I apply for a post and tell them I've been chief electrician in a diamond mine, they say they'll write to the manager for a reference. You don't understand, Bess. I'm a ruined man—I'm done for. It would be better if I were dead."

"That's wicked!" cried Bess. "It's stupid too. You're young and fit. We'll find a job for you . . . but the first thing for you to do is to give yourself a good shake and get rid of your inferiority complex. Stop feeling that everyone is looking at you and —— "

"How do you know I feel like that?" he interrupted.

"It's obvious, my dear. Now listen to me. You're innocent, so you've nothing to be ashamed of."

"I feel—ashamed."

"Why?"

"I don't know, really. I feel—dirty. I feel as if the mere suspicion that I could have played such a low-down trick had—had dirtied me. Angus and Pat both believed I was a thief. So did Stafford, the X-ray man. They all thought it. Angus said I had used my position as cover. I had betrayed my trust. He said I was a traitor not only to him but to every white man in Africa."

"But you're innocent," declared Bess somewhat impatiently. "You didn't betray your trust. You aren't a traitor. The whole thing was just a stupid mistake. I wish we could get to the bottom of it and find out the truth."

"We can't," said Gerald hopelessly.

"Well, in that case you must just accept it. You've got to accept the good and the bad in life and make the best of them. I don't mean you should knuckle down—anything but! I mean it's no good trying to row against the tide. Now just do as I say," she continued. "Take a taxi and fetch your luggage. You're coming to stay with me here until you find a job."

"Bess . . ." he began earnestly.

But it was no good. She had put her fingers in her ears.

5. Gerald in Clover

Gerald was in clover: he had never been so comfortable, never occupied such a comfortable room in all his life. It was furnished as a bed-sitting-room with a solid table to write on and a couple of easy chairs. The bed was as soft and springy as a cloud. There was an electric radiator and a fixed basin—a large basin in which a man could shave and wash without crouching or knocking his head against a glass shelf. There was a good light over the mirror and a small electric plug for a razor. When Gerald had unpacked his few belongings and put them away in the drawers and cupboards, he sat down and looked about him. It struck him quite suddenly that this room looked as if it had been carefully designed and furnished for a man. What man?

However, it wasn't his business and he had no intention of asking. If Bess wanted to tell him about her private affairs, she would tell him.

Gerald had expected the life of a "star" would be hectic, but apart from her work Bess led a very quiet life. She was showered with invitations, but she refused them firmly.

"I can't do both," she explained. "I used to go to lots of parties, but it wore me out and my work suffered. You may not think it, but Aurelia is hard work."

"Of course she is! You're on the stage all the time."

"Most of the time . . . so I was obliged to cut out social

engagements. Some people think it's a pose, but it isn't. Besides I'm happier leading a peaceful life. I take Gubby for a walk in the morning and have lunch at home—Matilda knows what I like to eat. I rest in the afternoon; then I have a light early meal and go to the theatre feeling fresh. You can fit in with my routine, can't you, Flick?"

Gerald fitted in quite easily. He got up early and took Gubby for a run. He breakfasted with Matilda in the kitchen; then, when Bess was ready, they had a cup of coffee together and went for a walk. After lunch, while Bess was resting, Gerald prowled about London searching for a job. The light meal was at six o'clock. In the evening, while Bess was at the theatre, Gerald settled down to write letters. He applied for posts in all sorts of businesses, suitable and unsuitable, and answered every advertisement in the daily papers.

After ten days of this routine he felt as if he had been pursuing it for weeks.

"You're settling down nicely," Matilda told him (they were having breakfast together). "It's good for Miss Burleigh to have you. You must get a post in London and then you can live here. That is what she wants."

By this time Gerald was aware that what Miss Burleigh wanted was all that mattered to Matilda.

"I must get any sort of post—anywhere," he said desperately.

"You worry too much," Matilda told him. "I used to worry until I learnt that it was useless. It was after I stopped worrying that I met Miss Burleigh."

There was more in this little piece of philosophy than was apparent on the surface. Gerald digested it thoughtfully. "What did you do before you met Bess?" he asked.

"I was in a children's hospital in the Midlands. I was happy there—I love children and they like me because I'm small—but I had no training of course, so I was just a 'helper.' It meant that I was at everyone's beck and call; I got all the hard work to do and it was too much for me."

"So you came to London?"

40

She nodded. "I thought I could get lighter work; I wanted a job with children. I tried and tried and answered advertisements—just as you're doing, Mr. Burleigh—but when people saw my back was crooked they didn't want me."

Gerald felt so sorry for her—and so ashamed of himself—that he was speechless.

"I worried terribly just like you," added Matilda.

"But you stopped worrying?"

"I saw it was useless, worse than useless to worry, so I used my last few shillings to go and see Miss Burleigh in *Monday's Child.*"

Breakfast was finished now; Matilda rose and began to clear the table. She continued, "I've been thinking about the daily papers, Mr. Burleigh. You said they were full of horrors and that it did us no good to read about people being robbed or murdered . . . but it's good for me. I'm so happy with Miss Burleigh that I might forget to be thankful for my blessings."

Gerald looked at her. What had she to be thankful for? She worked hard, cooking and cleaning; she never went out; she had no relations or friends. There was only one person in Matilda Meredith's life; it was "Miss Burleigh."

Gerald thought this was rather frightening . . . and the more he considered the matter the more uncomfortable he felt. After a few days of observation and deduction, he began to wonder if Matilda Meredith were quite sane.

"Bess," he said, "that woman worships you."

"I know," agreed Bess thoughtfully. "I'm very fond of Matilda, but I wish she had other things in her life besides me. It's a responsibility—and sometimes it's rather a burden. There's nothing horrid about it, Flick. It's like the love of a dog." She stooped down and fondled Gubby's ears.

They were sitting on a seat in the Park. It was a real October day, mild and misty. There were very few people about and those who had braved the mist were walking past quickly.

"How did you get her?" asked Gerald.

"It was an accident. She had come to see me in *Monday's Child,* and as she was going out of the theatre, she got pushed

41

over in the crowd. They brought her into the foyer and someone came to tell me what had happened; they thought I might know who she was. I didn't know her—but I was amazed when I saw her face. She's beautiful, isn't she?"

"Yes."

"By that time the theatre was empty and a doctor was there. Matilda was lying on a sofa, unconscious. I asked the doctor if she were badly injured and he replied that as far as he could tell there was no serious injury, but she was under-nourished, so he had sent for an ambulance to take her to hospital. He said not to worry, she just needed good food."

Bess paused for a moment and then continued, "I couldn't get her face out of my mind. I dreamt about her, Flick. The next day I took some flowers and fruit and went to see her in hospital. I hadn't realised before that she was a cripple. I went and saw her several times; she's interesting and well-read, so I enjoyed talking to her. The annoying thing is that I can't go anywhere or do anything without a fuss."

"Photographers waiting for you on the doorstep," suggested Gerald.

"Worse! I don't mind a few snap-shots; I'm used to it, and press-photographers have got to live. What happened was this: My publicity agent had heard about my visits to Matilda and the ward was full of camera-men. He was there himself to superintend the proceedings. I was to be photographed bending over Matilda's bed and giving her flowers. I couldn't refuse because it would have upset Matilda; she was delighted at the idea; she wanted her picture in the papers. The other women in the ward wanted to be photographed too, so I had to let them do it, but I felt I was making capital out of their misfortunes. I was a fraud."

"You weren't a fraud."

"I was! I was! What had I done except take them a few flowers—which had cost me nothing? I smiled and smiled, the lights flashed and the cameras clicked. 'Could we have another, Miss Burleigh?' 'Oh, thank you, Miss Burleigh!' 'Just one more, Miss Burleigh. Perhaps you could hold her hand?' 'Oh, that's perfect, Miss Burleigh!' Sickening!" cried Bess angrily. "Afterwards I got hold of Albert and told him I wouldn't have my private affairs used for publicity. He said I was crazy. He said if I wouldn't go to parties or race-meetings, I must be presented to the public as a ministering angel, visiting the sick. We had a frightful row."

"Were the pictures successful?"

"Oh, yes, they were in all the papers with a lot of rubbish about Elizabeth Burleigh bringing sunshine to a hospital ward. Matilda and the other women were pleased."

"What then?" asked Gerald.

"Then, when Matilda was better, I discovered that she had nowhere to go. She had no relations, no friends who could have her, so I had her to stay for a few days; I thought she could potter about the flat and help me with the flowers. As a matter of fact I had had awful trouble with housekeepers—I had an absolutely futile one when Matilda came—so Matilda suggested that I should sack the woman and she would carry on 'until I could get someone else.' I never got someone else. Matilda just dug herself in and she's been with me ever since. She does everything except for a daily and I'm more comfortable than I've ever been in all my life."

"Wrapped in cotton-wool," murmured Gerald.

"I know." Bess sighed and added, "I'm very fond of her, but I wish she had some other interest. I wish she would go out sometimes—but she never does unless I take her in the car. I wish she could find a boy-friend, but she never will because she's sexless."

"Sexless?" asked Gerald, frowning.

"Oh, I don't mean anything like that," said Bess quickly. "She's a woman all right, but she has no sex-appeal."

Gerald said nothing to this, but he disagreed. Matilda Meredith was feminine to the tips of her fingers.

6. "Do You Remember . . . ?"

It was fun staying with Bess. They talked about their childhood. The game of "Do You Remember?" can best be played with a brother or sister. Bess and Gerald found it so enthralling that they played it for hours on end.

"Do you remember Cannochbrae?" asked Bess.

It was a Monday evening (there was no performance of *Venus* on Mondays), so they had settled down beside the fire for a comfortable chat.

"I remember some of it," Gerald replied. "I remember my nursery. I remember helping Father to feed the pigs. I remember the woods where we used to play, and of course I remember you, dancing in the hay-loft."

"Oh, the hay-loft was a perfect stage! There was a spotlight where the sunshine fell through the sky-light."

"You told me wonderful stories and acted them as you went along. Most of your stories were about beautiful ladies and handsome princes—you used to say you were going to marry Prince Charming."

"Childish dreams," said Bess sadly. "Now that I'm older and wiser I should like to marry a Man: someone big and strong and full of integrity; someone older than myself—and much more clever! A Man I should be proud to obey."

"Proud to obey?"

She nodded. "But I shall never marry."

44

"Bess!" exclaimed Gerald in surprise. "In all our games you were always the mother of a family. You had seven children; I could tell you their names! You made them real to me."

"I shall never be the mother of a family."

"Do you mean you're dedicated to your career on the stage?"

"No, I don't mean that at all! I want a woman's life; I want love and marriage and children; I want fulfilment . . . but I can never have it, never!"

"Why not?"

Bess hesitated and then replied in a low voice, "My mother suffered from melancholia."

"But, Bess, that doesn't mean——"

"It's in my family," she interrupted. "Not in yours, of course, because you had a different mother. My mother's sister is still alive. She's in a mental home."

"You mean Aunt Anna?"

"Yes, Aunt Anna. I went and stayed with her when I was a child and she cried all the time. That was the beginning of her illness. After that she was miserable off and on. Then, as she got older, she became worse. I go and see her sometimes, but it upsets me dreadfully and it upsets Aunt Anna too."

"Why go at all, Bess?"

"Matilda thinks I should. Matilda says I should go more often, but the matron of the home doesn't agree. She told me that the patient is always more difficult to manage after one of my visits."

"You should take the matron's advice. She knows what's best."

"I've sometimes wondered . . ." said Bess doubtfully. "But, you see, Aunt Anna is my only relation on my mother's side and Matilda thinks it's good for me to go and see her. Oh, poor Aunt Anna! It's pathetic, Flick! She's like a lost soul wandering in a fog . . . and the dreadful thing is that I understand. I understand only too well! It could be me."

"Darling, what nonsense! You're the sanest person I know!"

45

"Most of the time," agreed Bess. "Most of the time I'm full of life and vim, but sometimes when things go wrong I find myself going down—down—down. Then I think of Mother and Aunt Anna."

"We all go down sometimes," declared Gerald. "Honestly, Bess, you're making mountains out of molehills. You're seeing ghosts."

She nodded, "Yes, ghosts. There's a germ in me."

"A germ?"

"A germ of madness. It could develop and grow and steal away my senses. Then I should be like poor Aunt Anna, frightened of shadows." She leapt to her feet and cried, "I could play Ophelia! I understand Ophelia. I've never seen Ophelia played as I could play her!"

Bess began to wander round the room, saying—not singing—Ophelia's lines in a soft, vague, tender voice. Sometimes her voice rose a little in a questioning way, sometimes it fell to a whisper and she held out her hands groping as if she were indeed "a lost soul wandering in a fog."

" 'He is dead . . . and gone, lady. . . . White his . . . shroud as the . . . mountain snow. . . . Larded with sweet flowers. . . . They say . . . they say the owl was a baker's daughter. Lord! we know what we are, but know not what we may be! . . . I hope . . . I hope all will be well. We must be . . . patient: but I cannot choose but weep . . . My brother shall know of it: and so I thank you for your . . . your good counsel. . . . There's rosemary, that's for . . . for remembrance. Pray, love, remember: and there is pansies, that's for thoughts. . . . There's fennel for you, and . . . and columbines; there's rue for you . . . we may call it herb of grace on Sundays. . . . There's a daisy; I would give you some violets, but they . . . they . . . they withered . . . they withered all when . . . when my father died. . . .' "

Gerald listened until he could bear it no longer, then he caught her in his arms and shook her roughly. "Bess, wake up!" he cried. "Bess, be quiet! You're making my blood run cold! I can't stand it! Wake up, Bess. It's all nonsense! Of course you

46

could play Ophelia, but that means nothing. It doesn't mean you've got the seeds of madness in you; it means you're a damn good actress, that's all!"

She came to herself slowly. Then she laughed. "Oh, Flick, you are good for me! Oh, Flick, you're so solid and sensible—and so terribly strong. Look what you've done to my arm!"

"What have I done?"

She rolled up her sleeve and showed him the red marks of his fingers. "Those will be bruises tomorrow," she told him.

"I don't care! You deserved it. If you do that again, you'll get worse than bruises. Come and sit down by the fire and behave yourself."

"Yes," she agreed. "Yes, you're right. I'll make a bargain with you, Flick. I'll promise not to make your blood run cold if you'll promise not to disappear again."

"Disappear?"

"Yes, you disappeared for weeks."

"I didn't mean to, Bess. I just wanted to get a job before I saw you. I wanted to make good. I didn't want to sponge on you—as I'm doing now."

"You aren't sponging!"

"Yes, I am. I must get a job," declared Gerald desperately. "If I can't get a decent job soon, I shall hire myself to a builder to dig drains."

"Do you mean that?"

"Of course I mean it!"

"You could go to Uncle Gregor as a farm-hand," suggested Bess with a twinkle in her eye.

"Uncle Gregor! Good heavens! Is he still alive? Does he want a farm-hand?"

"Don't be absurd! It was a joke, of course. You wouldn't be the slightest use as a farm-hand. I just mentioned Uncle Gregor because I had a letter from him last week."

"Do you mean you correspond with him?"

"No. It was the first letter I have ever had from him. I never was so surprised in my life as when I saw his signature."

47

"What did he want?"

"It was a 'fan' letter," said Bess chuckling. "At least I suppose you could call it that. He said he had been to London on business and had seen me in *The Girl from Venus*. He said it was a scientific fact that there was no life on the planet Venus . . . and, in any case, people from another planet would be unable to speak English."

"What an ass the man must be!"

"Not really," said Bess thoughtfully. "I mean some people enjoy fairy-tales, others don't. I haven't answered the letter yet. I couldn't make up my mind whether to answer jokingly or seriously. Do you remember him, Flick?"

"Very tall and thin—and old. He was older than Father, wasn't he? He must be about a hundred by this time! What else did he say?"

"He said he was sorry he hadn't written to condole with me when Father died, but as there was no notice of his death in *The Scotsman*, he had only just heard of it. Then he went on to ask if I had got his mother's writing-desk. He said that unless I was anxious to keep it, he would like to have it. I don't want it, of course, but how am I to send it to him?"

"We could pack it up and send it by carrier," suggested Gerald. He paused and then added, "Father and Uncle Gregor had a row about something, didn't they?"

She nodded. "They ran the farm together for years, but they had different ideas about things. Uncle Gregor wanted to jog along in his old-fashioned way and Father wanted everything up-to-date. He wanted fertilisers and new ploughs and a tractor—but, of course, Uncle Gregor was the boss, so they agreed to part company. They divided the furniture and Uncle Gregor bought Father's share of Cannochbrae and Father got a job in London with a firm that manufactured agricultural machinery. . . . But you remember that, I suppose?"

"Not really."

"Well, you were only five when we left the farm. I was eight, so I remember it quite clearly. I was miserable," declared Bess. "We lived in a horrid little flat—it was dreadful after the freedom of dear Cannochbrae! Then Father invented an improved hay-baler which brought him quite a lot of money, so we moved."

"I remember that!" exclaimed Gerald. "We moved to Beckenham. There was a nice garden to play in and Father gave me a bike. I remember my first day at my new school, wearing my new school blazer——"

"You were terribly proud of yourself!"

"You went to school too," continued Gerald. "It was a big building at the corner of the road. You liked it much better than the school you had been to in London."

"Of course I did! St. Augusta's was fun. The girls were nice and we had dancing and singing lessons and we acted plays. We acted——"

"Wait!" exclaimed Gerald. "I'm remembering now. I went with Mother and Father to see you acting in the school-play. It was *The Tempest*—and you were Miranda. The other girls were just girls, dressed up and pretending, but you were real."

Bess nodded dreamily. "That was the beginning of it. I really *was* Miranda. I knew *then* that I wanted to go on the stage. I knew it was the one thing I could do. Father was against it, of course, but your mother understood. Your mother was terribly good to me, Flick. She helped me and encouraged me; she believed I had it in me to be a success on the stage."

"Your mother died when you were a baby, didn't she?"

Bess nodded. "Yes. I don't remember her at all and nobody told me about her."

"What do you mean?"

"I always thought your mother was my mother. It wasn't until I was seven years old that an old woman in one of the cottages told me your mother was my step-mother. It gave me an awful shock. I ran to her in distress and she explained it to me. She hugged me and kissed me and dried my tears and said I was only a year old when she married Father and she had always loved me just as much as if I had been her own child."

"It was true!"

"Yes, it was true. She was a wonderful mother to me; I loved her dearly."

They were silent for a while.

"What else do you remember?" asked Bess at last. "Do you remember my white mouse? He lived in the loft. I had to keep him there in his little cage because Aunt Maggie wouldn't have him in the house. You were very small—you couldn't have been more than three years old—so it was difficult getting you up the ladder, but you always wanted to come with me and help me to feed him. He used to sit up and wave his little front paws. One day I took a chocolate biscuit to give him. You wanted it," said Bess smiling. "You loved chocolate biscuits—but I wouldn't give it to you. I said it was for Flick."

"Flick?"

"Yes, Flick," said Bess laughing. "But Flick wasn't at home. Flick had escaped from his cage and was scampering about in the rafters—he wouldn't come down, not even to get his bicky! So you sat up on your little behind and waved your paws. 'Me-Flick' you declared solemnly. Of course you got the biscuit!"

Gerald laughed. "And I got my name! I've often wondered how I got it."

"Don't you remember anything about it?"

"Not a thing."

"You remember the van, of course?"

"What van?"

"The huge green van which came to move our furniture from Cannochbrae to London. It was so enormous that it stuck in the gateway and knocked down the gate-post."

"Oh, yes, I do!" exclaimed Gerald. "Yes, I remember my bed being carried down and put into the van." He laughed and added, "I thought we were going to live in the van like gypsies. I thought it would be fun."

"Talking of vans," said Bess. "Just wait a minute." She rose from her chair and went away.

Gerald made up the fire and waited.

Presently Bess returned with a large mahogany box inlaid with mother-of-pearl. She put it on the table. "There," she said. "Awful, isn't it? And it weighs a ton. How on earth are we going to send it?"

"Grandmother's writing-desk?"

"Yes."

"Why is it so heavy? What's in it?"

"I don't know," replied Bess. "There's no key. I've tried all the keys I've got, but none of them fit. I don't suppose it has been opened since we left Cannochbrae more than twenty years ago, but I hate the idea of sending it away without knowing its secrets—and she was our grandmother, so we have every right to see what's in it before we send it to Uncle Gregor. It's ours, Flick."

Gerald agreed. The writing-desk must have been part of their Father's share of the furniture or he wouldn't have brought it to London in the huge green van which Bess remembered so well.

Bess was so anxious to see the contents of the writing-desk that Gerald borrowed a bunch of small keys from a friendly jeweller and spent some time wrestling with the lock—but in vain. Finally they decided that the desk must be despatched to Cannochbrae unopened.

"I suppose it must," said Bess. "It wouldn't do to break the lock, would it? But how are we to send it?"

"Ask Uncle Gregor," replied Gerald. "You've got to answer his letter, haven't you?"

"I hate writing letters," she declared. Then she smiled and added, "I know! You want a job, don't you? You can write to Uncle Gregor. Write a nice letter, Flick. It was kind of the old thing to come and see me in *Venus*—and we don't want to prolong the silly feud."

7. The Winged Steed

Somewhat to his surprise Gerald found Uncle Gregor's letter difficult to answer. He began by explaining that he had just returned from Africa and was staying with Bess. He went on to say that Bess was very busy, so she had asked him to write in her stead.

Gerald continued:

> Bess is very pleased to hear that you came to see her in *The Girl from Venus*. If she had known you were in town, she would have sent you a complimentary ticket. The play is not based upon scientific data. It is a fairy-tale—like Cinderella—and is merely intended as an evening's entertainment. Bess asks me to tell you that she has got the inlaid mahogany writing-desk which belonged to our grandmother. She is delighted that you should have it, but wonders how to send it to you. It is very heavy and has no key. If you are coming south again in the near future, perhaps you could take it back with you? We are both very pleased to hear you are in good form and able to walk for miles over the hills. No doubt it is the fine air of Cannochbrae which has kept you so fit and healthy.
>
> We both send kindest regards.
>
> Yours very sincerely,
> Gerald Burleigh-Brown.

When Gerald had finished the letter and read it over, he decided that it was rather stilted, but Bess was delighted with it.

"How clever you are!" she exclaimed. "You can answer some of my fan mail for me. Can you use a typewriter?"

"But you've got a secretary, haven't you? Doesn't she answer your letters?"

"Some of them require a personal reply," replied Bess. She fetched a large cardboard box and emptied it onto the floor. "There," she said, smiling. "You can answer those for me. They are from men who want to take me out to dinner or marry me, or from men who are married already and want to take me for a holiday to Paris. I can't give them to Miss Barling to answer because she would be shocked."

"What am I to say to them?" asked Gerald, looking at the pile of letters in distaste.

"Anything you like," replied Bess chuckling. "Say thank you, of course, and tell them I'm married and I'm too busy looking after my five children to accept their invitations. Tell them my husband is terribly jealous and always carries a revolver in his pocket. I don't mind what you say as long as you make them understand that it's No Good."

Gerald was reluctant to undertake the task, but he realised that it would be ungrateful to refuse. He was accepting the hospitality of Bess—she wouldn't allow him to pay a penny towards his keep—so the least he could do was to write a few letters for her. He typed the answers neatly and gave them to Bess to sign. They were quite short letters, polite but firm, and were designed to make it perfectly clear to the recipients that Miss Burleigh was not interested in their proposals, honourable or otherwise.

More letters arrived daily and it became a pleasant habit for Gerald to go to his famous sister's room while she was having her breakfast and to sit on her bed and open them for her. Most of them could be answered by Miss Barling; the "funny ones" were put aside for Gerald to deal with.

Gerald had noticed that Bess always wore a platinum chain round her neck—it was there every morning so, presumably, she even wore it at night—and one morning he asked what was at the end of the chain.

"Oh, it's just for luck," replied Bess casually. "I'll show it to you some time . . . if you're good. Look, Flick, here's your reply from Uncle Gregor! Read it and tell me what he says."

Uncle Gregor's letter was short but friendly. It consisted of an invitation to spend a week at the farm and "enjoy the fine hill air." He had added in a postscript, "Bring the desk with you" . . . which amused Gerald considerably, for obviously the invitation was prompted by Uncle Gregor's desire to obtain his mother's writing-desk in the easiest and cheapest way.

"What's the joke?" enquired Bess.

"He's a canny Scot, that's all. There, read it yourself!" Gerald replied, handling Bess the effusion.

"Oh!" cried Bess. "Oh, what fun! How I wish I could come with you!"

"Come with me? But I'm not going! Nothing would induce me to go!"

"Of course you must go! If I could get away from *Venus* for a week, we'd have a gorgeous time—but I can't, so it's no good thinking about it."

"But, Bess, I can't wander off to Scotland! I've got to find a job."

Bess took no notice. She continued dreamily, "Cannochbrae is lovely. It's a farm on the moors, miles from anywhere. There are sheep on the hills and salmon in the river. Father used to fish. Sometimes he took me with him—it was fun. You said you remembered the cave. You must go and see it, of course——"

"But, Bess——"

"And you must go and see Mrs. Inglis. She was our cook at Cannochbrae. I used to go into the kitchen and chat to her; she was very kind to me and I loved her dearly. Then, later, she married the grocer in the village and had two sons. I didn't see her after that, but she always sent me a card for my birthday. Now she has stopped sending me a card and doesn't answer my letters, so I want to know what's happened to her."

"She's probably dead . . . and anyhow I can't go. I don't want to go."

"You'll enjoy it, Flick. I'll lend you my car; that's the best way to take the writing-desk."

"I didn't know you had a car."

"Oh, I don't use him in town—parking is such a bother—but on fine Sunday afternoons (and sometimes on Mondays, when there's no *Venus*) I take him for a spin into the country. It will do you a lot of good, Flick. Once you are on the road, heading north, you'll forget all your worries . . . and it will be good for Grandpa to have a nice long run to Scotland."

"Grandpa is your car, I presume. May I ask how old he is?" enquired Gerald apprehensively.

Bess chuckled. "Don't worry! He's only a year old. I just call him Grandpa because he's such a pet. We'll take him out for a little spin next Sunday so that you'll get used to him before you go to Cannochbrae."

"Look here, Bess!" said Gerald. "If you're determined that I'm to go to Cannochbrae, I'll go—but not before I've found myself a job."

"Well, we'll see," replied Bess, smiling in a sphinx-like manner.

Sunday was a fine dry day, so they walked down together to the garage. Bess opened the big doors and displayed her "pet," which proved to be a long, low sports car with a sliding roof and the equivalent of forty horses beneath his highly polished bonnet.

"Good heavens, you must have paid a lot for that!" exclaimed Gerald in awed tones.

"Yes," replied Bess simply. She added, "I work hard and make a lot of money, so why shouldn't I spend some on something I enjoy?"

"No reason at all," Gerald agreed.

"I enjoy speed, Flick."

"So do I," he admitted.

While they were talking the garage-man came out of his house and Bess introduced him. "This is Leonard," she explained. "Leonard helped me to buy Grandpa and looks after him for me. Leonard doesn't approve of me calling him Grandpa."

"Cars are ladies," said Leonard. He started the engine and backed the car into the yard. "She's a beauty," said Leonard. "It's a pleasure to look after a car like this. You don't take her out often enough, Miss Burleigh."

"I'm so busy," lamented Miss Burleigh.

"Of course you're busy," agreed Leonard. "I've been to see *Venus* three times. You're super, Miss Burleigh—if you don't mind me saying so. I like the bit where the little dark chap tries to make up to you and you tell him there's nothing doing. It made me laugh fit to bust! My sister Ella that lives with me liked the sad bit at the end when the space-ship comes for you and you've got to go back to Venus. You've married the tall chap with the fair hair and you want to stay with him, but the two nasty bits of work won't let you. So you say goodbye.

" 'Goodbye to the World of Summer Flowers,' " carolled Leonard in a pleasant baritone.

"Why, you've got a lovely voice, Leonard!" exclaimed Miss Burleigh in delight.

"I sing in the choir at St. Rude's," replied Leonard, blushing with pleasure. He continued, "Then the tall chap that you've married picks a bunch of flowers for you and you walk away slowly and sadly and you get into the space-ship and off you go. You've dropped a rose on the way and the chap picks it up and kisses it. Ella cried buckets—everybody was crying—it was so real."

Miss Burleigh accepted the tribute graciously. "Yes, it's good theatre," she said.

"We were wondering what happened after that," said Leonard. "Ella was wondering. Most of the chaps that had dangled after you went back to their wives and sweethearts, of course."

"Yes, and lived happily ever after."

"Yes, but what about the tall chap who really loved you? Ella thinks you came back to Earth——"

"No," said Miss Burleigh. "No, I didn't come back."

"Never?" asked Leonard anxiously. "We thought perhaps someday——"

"No, Leonard," said Miss Burleigh, shaking her head sadly. "No, I never came back."

There was a short silence. The gentle purr of Grandpa's engine was the only sound.

"Are you going far this afternoon, Miss Burleigh?" asked Leonard.

"No," she replied. "It's just to let my brother try the car. He's going to Scotland soon; I don't know when, exactly."

"Scotland? Wish I were going! You get nice clear roads in Scotland. Traffic is bothersome in a big powerful car. What part of Scotland will you be going to, sir? I took an American family to John o'Groat's—that's as far as you can go."

Gerald said he wasn't going as far. (He had only a vague idea of where he was going, but he was aware that his uncle's farm was at a village called Haines and that the nearest town was Drumburly.)

"You should go to John o'Groat's," declared Leonard, adding reminiscently, "Lovely clear roads in Scotland."

Gerald was amused at Leonard's reaction to Scotland. The bens and burns did not appeal to him. It was the "lovely clear roads."

Bess settled herself comfortably in the driving-seat and fastened the safety belt. Gerald got in beside her. At first the traffic was dense and it was not until they had wound their way out of the bewildering mass of cars and buses that the driver could satisfy her craving for speed.

"Now I'll show you what he can do!" she said cheerfully and the car bounded forward like a greyhound released from the slips.

Gerald had said he enjoyed speed, but when the speedometer needle crept up to ninety, his toes curled up inside his shoes and he remonstrated mildly.

57

"I just wanted to show you," said Bess. "As a matter of fact I've been up to a hundred. Now we'll change places and you can have a go."

They changed places and Gerald had his first lesson in driving Grandpa. He found it much more difficult than he had expected and even a little alarming. His own old car (which he had sold in Capetown) had been a very different machine. It seemed to Gerald that his car was alive—and he said so.

"Yes, he's alive. He's a wingéd steed," agreed his owner.

"You should call him Pegasus."

"That's not a bad idea," she admitted. "We could call him Peg for short, couldn't we? Leonard would be pleased. You're smiling, Flick, but Leonard is very important to me, so I like to please him. He's as good as a private chauffeur—in fact he's better! Those Americans he told you about were so pleased with him that they gave him enough money to buy a second-hand Daimler. He had it done up—like new—and he got himself a uniform and he's on tap whenever I want him. He takes me to the theatre and brings me home and I have him for shopping sometimes . . . and he looks after Grandpa beautifully. Peg, I mean."

"Does he hire himself out to other people too?"

"Yes, he makes a good thing out of it," replied Bess.

Gerald discovered that it was quite easy to drive Peg on an open road, but the array of knobs and switches on the dashboard was extremely puzzling and Peg was so "alive" that he was apt to take the bit between his teeth and bolt. He was difficult to manage in traffic and not very easy to park.

Gerald decided to ask Leonard to give him a few lessons before starting off on his own.

"Yes, that's a good idea," agreed Bess. "You'll enjoy the trip much more if you're used to Peg . . . and I don't suppose it will matter to Uncle Gregor when you go."

8. The Stage Box

Gerald had been living at the flat for three weeks by this time and, in spite of the fact that he couldn't find a job, he felt a great deal better. It was Bess, of course. Bess was giving him back his self-respect. Perhaps his room had helped too. You couldn't occupy such a comfortable room and continue to feel dirty. On several occasions Gerald had been given a free seat for *Venus*—either in the stalls or the dress circle—and he had followed the plot with interest. It was quite a good plot and the songs were catchy, but it was Bess who "made" the play. The play wouldn't have been worth seeing without Bess as Aurelia.

One day Bess asked him if he would like the stage box. "You can have it on Wednesday night," said Bess. "It has been returned, so I asked Thwaites if you could have it. You can have it all to yourself. I thought it would be fun for you."

Gerald hesitated—but only for a moment. He had never sat in a stage box before; it would be amusing to sit there alone in his glory! He decided that he must "dress the part."

Bess had helped him to augment his scanty wardrobe. He had bought a good lounge suit, a dinner-jacket and so on but not "tails" of course. However, he could hire tails for the occasion and a white waistcoat and tie. He could buy a white carnation for his button-hole. It would please Bess to see him looking smart!

These plans were carried out in secret and when Gerald

was ready, he surveyed his reflection in the long mirror in his bedroom with approval. This was a very different person from the wretched creature who had cowered in his cabin reading *The Adventures of Robinson Crusoe!*

Just to complete the picture Gerald engaged a taxi to take him to the theatre and stopped on the way to purchase a sumptuous bouquet which he could hand to Aurelia from the stage box.

Mr. Thwaites was waiting for him in the foyer and obviously was impressed with his appearance. He shook hands and said, "It's a great pleasure to meet Miss Burleigh's brother. I was not aware that she had any relations."

"I've been in Africa for years," explained Gerald.

"Quite so," agreed Mr. Thwaites.

This little conversation being over, Miss Burleigh's brother was conducted to the stage box.

Gerald had come early on purpose to watch the audience arriving and finding their seats. He realised that a good many people were staring at him, but secure in his knowledge that he was looking his best, he rather enjoyed the interest he was arousing.

When the curtain rose, Gerald discovered that the stage box was a little too near the stage. He could see things that he was not meant to see and although it was amusing, it destroyed the illusion. However, he was not too near to see Bess for there was no illusion about her. Gerald could never think of her as Aurelia; she was just her own dear natural self.

Gerald wondered about this: Was Bess really an actress? Could she play a part foreign to her nature? He could "see" her as Shakespeare's Rosalind—she would make a very good Rosalind! He could "see" her as Portia . . . but, no, he couldn't "see" her as Lady Macbeth nor as one of Shaw's sophisticated ladies. Then suddenly he remembered he had seen her as Ophelia . . . and he shivered.

These reflections occupied Gerald's mind during the first interval, so he did not take much notice of the audience. The second interval was longer and he took the opportunity of looking round the theatre. There were three people in the fourth row of the stalls who seemed to be particularly interested in him. They were gazing at him through opera glasses.

Good heavens, they were the Harrimans! They were Mr. and Mrs. Harriman and Marion!

Gerald gasped and drew back instinctively . . . but then he realised that they did not know him (there were no signs of recognition on their faces); they were just looking at him, talking earnestly to each other, and then looking at him again.

The next moment there was a gentle tap on the door of the box and Penelope stood there, smiling rather shyly.

"Penelope!" he exclaimed.

"I had to come," she said. "It's a bit forward of me, but I just wanted to say 'Hullo.' "

"It's very nice of you," said Gerald, rising. "Come in and sit down, won't you?"

"I won't come in; the family might see me! They were interested in you—they couldn't think why they sort of knew your face—but I had promised to keep your secret, so I didn't tell them." Penelope giggled in an attractive manner and added, "Marion is sure she's seen you before—somewhere. Mother thinks you're an Earl."

"Thinks I'm an Earl?" asked Gerald incredulously.

Penelope nodded. "You look like somebody important, so she thinks she must have seen your picture in the papers."

"Oh, I see!"

"You look—quite different," added Penelope.

Gerald knew this already. "Fine feathers make fine birds," he suggested.

"But it isn't only the feathers—it's you. Have the clouds blown away?"

"No, not really, but I'm staying with Bess. She's good for me. She has made me see my troubles in the right perspective. She says you've got to accept good things and bad things in life and make the best of them."

"She's a lovely person," Penelope declared. "Mother thinks she's the most wunnerful thing that ever happened. We've

61

been to see *Venus* three times and Mother wants to come again, so we've got the stage box for Friday night. Mother is just crazy to meet Miss Burleigh," added Penelope, looking at Gerald hopefully.

Gerald hesitated. Then he said, "I'll ask Bess, but I can't promise anything. Aurelia is hard work, so she has to rest a good deal."

"Oh, I know!" agreed Penelope. "We don't want to bother her, but if we could just speak to her for a minute . . ."

"I'll ask Bess," repeated Gerald. "I'll write to you if I can arrange it. Are you staying at the Savoy?"

She smiled and shook her head. "We stopped at the Savoy last time we were over, but Father said we might as well have been at the Waldorf. He wanted to see 'the real England,' so he reserved accommodations at the Country House Hotel near Windsor Castle where there are fourteen bedrooms and three bathrooms."

"Local colour," suggested Gerald.

"That's right," agreed Penelope. "Father likes 'local colour' and Mother likes being near the Royal Family (we've seen the Queen twice driving through Windsor), so they're both happy. Marion isn't so happy; she likes a private bathroom with a shower."

"What about you?" asked Gerald smiling.

"I'm always happy," she replied.

Gerald thought this was true. She was a fairy-like little creature with a sunny nature. She was charming.

"I must fly!" exclaimed Penelope. "They'll wonder why I've been so long in the powder-room. Please try to fix it, Mr. Burleigh-Brown! Mother would be out of her wits with joy." She scribbled her address on the edge of her programme, gave it to Gerald, and fled.

"Now you've done it!" said Gerald to himself.

He could not think why he had done it—the last thing he had intended was to get involved with the Harrimans—but Penelope really was a dear, and it had seemed churlish to refuse! If Bess agreed to meet them, he could take them round to

62

her dressing-room on Friday night after the show; if not, a polite little note to Miss Penelope Harriman would end the matter.

Gerald had intended to ask Bess about the Harrimans on the way home in the car, but Bess was tired, so he didn't bother her. She was so exhausted that she lay back in her corner with closed eyes.

After a few minutes she said feebly, "I'm awfully tired, Flick."

"I know, darling. Don't talk," he replied.

"I never thanked you," said Bess, disobeying the command. "You looked marvellous and the flowers were lovely. There were more bouquets than ever tonight and we didn't deserve them. It was bad—bad—bad tonight. When it goes badly, it wears me out and I go down—down—down, like Aunt Anna."

"But, Bess, it didn't go badly!"

"It was Arnold. He was in one of his moods. He did everything just a little bit wrong. He did it on purpose. It put the timing out and upset everyone. I told him he was being a swine and he said it was because he loved me. He keeps on saying it. He says he's mad about me."

"He sounds an absolute bounder," declared Gerald, adding savagely, "I'll beat him up if you give the word."

"It wouldn't be any use," said the tired voice which was so unlike the voice of Elizabeth Burleigh.

Gerald found a hand under the rug and held it firmly.

"Nice Flick," said Bess with a sigh.

When they arrived at the flat, Bess went straight to bed with Matilda in attendance—Matilda fussing over her like a hen with one chick—but presently Matilda came into the dining-room where Gerald was having supper to ask if he had everything he wanted.

"Yes, thank you," he replied.

"I've given Miss Burleigh a glass of warm milk and one of her tablets," explained Matilda. "She'll be better in the morning. It was Mr. Knight who upset her."

"Yes, she said he was 'in one of his moods,' but I saw nothing wrong."

"Nobody would see anything wrong, but Miss Burleigh would know that it wasn't as good as it should be. Nothing must interfere with the play. That's why Miss Burleigh doesn't go out to parties." Matilda hesitated for a moment and then added, "I was worried about her, so I asked Dr. Ainslie. He's a very good doctor and often comes to see her."

"Dr. Ainslie?"

"He lives downstairs, so I can always get him at a moment's notice."

"What do you mean?" asked Gerald in alarm.

"She needs a lot of care, Mr. Burleigh. But I'm here so I can look after her. I shall never leave her, so you needn't worry."

Matilda would say no more . . . but Gerald spent rather a disturbed night.

However, the next morning when he went to his sister's room he found her in very good form; her cheeks were pink and her voice had regained its usual timbre.

"You're all right!" exclaimed Gerald in relief.

"I was tired, that was all," she replied. "You weren't worried about me, were you?"

"I was—a bit. Matilda said——"

"Oh, Matilda! She likes fussing. Sometimes her fussing becomes rather a burden, but she means well, of course. Last night I was angry with Arnold. When I get in a rage, it always makes me tired. It's silly, isn't it?"

"You had good cause to be angry, but honestly nobody could possibly have noticed that anything was wrong."

"It has got to be right, whether anyone notices or not."

"Elizabeth Burleigh is a perfectionist!"

"Yes, I suppose I am," agreed Elizabeth Burleigh smiling. "It seems to me that if you undertake a job, you should do your very best to carry it out successfully. Sometimes you don't feel like doing it, but you must do it just the same. In fact you must do it better."

"Is there no chance of your getting a little holiday, Bess?"

"Not till April. My contract ends in April. They want me to sign another, for a tour in the United States, but I refused. They're all very angry with me (and I feel rather a pig because they can't go without me), but by that time I shall be thoroughly tired of Aurelia and I must have a rest. I *must* have a rest, Flick."

"Of course you must," Gerald agreed. "Surely they realise that you're carrying the whole play on your shoulders. Just you stick to your decision and don't let them persuade you."

She nodded.

"Bess," said Gerald, "some people called Harriman were there last night. I met them coming home in the ship. They're terribly keen to speak to you—just a few words would do. They've been to *Venus* three times and they're going again on Friday."

"Oh, well, I don't suppose it would kill me to speak to them," said Bess cheerfully.

"It's just as you like. I told her I might not be able to arrange it."

"Her?" asked Bess enquiringly.

"Miss Penelope Harriman. They're Americans. Mr. Harriman is a millionaire."

"A millionaire?"

"Dollars, of course," said Gerald hastily.

"Oh, of course," agreed Bess, hiding a smile. "But even in dollars it's a good deal of money. Is she very pretty?"

"Yes, very—and very nice. I mean she isn't a bit spoilt; she's natural and friendly and kind."

"They're staying at the Savoy, I suppose?"

Gerald chuckled. "That's what I thought, but I had guessed wrong . . ." and he went on to tell Bess what Penelope had said about the Country House Hotel.

"They sound amusing," declared Bess, laughing. "I'd like to meet them, Flick. We'll have a party. That's the best plan."

"Oh, no, not a party!" exclaimed Gerald in dismay. "It would be much too tiring for you . . . and I don't want to meet people."

"Why? It's fun meeting people. You met lots of people during the voyage home, I suppose. Why have you suddenly gone shy?"

"I haven't suddenly gone shy. You don't understand, Bess."

"No, I don't."

"Don't you see that I can't meet people and talk to them because . . . well, because I should feel a fraud? I should know all the time that if they knew about me, they wouldn't want to speak to me. I can't tell everyone I meet my story and I can't talk comfortably to people who don't know it."

"Flick, that's nonsense! People just take you as they find you. They don't want to know your whole life-story; all they want is a friendly chat."

Gerald thought about this seriously. Perhaps it was true.

"Most people have secrets," added Bess. "Much worse things than being accused of something they didn't do. We'll have a party," she repeated firmly. "It will kill two birds with one stone . . . it will kill quite a lot of birds with one stone. We'll have it here, in the flat, on Monday night; there isn't a show on Mondays. Shall I send your friends a card or will it do to ring up?"

"Who are the other birds?" asked Gerald apprehensively.

Bess smiled and said, "You answer first—then I'll tell you."

"Oh, it will do to ring up. They'll be thrilled to bits. They're just crazy to meet the wunnerful Miss Burleigh!"

"Is that how Penelope talks?"

"No, she doesn't," replied Gerald. "She was at a school near Ascot for a year and most of the time she speaks like an English girl. Just sometimes when she gets excited she comes out with an American expression. It's very intriguing. I like the way she says 'wunnerful' . . . and she has an attractive giggle."

"A giggle?"

"It's a sort of chortle," explained Gerald.

"Well, you seem to have got yourself a job, Flick."

"Got a job? What do you mean?"

"The son-in-law of an American millionaire will have lots to keep him busy."

"Good lord, I'm not going to marry her!" cried Gerald. "I scarcely know the girl; she's just a chance acquaintance. Besides, you seem to have forgotten that I was sacked for stealing diamonds!"

"Does Penelope know your secret?" asked Bess with interest.

"Not really. I just told her I had lost my job; I was a failure—a man under a cloud."

"And she wasn't put off?"

"No, she didn't seem to be."

"Strange," said Bess, trying not to laugh.

"Oh, shut up!" Gerald exclaimed. "You're being silly. I've told you she's just a chance acquaintance. I've spoken to her twice: once in the ship, the night before we docked; the second time last night in the theatre. All she wanted was an introduction to you. There, that's the truth."

"You don't waste time, do you, little brother?"

"Oh, shut up!" repeated Gerald crossly.

"All right, all right! I won't tease you any more. Go and ring up Penelope and speak to her for the third time."

"But what about the other birds?"

"What other birds?"

"The ones you're going to kill with the same stone."

"Oh, yes, of course! Well, I want to introduce you to my friends."

"But, Bess, I've told you——"

"But I'm telling you," she interrupted. "Now listen, Flick. They all know you're staying with me and some of them are talking about it in a catty sort of way, so——"

"A catty sort of way?"

"Oh, *you* know," said Bess, chuckling. "'Her *brother* is staying with her, my dear!' 'I never knew Bess had a *brother*.

Funny, isn't it?' Then shrieks of ribald mirth. As a matter of fact," continued Bess, "that was why I asked Thwaites for the stage box for you. I thought if they saw you sitting there, they would believe in you and it would put a stop to the silly talk (I'm getting a bit sick of it) and then you turned up looking like a Prince of the Royal Blood with an enormous bouquet for me!"

"Oh, Bess, I thought you'd be pleased!"

"Darling, of course I was pleased! It was sweet of you to take so much trouble to please me . . . but you see what I mean, don't you?"

Gerald saw. "If you had told me——" he began.

"Oh, I didn't want to make a fuss about it! How could I guess that you would turn up looking like that? The girls all said you were gorgeous."

"So now they think——"

"They think the worst," said Bess cheerfully. "That's why I want to have a party and introduce you to everyone."

"But we aren't alike."

"No, but you look so respectable. You'll enjoy it," declared Bess earnestly. "I shall ask them from eight to ten, so they can't stay after midnight—and I shall get lovely eats from Fortnum's and lots of booze. I don't often give a party, but when I do, I like to do it in style. I shall lay on a couple of waiters (Matilda prefers to remain in the background on these occasions) and I shall——"

"Will they mix all right?" interrupted Gerald anxiously.

"Of course they'll mix. Anything new is a 'draw' and Americans are usually friendly and decorative. There," added Bess, smiling. "Now that you know about 'the other birds' you better go and ring up your little American bird and see if she and her family would like to come to our party."

"Wild horses wouldn't keep them away," Gerald declared.

He was right of course. The Harrimans accepted Miss Burleigh's invitation rapturously.

9. Miss Burleigh's Evening Party

On Monday night Gerald was ready in good time for the party. He had returned the tail coat, which had made such an impression on "the girls," and was wearing the dinner-jacket and etceteras, which he had bought "off the peg."

It was ten minutes to eight when he knocked on his sister's door to ask her if there was anything she would like him to do. He was surprised to find her in her dressing-gown.

"Oh, you're ready?" she exclaimed. "How nice you look! Almost too nice. It would really be better if you weren't so attractive—but of course you want to look nice for Penelope, so it can't be helped."

"It's five to eight," said Gerald. He was feeling to nervous and strung up to argue with Bess.

"Oh, they won't be here for ages. People never come to a party at the right time. It just isn't done. They'll drift in about half-past-eight and if they're enjoying themselves, they'll stay on until midnight." She sat down at her dressing-table and began to brush her hair.

"But the Harrimans won't know that," objected Gerald, frowning anxiously. "You told me to ask them at eight."

"Oh, I expect it's the same in America. Don't fuss, Flick. Anyhow if they *do* come early, you can cope with them can't you?"

"But Bess, it's you the Harrimans want to see!"

"They'll see me when I'm ready."

"There's the bell!" cried Gerald in alarm.

"Don't fuss," repeated Bess. "You're delaying me."

"It *is* the Harrimans," declared Gerald in anguished tones. "I can hear Mr. Harriman's voice. What am I to say to them? It will be embarrassing for them if they think they've arrived too early. What am I to say?"

"Oh," said Bess, listening with her head on one side. "Yes, you're right, Flick. You had better say I wanted them to come before the other guests so that we could have a quiet little chat."

"Yes, of course!" agreed Gerald. "Yes, that's what I'll say ... but *do* hurry up, Bess."

"I'm nearly ready, but I'm not going to hurry. I must get my face done properly. Make-up takes time."

"Why bother? Your face is much nicer without that muck all over it," retorted Gerald. It was a good "exit line," so he went out upon it.

The hired waiter had put the Harrimans into the drawing-room. Gerald hesitated outside the door. He was nervous of meeting them. In fact he was terrified (not of Penelope, but of the others). During the voyage his behaviour had been rude and ungracious. He had repulsed their advances and had refused Mr. Harriman's invitation to drinks. Now he would have to play the part of a welcoming host. They would think he was mad! However, it couldn't be helped.

Gerald opened the door and went in. Fortunately the Harrimans seemed to have forgotten his bear-like behaviour. Mrs. Harriman asked anxiously if he were better.

"Much better, thank you. So nice of you to come," said Gerald as he shook hands with them. He added, "My sister has been delayed—she's very busy, you know—but she will be here in a few minutes. She asked you to come at eight because she wants a quiet chat with you before the other guests arrive."

"I'm just longing to meet her," declared Mrs. Harriman.

"This is a beautiful apartment," said Mr. Harriman. "I've been admiring those cute little china houses. They're very unusual."

He was looking at the china houses, which were arranged on a broad shelf in an alcove with a light above them to show them off.

"Oh, Bess loves her china houses," replied Gerald. "They're Rockingham, you know."

"Rockingham?"

"Yes."

"Where can you buy them, Mr. Burleigh?"

Gerald didn't know.

"You can buy most things you want at Harrods," suggested Mrs. Harriman.

"I want a whole set," declared Marion. "I could give them to Clem."

"Good idea," said Penelope. "Then you would have them yourself for keeps."

They both laughed.

Gerald felt pretty certain that you couldn't walk into Harrods' china department and order "a whole set" of Rockingham china houses. He tried to explain this to his guests. "These are old," he said. "Bess picks them up at sales or in antique shops. She knows a lot about china. You want the real thing, not cheap imitations——"

There was a chorus of agreement. Quite definitely they wanted "the real thing."

"Well, you must ask Bess," said Gerald. He added, "And here she is!"

Here she was, in a simple evening gown of cream lace, her only ornament a large emerald on the platinum chain about her neck, and her marvellous copper-coloured hair shining like a halo.

"Beautiful," murmured Mr. Harriman under his breath.

The conversation, which had been a trifle sticky, became general. Bess was perfect. She was warm and friendly and charming. It was as if the sun had come out on a grey day. In a few moments she had made them feel comfortable; they were all talking and laughing as if they had known each other for years. Mrs. Harriman was explaining that the first moment she had

71

seen Miss Burleigh—in *Monday's Child*—she had fallen in love with her, straight off. Marion said it was wunnerful to meet Miss Burleigh and her only regret was that Clem couldn't be there to share the pleasure. Mr. Harriman said meeting Miss Burleigh informally in her own beautiful home was something he would never forget.

Penelope whispered, "She's like sunshine."

"Let's sit down while we can," suggested Bess.

They sat down. Gerald found himself sitting on a sofa beside Penelope. He wondered if Bess had arranged this. If so, she had done it with so much social aplomb that it had seemed a natural arrangement.

Penelope said in a low voice, "I just can't tell you how grateful I am. They're very happy tonight."

"Your parents?"

She nodded. "They're older now, and they don't really enjoy getting about. They sacrifice themselves for Marion and me! Next year they will be able to stop comfortably at home."

"You aren't coming over next year?" asked Gerald.

"Sure, we are!" said Penelope, smiling. "We're planning the trip already, but Marion and Clem will be married by that time, so Clem will bring us and look after us. Clem is a dear; he doesn't mind having me around."

"Who would?" said Gerald.

"Most men would," she replied. "Most men would sooner have a honeymoon *à deux* . . . but I'll do my best to keep out of the way."

Meanwhile Bess had given Mr. Harriman a great deal of information about Rockingham china (which had been eagerly absorbed) and was looking about for something else to interest him . . . but he had found something for himself. He was examining the fireplace.

"That's very pretty," he said admiringly.

"It's a copy of an Adam fireplace," Bess explained.

"Adam?" asked Mr. Harriman.

"The Adam brothers were architects, you know. They designed Charlotte Square in Edinburgh and the Adelphi and

72

Royal Crescent in Bath and big country houses: Kedleston Hall and Lansdowne House and—and many others."

"When did they live, Miss Burleigh?"

"Oh, about two hundred years ago. There was a lot of building going on in those days."

"They were famous men?"

"Yes, very. Robert Adam was buried in Westminster Abbey."

"Amongst the kings and poets," said Mr. Harriman, nodding.

It was obvious that he was impressed and would have liked to know more about the famous brothers, but Bess had just about come to the end of her information about them, so she turned and smiled at Mrs. Harriman. It was time Mrs. Harriman received a little attention.

Mrs. Harriman said she would like to see over the apartment—if it wasn't too much trouble.

"No trouble at all," replied Bess cheerfully. "I'd like to show you over."

They went off together; Mr. Harriman and Marion followed.

"They're terribly interested," Penelope explained. "You see, Mr. Burleigh, when we come over here we stop in hotels and look at cathedrals and castles and ruins, but very few of us see a home where people live."

Gerald took the point. He realised that if he were to go to America—or anywhere else for that matter—he would much rather see "a home where people live" than a ruin inhabited by owls and jackdaws. Other travellers might think differently, but that was his idea.

"Oh, we're interested in history too! Marion adores ruins," declared Penelope. She added, "But we're wasting time. They'll be back any minute and I wanted to ask if you have found a suitable post."

"No, and I'm afraid it will be very difficult. You see, Penelope," said Gerald earnestly, "I've been working in a diamond mine for three years. I went there as assistant electri-

73

cian and was given the post as chief electrician when my boss retired."

"That sounds pretty good."

"It was. I liked the work and I had a very nice little bungalow."

"Why did you give it up?"

"I was sacked for stealing diamonds," replied Gerald. He had decided to say it, for (as he had explained to Bess) he felt that it wasn't right to make friends with people until he had told them his story . . . but he waited somewhat anxiously for Penelope's reaction.

Penelope took the disclosure calmly. She said, "But you shouldn't have let them sack you. You should have told them you were innocent and made them find out who had done it."

"The diamonds were found sewn into the lining of my jacket."

"Someone must have put them there," Penelope pointed out.

"My best friend thought I had done it myself."

"The one who let you down," said Penelope, nodding. "You told me about him and I said he couldn't be a real friend. If he had been a real friend, he would have known you better."

"But, Miss Harriman——"

"You'd better go on saying 'Penelope.'"

"I didn't know I had begun!" he exclaimed.

She laughed. "You've done it several times—and it sounds friendly. Miss Burleigh calls you 'Flick,' but I guess that's a pet name?"

"Some of my friends call me 'Gerry.'"

"'Gerry' is nice," Penelope said. "Now listen, Gerry. Marion was a bit surprised when I told her you had asked us to the party. She wondered how I knew you—and why I hadn't told her before—so I said you had been sick and hospitalised for weeks. I said that was why you didn't want to talk to people. I said you were recovering now. I had to explain," she added, looking at him a little anxiously.

"Was she annoyed?"

"Not really; she was too excited about the party. I hope you don't mind my saying you were sick?"

"It was true. I was sick at heart."

"That's the worst kind of sickness," said Penelope, nodding thoughtfully.

Soon after half-past-eight the other guests began to arrive. Bess insisted that her brother should stand beside her to receive them and be introduced.

"The party is really for you," she told him. "Try to remember their names; it will be difficult for you, but people like it."

It was very difficult indeed, for they came in groups, several people at once—then a breathing space, and then another lot—and, in a curious sort of way, they all looked alike: the men in dinner-suits and the women in evening frocks, with bare shoulders and arms and painted faces—and they were all extremely gay. Bess introduced them as Joy and Sonia and David and Dick and Arnold and Cynthia and Myrtle . . . and so on. Gerald memorised the first few names, then came a surging crowd and he was completely baffled.

Some of the guests kissed Bess; others seized both her hands and exclaimed, "More beautiful every day!" or something equally fatuous.

They greeted Gerald in a friendly manner—or else facetiously:

"It must be fun staying with Bess!"

"Where have you been hiding?"

"Why haven't we been allowed to see you before?"

"Does Bess keep you locked up in the coal cellar?"

Gerald tried to play up. He laughed and said, "I've been abroad for years—just got home last week. Yes, it's tremendous fun staying with Bess. We talk for hours and hours about old times."

"Bess is marvellous as 'The Girl,' isn't she?" said Joy—or Sonia. (He wasn't sure which.)

"Yes, marvellous," agreed Gerald. "But I saw her in her first play—the very first."

"That was *Knock at the Door*," said Arnold. "Bess was the parlourmaid."

"No, it was *The Tempest* and Bess was Miranda," Gerald replied.

There were shrieks of surprise.

"Miranda!" squeaked Cynthia. "Oh, Bess I didn't know——"

"Bess was Miranda? When was that?" asked Arnold incredulously.

"He's being silly," declared Bess, laughing. "It was a school-play, of course. Gerald was eleven and I was fourteen."

They all laughed.

(That was clever of us, thought Gerald. Bess has the effect of making me clever. It's a nice feeling.)

"I haven't seen that before, Bess," said Cynthia, pointing to the emerald. "Did your brother give it to you? He was in Africa, wasn't he?"

"I got it at Woolworth's, darling," replied Bess, laughing merrily. "They had them in all colours; I got a green one to match my eyes."

(Gerald had another look at the stone, which was glowing like green fire on his sister's neck. If Bess had got that at Woolworth's, he was a Dutchman!)

"It's quite a good imitation, but you can always tell," said Arnold, with a supercilious smile. "Besides, it's much too big to be real."

"How right you are, darling!" exclaimed Bess. "I shall get a smaller one tomorrow—if they aren't sold out."

"Did you enjoy *Venus*?" enquired a tall fair man who had been introduced as "David."

"Yes, I did," replied Gerald. He added, "Oh, you're Giles, of course! Your duet with Bess is delightful."

"Bess is wonderful to act with," declared David. "Some leading ladies bag all the lime-light—but Bess doesn't. I suppose you've realised that Arnold is the nasty piece of work who threatens to blow up the world."

It would have been interesting to discuss the play with David, but this was neither the time nor the place. Gerald was a little worried about the Harrimans who were standing in a group at the other end of the room, looking—and probably feeling—like an audience at a modern society play. He touched Bess on the arm and drew her attention to them.

"Yes, I know," murmured Bess. "It's all right, Flick; Mrs. Harriman understands. I'll do something about them in a minute. I just want to introduce you to Marthe. She's going to play for us later."

"Not Marthe Sönnenberg?" asked Gerald, gazing in awe at the small slender woman in perfectly fitting black who had just come in.

Bess turned and said, "Marthe, this is my brother Gerald that I told you about. He can't believe you're really you."

"I've got some of your records," exclaimed Gerald, taking her hand.

"That is nice," said Miss Sönnenberg, smiling happily.

"Bess, who are your other guests?" asked David.

"Friends of Gerald's," she replied. "Come and be introduced, darling."

"Me too!" exclaimed Cynthia.

There was a general move.

"Not all at once!" cried Bess, waving them back. But in spite of her efforts the Harrimans were suddenly engulfed in the mob. Gerald watched a little anxiously . . . but there was no need to worry. It was apparent that his new friends were quite able to look after themselves. Mrs. Harriman was chatting to David—probably about *Venus*. Mr. Harriman was talking to one of the girls and laughing. Arnold had made a bee-line for Marion and, cutting her out neatly, was holding forth to her in a corner. Gerald felt glad that it was not Penelope. The fellow was too intense and much too handsome, with his dark eyes and curly black hair, and he was waving his long white slender

77

hands to point his argument in a manner which seemed to Gerald quite revolting.

The room was filling up now and the two waiters had begun to circulate with trays of food and drink . . . but Bess had told Gerald not to bother, so he left them to it and went to speak to Miss Sönnenberg, who was standing beside the piano.

"Yes, I shall play later," she replied in answer to his question. "I shall play Debussy; and, possibly, some Dvořak— if there is time. Does that please you, Mr. Burleigh?"

"Enormously!" declared Gerald with enthusiasm. "You must make time, Miss Sönnenberg." He added, "I told you I had some of your records. I've been in Africa for years in an out-of-the-way place. I had a very good Gramophone; it was the only way I could satisfy my craving for good music. I can't tell you what a joy it was to listen to you. Most of the chaps went in for pop music—if you can call it music—but there was a little German who used to come to my bungalow and listen with me. He gave me lessons in German and I gave him music," added Gerald.

"I am glad," said Marthe Sönnenberg. "If Germans are nice, they are very nice. I am a Dane, Mr. Burleigh."

"You have a lovely name," Gerald told her.

"But it is not my real name," she replied, smiling. "My real name I shall not tell you. Sönnenberg is the name of my birthplace." She was taking off her rings and bracelets and putting them down in a glowing heap. "You will keep these for me, Mr. Burleigh," she added. "They will make a jingle if I leave them on the piano. They are pretty toys, are they not?"

"They are perfectly beautiful," agreed Gerald. He took a clean handkerchief out of his pocket and made a little parcel of the jewellery. It was not until he had stowed the parcel safely in the inside pocket of his dinner-jacket that he saw the joke: Marthe Sönnenberg had chosen the man who had been sacked for stealing diamonds to be the guardian of her treasures!

"What's the joke?" asked a girl who was standing near. (Was it Joy or Sonia—or perhaps it was Cynthia? Gerald was completely muddled by this time.)

"Oh, nothing much," he replied. "It just seems funny that people keep on coming, but the room doesn't get any more crowded than it was before."

"There are so many parties," explained the girl. "Sometimes there are three or four on the same night. I'm just waiting to hear Marthe play and then going on to Sonia's."

"Don't you get tired?" asked Gerald.

"Absolutely exhausted, my dear," replied Joy—or Cynthia. It couldn't be Sonia, of course!

Gerald had hoped for a few minutes' respite—he was so unused to parties that his ears were buzzing with the noise—but no sooner had he finished talking to Cynthia (or Joy?) than there was a gentle tap on his back and a voice said, "I think you must be Bess's brother?"

It was a small elderly gentleman with grey hair and spectacles.

"Yes. How did you know?" asked Gerald, smiling.

"By a process of elimination. We have heard of you, of course . . . and you look a little out of your element in this gathering, so it wasn't difficult. My name is Ainslie."

"Dr. Ainslie, of course!"

The little old gentleman's eyes twinkled behind his spectacles. He said, "Well, Mr. Burleigh-Brown, now that we have found each other, by a process of elimination, I should like a few words with you. Shall we hide behind the piano?"

There was an empty space behind the piano, so they retreated to this refuge and, although they were by no means "hidden," they were able to converse without being jostled and interrupted by the other guests.

"You and Mrs. Ainslie have been very kind to Bess," said Gerald.

"Bess has been very kind to us," Dr. Ainslie replied. "We live in the flat below this one—perhaps Bess told you?—and Bess comes in to see us when she can. My wife isn't able to go about much and one of her chief pleasures in life is a visit from Bess. I retired some years ago, but I still see a few patients in a friendly way."

79

Gerald was aware of this. He said, "I hope there's nothing the matter with Bess?"

"Nothing whatever! She's a strong, healthy young woman with an excellent constitution. She's just suffering from an excess of solicitude."

"You mean Matilda?"

Dr. Ainslie nodded. "I wondered if you had any views on the subject."

"Well . . . yes," replied Gerald doubtfully. "I rather agree with you, sir. Matilda is extremely capable—and devoted to Bess—but I think Bess is finding it a bit too much. I mean Matilda is on her mind."

"Exactly."

"But I don't see what can be done about it."

"I might be able to solve the problem."

"How?" asked Gerald in alarm. "Matilda would die if she——"

"No, she wouldn't die," interrupted Dr. Ainslie. "As a matter of fact she would do better in different surroundings. She never goes out; she has no friends! Body and soul Matilda is concentrated upon Miss Burleigh. That isn't very healthy and may lead to trouble. It is just as much for her sake that a change is desirable."

"You would have to ask Bess."

"Oh, of course! I just wanted to know what you thought. You're staying here, so you know the situation better than a casual visitor."

Dr. Ainslie was looking at Gerald seriously. It was obvious that he expected a well-considered answer.

"I think . . ." began Gerald. Then he paused.

"What do you think?"

"Well, in strict confidence, I had begun to wonder if Matilda was a little—unbalanced."

"People who indulge in possessive love usually are. Rely on me," added Dr. Ainslie. "I shall be extremely careful—and tactful. Nobody will die."

Gerald looked at him and trusted him. It was good to

know that Bess had a friend like this. Her other friends were anything but trustworthy.

When her guests had all been fed, Bess clapped her hands to obtain silence and announced that Marthe Sönnenberg was going to play and everyone must sit down. The men must sit on the floor—cushions were provided for them to sit on.

Quite a number of people slunk away hastily; the rest settled themselves and prepared to listen.

Gerald put his cushion near the chair where Penelope was sitting.

"Gerry," whispered Penelope, "is it really Marthe Sönnenberg? I just can't believe it."

"Yes, really. I've been talking to her."

"Oh, Gerry, we've got *all* her records. I wish you could tell Mother that it's really and truly *the* Marthe Sönnenberg. She'd be thrilled to bits."

Gerald leapt up, crossed the room to the sofa occupied by Mr. and Mrs. Harriman, gave the message and returned.

"What did they say?" whispered Penelope.

"They said it was too wunnerful to be true."

Penelope smiled. "I guess I'd better stop saying 'wunnerful.'"

"I guess you'd better not. It's rather intriguing," Gerald replied.

Penelope giggled softly.

Gerald had told Bess that it was an attractive giggle— and it was.

Marthe Sönnenberg had settled herself comfortably at the piano, which had been opened for her by her hostess. There was complete silence in the room. Then she began to play.

10. Penelope's Story

"I look a hag," said Bess.

It was after midnight; the last guest had gone and Bess was surveying herself in the mirror over the drawing-room fireplace.

"You don't look quite as beautiful as usual," admitted her brother frankly.

"Parties don't suit me."

"But it was a success, wasn't it?"

"Yes, a terrific success. I like your Harrimans, especially Mr. Harriman. He's taking me to lunch at Bicester next Sunday. . . . You seem surprised, Flick."

He was surprised. "Do you mean you're going alone with him?"

"Why not?" asked Bess. "I shall be perfectly safe with Elmer Harriman. He's the sort of man who knows how to look after a delicate female. He said he would hire the most comfortable automobile in London and drive me himself, and he's sure to bring a fleecy rug which he will wrap carefully round my knees."

"You seem to know a lot about him."

"We had a little chat," explained Bess. "Mrs. Harriman and Marion are going to York; Penelope is going to stay with a school-friend in Devonshire, and Mr. Harriman wants to look for some cousins in Bucks. I couldn't let him go alone, so I offered to go with him. It will be amusing—and I can prevent him from being taken in by impostors."

"I don't know what you're talking about!"

"It's quite simple, Flick. His mother's name was Audley and her grandfather came from Bucks—about a hundred years ago, I suppose—so Mr. Harriman intends to tour the county looking for Audley cousins. It isn't as mad as it sounds," added Bess.

"I'm glad of that!"

"Satire isn't your line," said Bess, smiling.

"Well, go on," said Gerald impatiently. "Why isn't it mad?"

"He has been making preliminary enquiries and has got a list of Audleys, living in different parts of the county."

"None of them may be *his* Audleys," Gerald pointed out. "His Audleys may have moved somewhere else—or they may all be dead. It is mad, Bess."

"Well, we shall see," she replied.

"And Bicester isn't in Bucks," added Gerald.

"No, but it's not far—and there's a good hotel there. At any rate it will be a pleasant little excursion and if it's a fine day, I shall enjoy it. I intend to make certain that he isn't swindled."

"It would be difficult to swindle a hard-headed American business man!"

"Not really. There's a romantic streak in Elmer Harriman."

"A romantic streak?"

"Oh, I don't suppose you could swindle him in business matters, but he's very romantic about his Audleys. However, I shall be there and it will be exceedingly difficult to swindle me. I know about people." Bess sighed and added, "Goodness, I'm tired! I wish I could just lie down and go to sleep like Gubby without bothering to undress and wash my face. I shall stay in bed tomorrow until tea-time, so you can entertain Penelope."

"What do you mean?"

"She's coming tomorrow—it's today, really—at eleven

83

o'clock, so you can give her a cup of coffee and you can have her all to yourself. She asked if she could come; she wants to talk to you about something very important," exclaimed Bess, stifling a yawn.

"But Bess, what does she want?"

"It's Leap Year so she'll probably ask you to marry her."

Gerald thought it unlikely.

"You might do worse," declared Bess. "She's a delightful little creature."

It was five minutes past eleven when Penelope arrived. Gerald had been waiting for the bell and opened the door himself. Coffee was ready on a little table beside the fire.

They sat down.

"Bess is tired," explained Gerald. "She's staying in bed until tea-time. Did you enjoy the party?"

"Oh, yes, it was a lovely party!" Penelope's face was rather pink and her eyes were shining. "Listen, Gerry," she continued. "I wanted to talk to you, so I asked Miss Burleigh if I could come. I'm going to Devonshire tomorrow for a week, so this was the only chance. I guess you think I'm crazy, but I want to tell you what happened to me when I was at school."

Gerald gazed at her in surprise.

"Just to show you," Penelope explained. "There was a girl called Joan; she had a brooch with diamonds in it. She had got it for her birthday. Then she lost it. There was a lot of fuss—everybody looked for it—and at last it was found in my drawer. It had been pushed down under my clean pyjamas. Some people thought I had stolen it."

"You hadn't, of course."

"No, I hadn't. I didn't know anything about it. And anyhow," added Penelope naïvely, "anyhow, if I'd wanted a diamond brooch, Father would have given me a much better one than that."

Gerald nodded. "Yes, of course."

"But it looked bad, Gerry. I was very unhappy about it. The worst bit was people thinking I was a thief. Miss

Clouston didn't think it, but Joan did—and lots of other people. That was the worst."

"I know," said Gerald sympathetically. "Poor Penelope, it was horrible for you. What happened next?"

"May confessed," replied Penelope, looking up and smiling. "May confessed and it was all cleared up in ten minutes. She had taken it. Then she got scared at all the fuss and she slipped it into my drawer. They discovered that she was a klepto, so she couldn't help it. She didn't mean any harm, Gerry. It was just a sudden temptation. I was sorry for her—everybody was sorry—so it was all right in the end. It just shows how easily things can happen."

Penelope was looking at him anxiously to see if he understood.

"Yes, I see," he said. "But it isn't quite the same."

"Not *quite* the same," she admitted. "But I thought I'd tell you about it. You ought to go back to that diamond mine and get all the trouble cleared up. It would be better for everybody."

"It would be better," Gerald agreed. "But I can never go back to Koolbokie because the manager would have me put on trial and I should be sent to prison. I couldn't bear it—I couldn't really."

"Prison?"

"Yes. He sacked me—I told you that. He said I could go at once—that very minute—and he hoped he would never see me again."

"Oh, Gerry! Then it's no good."

"No, I'm afraid it isn't."

"It was silly of me to tell you!"

"No, it wasn't silly, it was kind. It was *very* kind of you to tell me."

Penelope had risen and was putting on her gloves.

"Must you go?" asked Gerald.

"Yes, I must. Marion is waiting for me and I've got a lot of things to do. I'm going to Devonshire tomorrow to stay with Joan; that's the girl who lost the brooch."

"I'm going to Scotland," Gerald told her. "Shall I ring you up when I get back?"

"Yes, we'll fix a date."

She was standing there, smiling at him; and he had a sort of feeling that she would like him to kiss her . . . and he would have liked to kiss her . . . but he wasn't used to girls . . . so he wasn't quite sure . . .

The moment passed before he could make up his mind.

"Don't forget to give me a ring," said Penelope, holding out her hand.

"I shan't forget," he replied, taking the hand and giving it a gentle squeeze. "I'll ring you up at the Country House Hotel when I get back from Scotland."

"That's right," said Penelope.

Then he opened the door for her to go out.

"Au revoir, Penelope," he said.

She looked back and waved. "Have a good time, Gerry!" Then she was gone.

Gerald stood at the door and thought about Penelope's story for quite a long time. Her experience and his own were different . . . and yet there was a curious sort of resemblance between them. She had said, "It shows how easily things can happen."

Could the stones have got into the lining of his jacket "easily"? No, of course not! All the same he was glad that Penelope had felt she wanted to tell him her story.

11. The Great Man

On Wednesday night Gerald went to bed early and set his alarm for five o'clock. It would still be dark at five, but there wouldn't be much traffic and he would stop somewhere on the way for breakfast. He had been out several times with Leonard, so he was quite used to Pegasus, and Leonard had lent him a good map for his trip to Scotland.

Gerald went to sleep almost at once; he was dreaming of cruising up the Great North Road, when he was awakened by a gentle touch on his shoulder and opened his eyes.

"Just to say au revoir, darling," said Bess, kissing him on the forehead. "I shan't be awake when you go, but you don't mind, do you?"

"Of course not!" he murmured sleepily.

"I want you to deliver this letter personally," she added, propping a bulky envelope against his bedside lamp. "It's important, so you won't forget, will you?"

"All right," said Gerald, yawning. Then he glanced at the address. "But it's Glasgow!" he exclaimed, waking up properly. "I'm not going to Glasgow, Bess!"

"Yes, you are," said Bess firmly. "I want you to give it to him with your own hands, see?"

"But, Bess——"

"It won't take you much out of your way."

"Leonard said——"

"Never mind what Leonard said. You turn west at Scotch Corner and take the hill road over to Penrith. It's a lovely road. You'll enjoy it. Then, when you're through Carlisle, there's a dual clear-way to Glasgow."

"Listen, Bess. If I post the letter in Carlisle and register it——"

"No, darling," she interrupted. "You must give it to him with your own hands. It's *assential*."

This was a little unfair. He grunted rather crossly and agreed.

"I knew you would! You're my own darling Flick. Have a lovely time—but don't go too fast, will you?"

"Is that *assential* too?"

"Absolutely *assential* . . . and listen, Flick. Matilda wants you to knock on her door at five so that she can get up and make you some coffee."

"Very kind of her," said Gerald. But as this command was not *assential*, he intended to disobey it.

Gerald was cruising up the Great North Road; Peg was going like his namesake, the wingéd steed, and away to the east dawn was breaking. What Bess had foretold had come to pass: Gerald had left all his worries behind him. He found himself humming cheerfully.

His mind had been busily engaged with getting himself dressed and creeping out of the flat without making a noise and in driving Peg through the London streets (which already were waking up), so he had not had time to think about the letter, but he had put it carefully into his breast-pocket. He took it out now and looked at it. It was addressed to Sir Walter MacCallum, West George Street, Glasgow, and was very fat and crackly. He decided that the envelope must contain three sheets of the thick cream-wove paper which Bess used for important letters. It surprised him that Bess had written such a bulky epistle; Bess never wrote a letter if she could possibly avoid it. Sir Walter MacCallum was a new name to Gerald— Bess had not mentioned the man. Could this be the "Sir Walter" who sent roses twice a week? But how could he, since presumably he lived in Glasgow? The strangest thing of all was the command that the letter was to be delivered personally, by hand. It would be perfectly safe if sent by registered post. However, he owed Bess so much that the command was binding.

Bess had said, "Don't go too fast." That was rich, coming from Bess, thought Gerald smiling. All the same, when he glanced at the speedometer, he saw with surprise that he was doing 80 m.p.h. Eighty was Peg's cruising speed—he was purring like a contented cat—but Gerald slowed down to seventy.

It was just after two o'clock when Gerald arrived in Glasgow; he had stopped on the way for snacks. The city was strange to him, of course, so he showed the letter to a policeman and asked the way to West George Street.

"Sir Walter MacCallum? I ken him fine," said the policeman cheerfully. "Ma brither wurrks in MacCallum's yaird."

"What yard?" asked Gerald.

"MacCallum's Ship-building Yaird. West George Street will be his office, no doubt."

"Yes, I expect so," agreed Gerald. (The unfamiliar turn of phrase was intriguing.)

Having received clear and detailed directions from the policeman, Gerald pushed on and found the office, an imposing building with a brass plate on the door. However, it was a busy street, so he went on farther, found a parking place for Peg, locked him up securely, walked back to the office and rang the bell.

The door was opened by a uniformed door-keeper, who looked at Gerald disdainfully. Gerald showed him the letter.

"Sir Walter is out. I'll give the letter to his secretary," said the man, holding out his hand.

"I've got to deliver it personally."

"He's down at the yard—and anyway he never sees people without an appointment. I'll make an appointment for you to see him tomorrow morning if that will suit."

It didn't suit. Gerald intended to push on to Cannochbrae tonight.

Uncle Gregor was expecting him. "I'll go to the yard," said Gerald.

"Is it all that important?"

"Yes."

"He'll not be best pleased," said the man.

Gerald hesitated. He had no wish to stay the night in Glasgow, but perhaps it would be better to do that rather than to risk the Great Man's displeasure. Obviously Sir Walter Mac-Callum was a Great Man.

"I'd better go," said Gerald at last. "It's very important." (He had almost said it was *assential*.)

"It doesn't look to me like a business letter," said the door-keeper. "If it's not important, he'll be vexed—but you know best. You can get a bus that'll take you down in fifteen minutes."

This was a much better plan than manoeuvring Peg through the Glasgow traffic (Gerald was terrified of getting a scratch on Peg's gleaming paint), so he found the right bus and was deposited safely at the huge archway which was the main entrance to MacCallum's Ship-Building Yard.

Two men in uniform barred his way.

"I've come from London to deliver this letter personally," said Gerald.

The men looked at one another doubtfully . . . and Gerald walked past with a lordly air. He didn't look back, but he wouldn't have been surprised if he had felt a hand grabbing him firmly by the collar. Fortunately this indignity was spared him, but even now his troubles were not over for the ship-yard was surprisingly large and Sir Walter was difficult to find. It was not until Gerald had gone down to the slip where the keel of an enormous vessel was under construction that he was successful.

"That's him," said one of the workmen, pointing. "There's few days that he's not here. He likes keeping his eye on things."

Gerald stood and looked at Sir Walter for several minutes. He was tall and slender, and surprisingly young to be so important—about forty perhaps. He was standing at the side of the dry dock speaking to a foreman. He spoke eagerly, waving his arm and asking questions and making notes of the replies.

Obviously "he would not be best pleased" if he were interrupted. Presently he nodded, closed his notebook and turned away.

"Sir Walter MacCallum?" asked Gerald.

"Yes, what do you want?" asked Sir Walter sharply. "I don't know your face. Strangers aren't allowed here. You should have left a message at the gate."

"I was told to deliver a letter personally, sir," replied Gerald.

"Let me see it."

Gerald produced the letter and handed it to him.

"Oh!" exclaimed Sir Walter in surprise. His somewhat stern face broke into a charming smile and he added, "Sit down here for a minute while I read it."

Here was a baulk of timber behind a shed. Sir Walter sat down and opened the letter, but Gerald walked on. Gerald was of the opinion that it would take more than a minute for Sir Walter to read the letter, so he was surprised when Sir Walter called him back.

"Come here," said Sir Walter. "Have you read the letter, Burleigh-Brown?"

"No, of course not!"

"Well, there you are! Read it."

There were three sheets of thick cream-wove writing paper. Two of them were blank. On the third sheet was a pencilled scrawl: "This is Flick."

Gerald turned the sheets over, but that was all. He looked up in bewilderment.

"That's Bess," said Sir Walter, laughing. "Bess doesn't write letters, she lies in bed and chats on the phone. That's why I was surprised to get a letter from her."

"But why three sheets? One would have done."

"Oh, no," chuckled the Great Man. "One sheet wouldn't have done. The letter had to be bulky to show its importance."

"But why——" began Gerald and paused.

"Why what?"

"Why—everything? I don't understand."

"Bess chats to me on the phone. Then she sends me a

91

letter which must be delivered personally. It tells me all I need to know: This is Flick."

"I see," said Gerald thoughtfully. He saw a good deal.

"Yes, that's Bess," said Sir Walter gazing into the distance and smiling.

Gerald took the opportunity of looking at him closely: a man of about forty—possibly a year or two older—with a thin face, a firm chin and dark grey eyes. His ears were well shaped; his hands were rather large with unusually long fingers. His hair was thick and dark; his eyebrows strongly marked. Gerald's first impression had been that the man was somewhat alarming, but now his mouth was smiling.

"Look here!" he exclaimed, waking from his trance. "I've got an appointment at three-thirty—it's almost that now—so you had better come and have dinner with me. I live with my mother at Bearsden."

"I haven't got a dinner-jacket with me," objected Gerald.

"It doesn't matter. I want to talk to you, that's all. We have dinner at seven-thirty. Here's my address. Sorry I have to go, but we can talk more comfortably in my study. You can look round the yard if you're interested." He took out a card, wrote on it with a gold pencil and handed it to Gerald, who put it in his pocket.

Gerald had begun to thank Sir Walter for the invitation when his words were drowned by the shrill scream of a pneumatic drill.

"See what I mean?" bellowed Sir Walter, raising his hands in despair. "Can't—hear—oneself—speak."

Gerald nodded. It meant that he would have to stay the night in Glasgow after all . . . but it didn't matter. He could find a room somewhere, and as a matter of fact he wanted to see more of this man. He would have to find a garage for Peg and ring up Uncle Gregor, but first he would look round the yard.

Sir Walter was striding away rapidly. Although he was slender, he looked extremely wiry. It struck Gerald that he might be a good runner.

Gerald rose and began to walk along the edge of the dry dock. There were three men painting the hull of a ship with red lead.

"Hi, you! What are you doing?" exclaimed a foreman. "Nobody is allowed here except on business—not unless they've got permission."

Sir Walter's card was in Gerald's pocket. He took it out and gave it to the man.

"Oh, sorry, sir!" said the foreman, handing it back.

Gerald had not read it. He looked at it now with interest. It certainly had produced an interesting reaction. On the front of the card was Sir Walter's name and his address: Birkhill, Bearsden. On the back was a pencilled scribble: *"Mr. Burleigh-Brown has my permission to walk round the yard. Please give him every facility to see what he likes. W. McC."*

"I didn't know," explained the foreman. "We've got to keep people from wandering about here. It's orders."

"Yes, of course," agreed Gerald. "Of course you didn't know. How could you?" He put the talisman back in his pocket.

"Is there anything special you'd like to see, Mr. Burleigh-Brown?"

"Well, if you aren't too busy . . ." replied Gerald, smiling at the man in a friendly manner.

The foreman was not too busy to carry out the orders of the boss, so they spent an hour together going round the yard. It was interesting and instructive and Gerald was greatly impressed. Also—which was quite as important—he made a new friend in the person of his conductor whose name was Dickenson.

"Thank you, sir," said Dickenson when they parted at the gate. "It's easy to see you know a good deal about ship-building."

Gerald knew nothing about ship-building, but he knew about diamond mines and for this reason he had been able to show an intelligent interest in Dickenson's information. He would have liked to see a great deal more, but it was getting dark and he had a lot to do before his dinner engagement. Fortunately he had got the name of a garage and a hotel from Dickenson—which would save time.

93

12. Birkhill

Sir Walter's house was at Bearsden, a suburb of Glasgow, twenty minutes in the bus from the hotel where Gerald had found a room. As he walked up the drive to the front-door, he looked at the house in admiration. It was a long, low building with cream-coloured walls, a red-tiled roof and bow windows, and it stood in a large garden surrounded with trees and bushes. Gerald had discovered from the hall-porter at the hotel that Sir Walter had built it himself about ten years ago, when he was married.

"Married?" asked Gerald. "I thought he lived with his mother?"

"Yes," agreed the man, pocketing a tip. "Young Lady MacCallum died about four years ago—maybe five—so old Lady MacCallum sold her house and went to live with him. It was Sir Walter's father that was made a baronet—in the war, that was. Sir Walter has a son, about eight years old. He's a chip off the old block—interested in ships—and often goes down to the yard with his father. They all like Master Alastair down at the yard. They're busy at the yard," added the hall-porter. "There's a new ship on the stocks. She's a big passenger-ship for a firm in Hamburg."

"You know a good deal about it," Gerald suggested.

"I've a cousin that works in the yard," explained the man.

(Bess could have told Gerald all this—and more—but she had not said a word.)

There was nobody in the drawing-room when Gerald was shown in, so he had time to look about. It was a well-designed room, but too lavishly furnished—not a restful room. The pictures were good, some of them valuable, but there were too many. Gerald was looking at a still-life by S. J. Peploe when his host came in, wearing a lounge suit.

"Here you are!" exclaimed Sir Walter. "I'm glad to see you, Burleigh-Brown. I'm sorry I had to dash off and leave you this afternoon, but it was important. Did you have a look round the yard?"

Gerald explained what had happened.

"Good!" said Sir Walter. "Dickenson is a splendid chap; you couldn't have had a better guide." He added, "My mother will be down in a minute. I told her not to dress for dinner, but she can't eat her dinner comfortably in day clothes, so you'll have to excuse her."

"I hope she will excuse me, sir. I came north with a small suitcase. I'm going to stay at my uncle's farm, so——"

"Yes, I know," interrupted Sir Walter. "It isn't your clothes I want to see. We can have a private talk later."

The last statement was added in a low voice as Lady MacCallum came in. Gerald took it to mean that nothing important was to be said at the dinner-table.

Sir Walter made the introduction and added, "He's Elizabeth Burleigh's brother. You remember her, don't you? You saw her last time you were in London."

"Oh, yes, she's an actress, isn't she?" said her Ladyship vaguely. "The play was called The Girl from Somewhere or Other. I didn't like it much. I can't remember why."

"You like plays with happy endings," Sir Walter said.

They went into the dining-room and sat down.

At first they discussed the weather; it had been a fine day and the forecast for tomorrow was reasonably good. Then Lady MacCallum began to describe a sale of work which she had attended and to enumerate various people who had been present. Sir Walter ate his dinner and made a few remarks, but he did not seem to be listening very carefully.

The account of the sale was dull (all the more so because Gerald did not know any of the people mentioned by his hostess), but he was not bored. He was interested in his companions and was enjoying the excellent meal; he had not had much to eat all day. Could it be this morning that he had crept out of the flat in Molyneux Mansions? He had done and seen so much that it seemed like a week!

"Do you live in London, Mr. Burleigh?" asked his hostess suddenly.

"I've been staying there with my sister," Gerald replied.

"What do you do?"

"He's an electrical engineer, Mother," said Sir Walter. "His name is Burleigh-Brown. I told you that."

"I thought you said he was Elizabeth Burleigh's brother?"

"Yes, he is, but——"

"How muddling!" said Lady MacCallum fretfully. "I had got it into my head that he was Mr. Burleigh."

"It doesn't matter at all!" said Gerald, smiling. "As a matter of fact all my sister's friends call me Burleigh."

"Actresses often change their names, don't they?" said Lady MacCallum. "Not always, of course. Ellen Terry was Ellen Terry. I was taken to see her when I was a child. She was supposed to be a very good actress."

"Yes," said Gerald. It had become obvious why nothing of importance was to be said at the dinner-table.

"I saw Sarah Bernhardt too," continued her Ladyship. "It was in the First War, I think—because I was quite young and it made a great impression on me. She was a wounded soldier, lying under a tree. It was very moving. Then she died and everyone in the theatre was in tears. Was that her real name, I wonder?"

"Her real name was Rosine Bernhardt," said Gerald. This surprising piece of information had popped up into his head quite unexpectedly. He had no idea how he knew. He had no idea that he had known until he heard himself saying it. He explained this.

"The brain is very mysterious," said Sir Walter. "We don't know how to use it. Perhaps someday somebody will discover how to use his brain correctly. He will be a super man—as much above ordinary modern man as modern man is above the apes."

Gerald said, "Do you think it's bound to come as a process of evolution, sir?"

"No, I don't think so. Mind you this is just my own idea . . . but it seems to me that we're not becoming more intelligent. I haven't as good a brain as my father had, and although my son is more intelligent than I was at his age, he's very far from being a genius."

"What are your views about modern education?" asked Gerald.

"All wrong," replied Sir Walter. "Children are stuffed with facts to enable them to pass exams. If I had the courage of my convictions, I wouldn't send my son to school. I'd have a tutor for him."

"Like William Pitt the younger."

"Exactly. But would it be fair? He'll have to live in this modern world, so would it be fair to make him a freak? William Pitt was brilliant—head and shoulders above the crowd—but he didn't get on very well with his fellow-creatures; he didn't bear fools gladly; worst of all he wasn't a happy man."

Gerald was interested. He nodded and said, "The world is in an awful mess, isn't it? I wonder if a man like Pitt could help us."

"Oh, yes, we could do with a Pitt," replied Sir Walter.

"Mackenzie wants a pit," said Lady MacCallum. "He was asking me about it this morning. If he had a pit, he wouldn't need to take the cars to the garage to be serviced. He could service them himself. It would save money, Walter."

"Would it?" said Sir Walter with a sigh.

Gerald was sorry too. He would have liked to continue the conversation. He had intended to mention Shakespeare (who, like Pitt, was "head and shoulders above the crowd" and, like Pitt, had never enjoyed the benefits of a modern education). But it was useless.

Gerald came to himself to hear his hostess enquiring how he liked Glasgow.

"I only came to Glasgow this afternoon, so I really haven't had time to see it properly, but I'm sure——"

"It isn't what it used to be, Mr. Burleigh. My sister lives at Bournemouth. Have you ever been to Bournemouth?"

"No, never."

"It's a delightful place to live . . . but, of course, I shall never desert Walter and his motherless boy," declared her Ladyship with the air of an early Christian martyr—or possibly Mrs. Micawber.

"No, of course not," agreed Gerald uncomfortably.

"Why not go to Aunt Mildred for a month?" suggested Sir Walter. "A change of air would do you good, Mother."

"I might," replied Lady MacCallum thoughtfully. "I might go after Christmas. January is always rather a trying month—and Miss Young is really very good with Alastair. February is rather unpleasant too."

"Very unpleasant," agreed Sir Walter. "It was last February that you had bronchitis, wasn't it?"

"No, that was *before* Christmas, Walter. I remember because I had to write my Christmas cards in bed. All the same January and February are very trying, so perhaps I should write to Mildred. Glasgow isn't what it was," declared her Ladyship, turning to Gerald. "When I was young, it wasn't nearly so crowded and the weather was much better. I used to enjoy shopping, but this morning it was no pleasure at all. Mackenzie couldn't wait for me outside the shops and I couldn't get anything I wanted. Nowadays the saleswomen are so stupid and unhelpful. They don't care whether you buy the thing or not. In fact they would rather you didn't buy it because it saves them the trouble of wrapping it up."

The topic of inefficient and unhelpful saleswomen kept her Ladyship going until dessert was put on the table. Sir

Walter chose an apple, peeled it carefully and gave it to his mother.

"We'll leave you now, Mother—if you will excuse us," he said. "Burleigh-Brown and I have some business matters to discuss."

"Oh, Walter, you're always in such a hurry! It's most inconsiderate. Perhaps Mr. Burleigh would like an apple. You never asked him."

Gerald was about to say he didn't want an apple when his host handed him the dish. "Take one with you. They're good apples. We grow them ourselves," said Sir Walter.

"Thank you, sir," said Gerald and took one.

Sir Walter's study was a comfortable room with large brown leather chairs, a big desk and bookcases full of books. There was a log fire burning in the grate. Having been up at five, Gerald was tired; he was full of good food and was glad to sit down in a big chair and relax. He refused a cigar and began to eat his apple, biting it with his strong white teeth.

"That's the right way to eat an apple," said Sir Walter approvingly. "It spoils them to be peeled and cut up."

"It's a very good apple, sir," said Gerald.

"Yes, I put in the trees ten years ago when I built this house," Sir Walter replied. He sat down and added, "I expect you're wondering why I want to speak to you. I'll tell you. My greatest ambition in life is to become your brother-in-law. Have you any objection?"

Gerald was a little surprised—but not unduly. He smiled and replied, "No objection at all. I think it would be very nice indeed."

"You don't think I'm too old for Bess?"

"No, I don't."

"Good," said Sir Walter, nodding. "Now tell me if there is any hope."

This was more difficult to answer. Gerald thought about it seriously before he spoke. "Bess is very fond of you," he said.

99

"What did she tell you about me?"

"She never once mentioned your name."

Sir Walter gazed at him in dismay.

"But that's just the reason," explained Gerald. "She doesn't talk about you; your roses are the only flowers in her drawing-room; she lies in bed and chats to you on the phone. She sends you a letter with a cryptic message, knowing that you will enjoy the joke."

"Yes," said Sir Walter gravely. "You're right, of course. Bess loves me—I know that. I've asked her to marry me several times, but she won't. I really meant is there any hope of persuading her to change her mind?"

"You know about her aunt, I suppose?"

"Yes, I know about Aunt Anna. She's hopelessly deranged, I'm afraid. But it doesn't mean that Bess——"

"Of course not!" interrupted Gerald. "I told her! I told her she was seeing ghosts. Bess said that her mother was—was not quite—like other people," he added uncomfortably.

"That's the trouble," Sir Walter agreed. "We don't know whether her mother's mind was affected. Bess doesn't know for certain. Bess was a baby when her mother died."

"Who told Bess about her mother?"

"Aunt Anna told her—and poor Aunt Anna might easily have imagined it. I went to see the old lady (hoping that I might find out something more about Bess's mother), but it was useless. I didn't tell Bess I had been to see her aunt because I had no news, good or bad."

"I see," said Gerald.

"And listen, Gerald," continued Sir Walter earnestly. "Even supposing Bess's mother was a little queer, that doesn't mean her brain was affected—not really. She had a great deal to bear; enough to make a sane woman nervous and melancholy. She was a Londoner, not a countrywoman, so probably she was miserable on a little farm. It's a very isolated place, you know. She wanted a child, but she was delicate, so she had two miscarriages. Then, once more, she became pregnant and this time all went well for seven months, but at seven months she was suddenly taken ill. They rushed her off to a Glasgow hospital and the child was born in the middle of an air-raid."

"Goodness! How do you know all that?" asked Gerald.

"I made it my business to find out as much as I could. I have my spies," said Sir Walter with the ghost of a smile. "But it wasn't for my own sake I made these enquiries; it was because I wanted to comfort Bess. For my own part I'm perfectly willing to take the risk—if there is a risk. I want to marry Bess. I would marry her tomorrow without the slightest hesitation. I would do my best to make her happy. If she were happy, there would be no fear of melancholia."

Gerald nodded.

"I want to marry Bess," repeated Sir Walter. "If she's afraid of having children, we needn't have any."

"You've got a son."

"Yes, I've got Alastair. I'd like to have more children, of course, but we could be quite happy without them—or we could adopt a child."

By this time Gerald was quite certain that this was the right man for Bess. He said earnestly, "I'm sure you would be happy. If there's anything I can do——"

"You can," interrupted Sir Walter. "I've found out a good deal, but you're going to stay with your uncle—you're one of the family—so people might talk to you more freely than they would to a stranger. One of my reasons for asking you to come tonight was to tell you what I've done and to find out if you were willing to help."

"Of course I'm willing! I would do anything for Bess."

"A few tactful enquiries at Cannochbrae——"

"I see what you mean! If we could establish the fact that Bess's mother was normal, it wouldn't matter about Aunt Anna."

"It wouldn't matter so much," agreed Sir Walter cautiously. "Quite a number of families have one peculiar member, one poor thing who isn't like other people for some reason or other. It may be a love affair gone wrong or the loss of a dearly-loved child or possibly an unhappy marriage. Some people have the courage to accept hard blows. They will pick themselves up and march on. Others can't."

There was a short silence.

"Tell me about Bess," said Sir Walter, changing the subject. "She has a very arduous role in that new production. I hope she isn't finding it too much of a strain."

"She's all right when things go well. One night she was very tired; things had gone wrong—or she thought they had—and it upset her. She was all right next morning."

"You had a party on Monday night."

"Oh, you heard about that?"

"A little about it," admitted Sir Walter.

"Bess looked marvellous. She wore a cream-coloured frock and a single emerald on a chain round her neck. It was a magnificent emerald. One of her friends asked where she had got it."

"Did she say where she had got it?"

"She said, 'I got it at Woolworth's, darling. They had them in all colours. I got a green one to match my eyes.'"

Sir Walter chuckled with delight.

"I said nothing, of course," continued Gerald. "But as a matter of fact I know a bit about stones . . . and you don't get green fire in a bit of glass."

"There was green fire in the emerald, was there?" said Sir Walter, smiling to himself.

"Yes," said Gerald. He had wondered about the emerald. Now he knew!

Gerald had decided that he must not stay too long (already he had stayed longer than he had intended), so he rose and said he must go, adding that there was a bus at ten-thirty.

"Sit down, Gerald," said Sir Walter. "I've talked for hours about my affairs. It's time to talk about yours."

"My affairs aren't worth talking about," said Gerald bitterly. "I don't know whether Bess told you. Probably not. I was in a diamond mine in South Africa and was sacked for stealing diamonds. The stones were found sewn into the lining of my jacket."

"Was it unprecedented?" asked Sir Walter, without turning a hair.

"I don't know what you mean!" exclaimed Gerald in astonishment.

"Just exactly what I said. I wondered whether the individual who sewed the stones into the lining of your jacket had invented the hiding-place himself. It doesn't seem a very clever idea."

"You know about it!"

"I'd like to know more, but we haven't time tonight if you're going to catch that bus."

"Bess told you!"

"Bess tells me most of her troubles," explained Sir Walter. "She told me Flick was looking for a job—any sort of job. She said Flick spent hours trudging round the town. Then she sent me a letter which was to be delivered by hand. The letter said, 'This is Flick.' What do you suppose Bess meant me to do?"

"I don't know," murmured Gerald.

"You don't know?" asked Sir Walter in surprise.

"But you couldn't! You couldn't take a man without a reference!"

"No, I couldn't. I have to be careful. A man who turned up at MacCallum's without a reference would soon find himself in the street. You brought your reference with you. It tells me all I need to know—or nearly all," said Sir Walter, qualifying his statement. "Before I decide what to do I should like to ring up the headmaster of Marlborough College and get in touch with the establishment where Flick obtained his diploma in electrical engineering. Will that be all right?"

Gerald moistened his dry lips and managed to reply in the affirmative.

Sir Walter nodded. He said, "You can speak German, can't you?"

"Yes," said Gerald. "There was a German interpreter at Koolbokie. I had lessons from him."

"That will be very useful," declared Sir Walter. "The new ship is being built for a German firm. They write to us and send representatives to see how we're getting on. You'll be able to cope with them, I suppose?"

Until this moment Gerald had not really believed that he was being offered a post in MacCallum's. He had been too dazed to see where the questions were leading. Now, suddenly, he realised that it was true. He began to try to thank Sir Walter.

"All right," said Sir Walter, waving his hand.

"You're doing this to please Bess," said Gerald.

Sir Walter smiled. "It would be useless to say 'No,' wouldn't it? I like to please Bess—but apart from Bess, I shall be glad to have you, so don't worry about it, old chap."

Quite suddenly Gerald's eyes were full of tears; it was an extraordinary thing to happen; it was a thing that had never happened to him since he was a child—it was shameful!

"You want a cool drink," said his host, rising and pressing the glass into Gerald's hand. "When did you get up this morning?"

"Five."

"Eighteen hours ago! No wonder you're tired. I'll send you back to your hotel in the car. Can you come and see me at the office tomorrow at eleven-thirty, or do you want to press on to Haines?"

"Of course I'll come!"

"Just to fix up the details," explained Sir Walter.

13. The Job

It was not until Gerald had crawled into bed that he realised how tired he was. . . . But I shan't sleep, he thought. I'm too excited to sleep a wink. I've got a job. I've—got—a—job!

Sir Walter had not said what the job was to be (except that he was to cope with the representatives of the German firm), but that didn't matter. I can work for that man, thought Gerald. I don't care what I do. I would be happy to clean his shoes.

Gerald was still brim full of gratitude when sleep descended upon him like a soft brown blanket and he knew no more until the chambermaid came in to waken him.

"It's a fine day," she said as she pulled back the curtains and shut the window.

"It's a marvellous day," declared Gerald. "It's the most marvellous day for months and months."

"I wouldn't say that," replied the girl. "Last Thursday was bright and sunny. It was my day off."

"Today is better," said Gerald firmly.

The girl had no objection to a little chat with the nice young man who was sitting up in bed with his hair rumpled. He had nice teeth too. His wide grin showed them to advantage.

"Well, it might be a better day for you," said the girl, smiling. "But the washing goes out today and I have to count it: dirty sheets and towels and all the rest. Maybe you're meeting your girl-friend?"

"I'm meeting a man who's going to give me a job!" cried Gerald joyfully. He sprang out of bed and the girl vanished.

It was twenty-five minutes past eleven when Gerald presented himself at the office in West George Street. He had been much too early and had walked up and down until the right moment arrived. The door-keeper was expecting him, so there was no delay; he was taken up in the lift to Sir Walter's room.

Sir Walter was dictating letters to a dictaphone. He switched it off and told Gerald to sit down.

Gerald had thought a good deal about the manner in which he should address the man who was anxious to become his brother-in-law, and had decided to address him with circumspection. Someday (if the man became his brother-in-law) Gerald would have to address him as "Walter" . . . but Gerald could not imagine himself doing it, not even in private.

Gerald sat down. He said earnestly, "I just want to explain that I know nothing about ships; but I don't mind what I do. I saw some chaps painting the side of a ship with red lead so——"

"No," interrupted Sir Walter. "In MacCallum's yard we don't use skilled electricians to paint hulls."

Sir Walter had everything arranged satisfactorily. He explained that the chief electrical engineer had been in the business for years and knew his job thoroughly. His name was Carr. Gerald would be one of the team working under his direction on the electrical equipment of the new ship, but as the new ship was still in embryo—so to speak—Gerald's services would not be required until January or February, depending on the weather. The weather played an important part in a ship-building yard.

"It rains a good deal here," suggested Gerald.

"The actual rainfall is not very much higher than it is in other places, but we have long periods of drizzle," Sir Walter replied. He added, "So much for your main job—you can spend

Christmas with Bess—but if one of those German chaps comes over, you must be ready to fly up here at short notice. I suppose you will be able to talk to them quite easily?"

Gerald nodded. "I'm quite good, really. If two Germans chat to each other quickly, I might not be able to understand every word, but I can carry on a conversation without any trouble and I can read and write German. Steiner was very thorough."

"Good. I'm engaging you here and now. You'll be paid your salary, of course."

"That doesn't seem fair, sir!" Gerald exclaimed. "I shall be only too glad to wait until you want me. I can easily——"

"I want you now," interrupted Sir Walter. "Letters from Germany will be forwarded to our London office and you can deal with them there . . . or, if necessary, you can fly up here and discuss them with me." He smiled and added, "What are you worrying about? This arrangement suits me, Gerald. I want you at my beck and call."

"I'm not worrying, sir. I just feel that it's—unfair."

Sir Walter did not reply to that. He hesitated and then added in a confidential tone, "You won't like Carr. He's difficult. In fact he's so difficult that we've lost quite a number of good men on his account. They couldn't stand him. If he were not extremely efficient, I wouldn't keep him a week. He's been here so long that he thinks he's indispensable. That's the trouble."

Gerald was almost pleased to hear that Carr was a tartar. There had to be a snag somewhere. He said, "I'll do my best to keep on the right side of Mr. Carr."

"That's the idea . . . and that's all, Gerald. Do you know your way to Haines? The road is very good as far as Drumburly. Haines is beyond that; it's a small village amongst the hills."

Gerald nodded. He wondered if Sir Walter had been there himself, but he didn't ask.

"Look in at the office on your way out and sign the contract," added Sir Walter.

They stood up and shook hands. A few minutes later

Gerald was in the street. The interview had lasted less than half-an-hour, but the cloud which had shadowed his skies for months had vanished. He had got a worthwhile job which he knew he could tackle. He walked up the street with his shoulders back and his head erect. The fact that the weather had deteriorated and it had begun to drizzle made no difference to Gerald. He scarcely noticed it.

Gerald returned to his hotel and changed out of his "good suit" into slacks and a high-necked pullover which was more comfortable for driving. He was brushing his hair when he noticed a face grinning at him in the mirror. The face looked so different from the face he had been shaving every day for months that it gave him quite a shock. He threw back his head and roared with laughter. He was still laughing—perhaps a trifle hysterically—when the door opened and the chambermaid came in.

"You got the job!" she exclaimed, smiling in sympathy. "I thought of you when I was stripping the beds. I kept my fingers crossed."

It was a pity Gerald couldn't say he had thought of her. He gave her a pound instead.

"That's too much for just the one night," she told him.

"It's for keeping your fingers crossed," he replied. "Go on, take it! What's your name?"

"Penny MacTavish."

"Penny? That's short for Penelope!"

She nodded. "But my granny is the only one that calls me Penelope. It's a silly name anyway. They called me Penny-loaf at school."

"Penelope is a nice name," said Gerald.

"Maybe your girl-friend is called Penelope?" she suggested with a mischievous twinkle.

"I haven't got a girl-friend, but I know a girl called Penelope."

"I just wondered," explained Penny. "Well, I'll need to get on. I came to strip the bed. I've got five more to strip before dinner. It'll take me all my time." She added, "Good luck to the new job. We'll just need to hope for the best."

"What do you mean?" asked Gerald, looking up from the task of packing his suitcase.

"You never know," Penny explained. "This job looked all right—and the money's all right—it's the head-chambermaid. She's a fiend! But I couldn't know that, could I? Not till I came."

"No, of course you couldn't," Gerald agreed. He paused, suitcase in hand and watched her stripping the bed, tearing off the sheets and folding them in an expert manner which told of long practice. Then he said, "Well, good luck, Penny."

"Same to you!" replied Penny, blowing him a kiss.

The Glasgow streets were full of heavy traffic, and puzzling to a stranger. Gerald took a wrong turning and found himself in a cul-de-sac, so he was obliged to back. Then he fell foul of a policeman whose signal he had not seen. The policeman marched across the street and paused at the open window.

Gerald, aware that he was in the wrong, said meekly, "Sorry! I didn't see your signal. I'm not used to traffic."

"You'd be better driving a mini," said the policeman crossly. "A car like this is too big for busy streets."

"Sorry!" repeated Gerald.

The policeman stood back and waved him on. ("A soft answer turneth away wrath," thought Gerald in relief.)

All the same he was hot and bothered and was thankful when he got Peg safely onto the open road.

Now that he had time to think, he thought of Penelope Harriman. He had been thinking of her quite a lot. Penelope was a dear—he was very fond of her—but despite Bess's advice, he had no intention of asking her to marry him. He wondered what Penelope thought about it . . . but, whatever she thought, it wouldn't work! Penelope was used to luxury; she enjoyed a social life; she liked lots of fun; she liked travelling, seeing the world, and she would expect the man she married to trot after her like a poodle on a string. Gerald wanted a worthwhile job, a job which would use his superabundant energy—and he had got it! His future was assured. Therefore it was madness to think of Penelope.

There was no need to think about her, of course. Quite soon she would go home to America and he would never see her again. The idea that he would never see her again was remarkably unpleasant! She was so pretty—and sweet; she was clever and understanding; she was kind.

"What's the matter with you?" said Gerald to himself. "There you go—thinking about her. You're an absolute fool, Gerald Burleigh-Brown. Think about something else. Think about Penny MacTavish. It was funny about the head-chambermaid—I wonder if Carr will be 'a fiend.' I don't care if he is. I shall keep on the right side of Carr. He can't eat me."

Gerald was now weaving his way through a town. It was quite a small town but troublesome all the same. Peg was not at his best in towns, he was impatient when he was obliged to crawl behind a lorry. It was like reining in a mettlesome horse.

After that the road was clear, it stretched before him over a wild moor, so Gerald gave Peg his head and spun along happily. He thought of Bess. Bess had said she wished she could come with him. What a pity she hadn't been able to come! It would have been delightful to have Bess sitting beside him; everything was more fun when Bess was there. He thought again, as he had thought on Monday night, "The sun comes out when Bess comes in."

Penelope had thought so too. Penelope! Good heavens, here she was again! Penelope kept on popping into his head—and smiling. It's an obsession, thought Gerald. I shall have to get over it somehow or other . . .

Drumburly was a small town with one main street and a surprisingly good hotel, which stood near a bridge beside a little river. He would have stopped for a meal, but as it was only about ten miles to Haines, he decided not to. He filled up Peg's tank with super-grade petrol and set out over the hills. The road was less good now, but the skies had cleared and the air was delightfully fresh.

110

The village of Haines lay in a bend of a little stream. The road was steep, running down to the bridge from a gap in the hills. Gerald stopped at the top of the hill and looked about him. There were several farms, some large and some small. Which of them was Cannochbrae? Then he saw a farmer, riding a horse and called out to ask his way.

The farmer, who was wearing a tweed jacket, breeches and leather gaiters, dismounted and came to speak to him . . . and Gerald realised that it was a woman.

"Cannochbrae?" she said. "Oh, I suppose you're old Gregor's nephew?"

"Yes," replied Gerald. He was surprised that she should know him (or know about him), for he was unused to country places and country ways. Now that he could see her properly, he noticed that her hair was cut short like a man's; she looked strong and healthy and weather-beaten, as if she were used to working in the fields, but she had a well-bred voice without a trace of the local dialect. He wondered who she was.

"Is that Cannochbrae?" he asked, pointing to the near-by farm.

"No, that's Nethercleugh. It belongs to me. Anybody you like to ask will tell you about Freda Lorimer of Nethercleugh. I suppose you're surprised to hear that a woman can be a farmer?"

There was a curious sort of defiance in her manner, which made Gerald feel uncomfortable. "Well, it's—unusual—isn't it?" he said.

"It seems quite natural to me. I started to manage the place when my father was ill and went on with it after he died. It's mine now. I've been a farmer for years—and there isn't a better-run farm in the district."

"It looks very prosperous."

"And there isn't a worse-run farm than Cannochbrae. You can tell your uncle I said so," added Miss Lorimer.

It was her tone, even more than her words, that riled Gerald. He wouldn't have stood it from a man, but this was a woman—so he was silent.

"Everything is going to rack and ruin," she continued.

"The fields are starved and waterlogged. It's a shame! Men like Gregor Burleigh-Brown shouldn't be allowed to own land."

"The place belongs to him," Gerald pointed out.

"It should be taken away from him. It should be sold to somebody who can look after it properly."

Gerald had had enough. He wanted to push on, but Miss Lorimer was standing beside the car with her hand on the door, so he was obliged to wait until she had finished with him.

"Are you a son of Robert Burleigh-Brown?" she asked.

"Yes. Did you know him, Miss Lorimer?"

"I remember him vaguely. My father knew him, of course. My father used to say, 'You can't plough a straight furrow with an ill-matched team.' Robert was a live wire and Gregor has always been a lazy devil, so nobody was surprised when Robert got out and went to London with his family. Are you going to live with your uncle?"

"No, I've got a job in Glasgow."

"Well, if you take my advice, you'll have nothing to do with Cannochbrae. It would take years of hard work and a mint of money to put the place in order."

"I don't intend to have anything to do with it. I'm not a farmer."

"What about Matt? Your cousin Matt arrived this morning."

"What about him?" asked Gerald.

"I wondered why he had come."

"I haven't seen Matt since I was five years old—nor Uncle Gregor either. I'm staying here a week, that's all." Gerald added impatiently, "I must go now, Miss Lorimer. Perhaps you would be kind enough to tell me how to get to Cannochbrae."

She smiled quite pleasantly and replied, "Down the hill and over the bridge. It's the first turning to the right after you've passed the church. The road is full of holes, so you had better be careful. When you've had a look round your uncle's farm, you can come and see Nethercleugh. I'll give you a cup of tea and show you. a well-kept farm." Then, before he could reply, she mounted her patiently-waiting horse and trotted off up the hill.

What a strange woman! thought Gerald. She had been unpleasant at first and then suddenly her manner had changed and she had become quite agreeable—and had asked him to tea —but all the same he didn't like her. In fact, if the truth were told, he found Miss Freda Lorimer somewhat alarming.

14. Cannochbrae

When Gerald had passed the church and taken the first turn to the right, as directed by Miss Lorimer, he found himself on a very bumpy rutty road. He wasn't surprised, for he had seen worse in Africa, but he slowed Peg down to a walking pace. This gave him the opportunity to look about and he noticed other evidences of neglect in the straggling hedges, ditches full of dead vegetation and gates hanging askew on rusty hinges. There was a low wall round the garden, and tall gate-posts, one of which had fallen in a heap of stones. It seemed to have been lying there for some time, for the stones were covered with ivy. As there was nobody about, he drove on to the farmyard and found an empty barn which would do as a garage for Peg.

Gerald had hoped that, when he arrived, he would remember Cannochbrae—he had been five years old when the family had moved to London—but he had no recollection of it at all. It had just occurred to him that he might have come to the wrong place when he was hailed cheerfully and looked up to see Uncle Gregor standing in the doorway. He remembered Uncle Gregor quite well: a tall, thin old man with reddish hair. The reddish hair was going grey—so were the eyebrows—but apart from that Uncle Gregor looked exactly the same.

"Hullo, Gerald!" he exclaimed. "I see you've arrived at last. It's taken you a long time, but you're welcome."

"I phoned and explained the delay," said Gerald as they shook hands.

"I know that. I got the message, but it's a fortnight since I sent you the invitation. Well, never mind, you're just in time for tea."

As it was six o'clock and Gerald had had no lunch, he was ready for a square meal, but he need not have worried, for "tea" at Cannochbrae was extremely solid. There were sausages and bacon, a loaf of brown bread, scones and butter and strawberry jam. It was served by a small stocky man, who looked like a sailor.

"That's Man," explained Uncle Gregor. "We don't have women in this house. It's women who cause all the trouble. This is my nephew, Mr. Gerald," he added.

Man acknowledged the introduction with a grin. "His room's all ready, Mr. Gregor. It's been ready for ten days—ever since you said he was coming. I put Mr. Matt in the back room. He's not best pleased."

"He never said he was coming," grumbled Uncle Gregor. "If we'd known he was coming, we could have cleared the west room and had it ready. Where has he gone, Man? Why is he not here for tea?"

"He's gone to the village."

"M'h'm, that means The Black Bull. Well, if he's not here in time for tea, he'll need to go without."

"Och, he can have his tea when he comes in," said Man. Then he went away and shut the door.

"He never said he was coming," repeated Uncle Gregor. "That's Matt all over. He's been in Australia and Africa and goodness knows where else! He's a rolling stone, Gerald. He's never done an honest day's work in his life. His mother spoilt him, that's the trouble."

Gerald felt a little sorry for his cousin Matt. After all, this was his home and this was his father. Surely he deserved a welcome? "It would be nice for you if he settled down and helped you with the farm, wouldn't it?" suggested Gerald.

"Maybe it would—and maybe it wouldn't," replied Uncle Gregor. "But we'll not talk about that. Did you get the job you were after, Gerald?"

"Yes," replied Gerald cheerfully. "I saw Sir Walter MacCallum this morning and it's all fixed up."

"Let's hope the man will not be inconsiderate."

"Inconsiderate?"

"These big business men are all the same," explained Uncle Gregor. "They expect their employees to toe the line. However, it's a good sound firm, so maybe you're lucky to get into it."

"I'm very lucky."

"M'h'm," said Uncle Gregor.

Already Gerald had discovered that this curious exclamation, which he had never heard before, could mean various different things, depending upon how it was said. It could mean agreement or disagreement, pleasure or displeasure, or doubt. He was thinking about it and smiling to himself when the door opened and his cousin Matt walked in.

Gerald had remembered Uncle Gregor, but he had not the slightest recollection of Cousin Matt. He was an enormous man, well over six feet and considerably overweight—a positive giant—but he did not look strong and healthy. There was a softness about him; he was flabby. Gerald found himself thinking that it would be easy to knock him down! (It was a curious thought, for Cousin Matt was smiling pleasantly and it seemed unlikely that Gerald would ever want to knock him down.)

"Hullo, little coz!" said Cousin Matt. "You've grown quite a bit since the last time I saw you. I used to call you Tom Thumb. You didn't like it."

"You tormented him," said Uncle Gregor crossly. "You teased wee Bessie too—but she was a match for you. There was plenty of spunk in the lassie."

"It's good for children to be teased," said Matt, laughing.

Quite suddenly Gerald remembered the big boy who came home from school in the holidays. Matt used to twist his arm—and it hurt! Matt used to pull Bess's hair. Matt hid behind doors and pounced upon them, scaring them out of their wits. Bess was scared too, but she was too proud to "tell."

Gerald remembered hiding with Bess amongst the branches of a big oak-tree in the wood and watching the

116

ungainly schoolboy go lumbering past, looking for them, beating the bushes and calling out that he was the giant who would have their blood.

Bess had giggled, but Gerald had shivered all over with terror and excitement.

"What are you thinking about, coz?" asked Matt.

"I remember you now," replied Gerald, smiling.

Uncle Gregor went to bed early. It was his usual routine. He was up early in the morning; he walked miles over the hills, looking at his sheep, and did various jobs about the farm, so by half-past-eight or nine o'clock he was ready for bed. Gerald was quite pleased to follow his example; he had a book to read and he intended to get up early and accompany Uncle Gregor round the place. As he was to be here only for a week, he wanted to see all he could.

They went upstairs together and left Matt dozing by the fire.

15. Saturday

It was a fine dry morning. Gerald was awakened by the smell of frying bacon; he got up, had a bath, put on his oldest clothes and walked into the dining-room as Uncle Gregor was sitting down to breakfast. The old man was pleased to see him, and after a good solid meal they set off over the hills with a sheep dog.

Uncle Gregor didn't seem to be walking fast, but his long lounging stride took him over the ground at a surprising rate. Gerald fell into step beside him and listened to him talking.

"It's the beasts I like," said Uncle Gregor. "I've pigs and sheep and cows. There's money in beasts, Gerald. I grow some feeding stuff, but there's too much work in ploughing and sowing and reaping. I can't be bothered with it—and I've only the one man. He's lazy, but we get on well enough."

"If you got another man, you'd be able to get the place into better order, wouldn't you?"

"I'd have to pay him and it wouldn't be worth it. The more men you have about the place the more bother you have."

"If the fields were properly drained and fertilised . . ." began Gerald. Then he stopped and smiled at his own folly. Uncle Gregor was old and set in his ways. Was it likely that anything Gerald could say would change Uncle Gregor overnight from a bad farmer into a good one? Better to humour the old man! thought Gerald.

Gerald was all the more ready to humour him because he discovered that where his "beasts" were concerned Uncle Gregor was not lazy. As they walked over the hills, he kept a sharp look-out and worked his dog with remarkable skill. Little groups of sheep were rounded up and examined. A ewe which was lame was found to have a hard ball of mud in her cloven hoof. Gerald was shown how to hold the struggling animal while Uncle Gregor removed the plug and swabbed the cleat with disinfectant, a bottle of which he produced from a pocket in his shapeless tweed jacket.

"There's a lesson for you, Gerald!" said Uncle Gregor as they watched the creature bounding away up the hill. "If I'd not noticed that the beast was lame, yon wee plug might have caused a deal of trouble."

"Could you have done it by yourself?" asked Gerald.

"I'd need to have done it myself, but it would have taken longer. I'd have roped the ewe, of course," replied Uncle Gregor. He added, "It's well worthwhile to take a walk round the hirsel two or three times a week; besides I enjoy it. It's grand to walk over the hills and know they're your own—every stone and blade of grass, Gerald. See what I mean?"

"Yes, of course," agreed Gerald.

They walked on. Uncle Gregor continued. "Cannochbrae has been in the family more than a hundred years. I was born here, so I've a feeling for it. A man has a fondness for the place where he was born. You were born here, so you must have a feeling for it."

"Yes," said Gerald. What else could he say?

"Farming is a good life. There's no hurry about it—and you can do as you please. There's nobody to make you toe the line. You're your own master, Gerald. The soil is poor, so there's little enough money in it, but I do well enough. There's enough to live on. That's all a man needs in this world."

"Yes," said Gerald.

"I'll leave it to you in my will. It's to be yours, Gerald, but don't mention it to Matt."

"But you can't!" cried Gerald in dismay.

"I can," said Uncle Gregor. "I can do what I like with Cannochbrae. It's my own property——"

"But you mustn't, really! It wouldn't do! You must leave it to Matt."

"Not me!" declared Uncle Gregor. "Matt would sell it. The place has been in the family more than a hundred years. It's not to be sold! Matt would sell it to yon besom on the hill. Freda Lorimer of Nethercleugh she calls herself! She's after it, but she'll not get it! I'm leaving it to you, Gerald. You've a fondness for Cannochbrae—you said so. You'll not sell it."

"Listen, Uncle Gregor," said Gerald earnestly. "Cannochbrae is a lovely place. I like it immensely, but I'm not a farmer—and never could be!"

"You can learn."

"I've got a job in Glasgow. I told you that!"

"You don't want to spend all your life in Glasgow."

"I'm not a farmer," repeated Gerald. "I don't want to be a farmer, so it isn't the least use leaving it to me. I don't want it."

"You don't want Cannochbrae?" asked Uncle Gregor incredulously. "Och, Gerald, I'm disappointed! I thought you liked the place. I want you to have it when I'm gone!"

"When you're gone?" said Gerald. "Goodness, Uncle Gregor! What are you talking about? You're fit and well. You're a strong healthy man. I shouldn't be surprised if you see us all out."

"Well, that's true enough," replied Uncle Gregor, smiling. "There's nothing much wrong with me. I can still walk five miles over my hills without any trouble; it's more than Matt could do. You're a good lad, Gerald. I like you and I was fond of your father. Robert and I would never have parted company if it hadn't been for the women-folk."

"The women?"

"Just that. Maggie (your aunt Maggie) was a good creature, but she liked to be the boss. That was the way of it, Gerald."

"I don't understand."

"There was no trouble when Joan was here, but then Joan died and Robert married Alice."

"My mother," said Gerald, nodding.

"I liked Alice. She was bright and cheery—very different from poor Joan—and Maggie liked her too. They had jokes together. At first Alice was taken up with Bessie; she was a dear wee mite. Then she had her own child—that was you, Gerald—but then you and Bessie got older and ran about together, so you were off her hands. She hadn't much to do and she started taking an interest in the house. She wanted to do a bit of cooking, she wanted a say in things, she wanted new curtains in the sitting-room—and Maggie wouldn't have it. That was the way the trouble began. The fact is you can't have two bosses in the house."

"No, I suppose not," said Gerald uncomfortably.

"No, not if they're women. Mind you, I don't blame them. They were good women, both of them, but Maggie had been the boss for years and she couldn't thole interference. That was the trouble. See?"

Gerald saw. He remembered his mother, of course. She wasn't really bossy, but she was a good manager and she enjoyed running her house. The house at Beckenham had been spick and span—very different from Cannochbrae! She was a very good cook and was never happier than when she was in the kitchen. He remembered her beating up eggs and baking cakes and filling dozens of glass jars with home-made preserves: marmalade and strawberry jam and tomato ketchup.

It was queer, thought Gerald. Three different people had given him three different reasons for the break-up of the partnership between the brothers . . . but perhaps they were all true! Life was a muddle; little things piled up and made a big thing.

By this time Gerald and Uncle Gregor had finished their round of the hirsel (it had taken the whole morning), so they went in and sat down to a mid-day meal of steak and kidney pie and a steam pudding. Matt had spent the morning in bed and came down looking tousled and sleepy; he complained of a headache.

"You should have been out with us," his father told him.

121

"We've had a good walk over the hills. Gerald likes Cannochbrae, don't you, Gerald?"

"The place is going to pot," said Matt crossly.

"It needs a bit done to it," admitted Uncle Gregor. "Maybe I'll get an extra man in the spring."

"Look here, Matt," said Gerald. "Why don't you settle down here and give your father a hand?"

"Settle down here!" exclaimed Matt scornfully. He hesitated and then changed his tune. "Well, I might, of course. I might try it for a bit . . . but I've got a heart, that's the trouble. The doctor said I mustn't exert myself unduly. I can't dig or——"

"But you're not ashamed to beg," interrupted Uncle Gregor.

It was obvious that Cousin Matt didn't understand the scriptural allusion. Gerald did—and hid a smile.

"I don't know what you mean," mumbled Matt. "I want a loan, that's all. I'd pay you back, of course."

"M'h'm," said Uncle Gregor incredulously.

16. The Broken Door

It was raining in the afternoon. Uncle Gregor and Matt had settled down by the fire in the dining-room, but the atmosphere was so unpleasant that Gerald put on his waterproof and went out.

The rain was not heavy—it was little more than a mist—and he wanted to look round the place by himself. Alas, the more he saw of the farm the more he realised that Miss Lorimer's dictum was justified. It was in a frightful condition. The barns were leaking, some of the windows were broken and there were piles of rubbish everywhere. It would take years of hard work and "a mint of money" to put it in order . . . and he had a horrible feeling that, in spite of what had been said, he would sooner or later become possessed of the white elephant. He wondered if it were true that Miss Lorimer wanted it.

Man was in the farmyard (which Gerald had learnt to call the steading). He was trying to mend a broken door.

"It's a shame to see the place like this," said Man. "I do what I can, but it's pretty hopeless."

Gerald agreed.

"Mr. Gregor likes his beasts," continued Man. "He makes money out of the pigs and sheep, but he doesn't seem to notice that the barns are falling to pieces. They were good barns too. I was trying to mend this door, but the wood is rotten, so the nails won't hold."

123

"There's another man on the place, isn't there?"

"There's Macfarlane, but he's lazy. You can't blame him. I mean if the boss takes no interest——"

"No, you can't blame him," agreed Gerald.

"His sister used to be cook here," continued Man. "That was before I came, of course. Jean Macfarlane was her name. Then she got married. She's Mrs. Inglis now."

"Mrs. Inglis?" asked Gerald, pricking up his ears.

"Yes, she's got a nice little cottage in the village. Her husband died some years ago, so she lives by herself."

"Didn't she have two sons?"

"Yes, one of them is in the Merchant Navy and the other has a job in Glasgow. They're nice lads, both of them."

"My sister remembers her."

"You should go and see her, Mr. Gerald. She'd like that. Her cottage is next the Post Office."

"Yes, I must go and see her," agreed Gerald.

It was beginning to get dark now, so Man abandoned his hopeless task and they walked back to the house together.

"Look at that gate-post!" exclaimed Gerald, pointing to the heap of fallen stones. "If you had a bag of cement, I could build it up quite easily. It wouldn't take long."

"I'll see if I can find some, Mr. Gerald. I've spoken about it several times, but Macfarlane doesn't bother—nor Mr. Gregor either! It's been like that ever since I came. Mr. Gregor said it was a big van that knocked it down."

"In that case it has probably been like that for over twenty years," said Gerald, smiling at the thought.

Gerald was interested in people, so he encouraged Man to talk about himself and learnt that Man had been born and bred on a farm in Yorkshire. He had served in the Merchant Navy and had "seen the world a bit." He had spent several years in New York and then had become homesick and returned to London where he had got a job in a grocer's shop. It seemed strange that having travelled so much he should be content to settle down at Cannochbrae.

"Well, I got a bit tired of being ordered about," ex-

124

plained Man. "I can do as I like here, more or less. Mr. Gregor doesn't bother. I do the catering and get what's necessary. I've got a motor-bike. I can get a day off and go to Glasgow if I want. I'm free, Mr. Gerald. See what I mean?"

"You're a good cook," said Gerald.

"I like my food," explained Man. "If you like good food, you soon learn to cook nicely."

They had got to the back-door of the house by this time, and it had begun to rain quite hard, so they went in. The front-door had sagged on its hinges and was difficult to open or shut, so nobody ever used it.

Tea was at six-thirty as before. It was fish and chips tonight, and nicely cooked. Uncle Gregor enjoyed the meal—so did Gerald—but Cousin Matt seemed to have little appetite. He prowled about the room restlessly and grumbled at the weather.

"Sit down, Matt," said Uncle Gregor. "It'll be a good day tomorrow. We'll go to the kirk, the three of us. You'd like that, wouldn't you, Gerald? You're a 'Pisky,' I suppose, but it'll do you no harm to hear a decent sermon for once in your life."

Gerald had no idea what a 'Pisky' was, but he agreed to go to church with Uncle Gregor.

"Well, I'll away to bed," said Uncle Gregor, rising.

Gerald was left with Matt.

"This place is dead," said Matt scornfully. "You won't catch me settling down here. The old man can't live forever, so I'll sell the place, of course. Freda Lorimer wants it—and I'll see she gives me a good price for it. She's well-heeled, so she can afford to pay for her whims."

Gerald let him talk. He went on talking while Man cleared the table and said "Goodnight."

For a time they could hear sounds of Uncle Gregor stumping about upstairs. Then, when all was quiet, Matt rose and went to a box on the chimney-piece and took out a key.

"The old man hides it," explained Matt with a grin.

125

"Hides what?"

"I'll show you, coz." He opened a locked cupboard in the corner of the room and produced a bottle of whisky and two large tumblers. Then he fetched a jug of water from the pantry and sat down.

"Keep it under your hat, coz," continued Matt. "He doesn't know I've discovered his secret hoard. He's an old skinflint. Do you want water in yours?"

"I don't want it at all."

"You don't want it?" asked Matt incredulously.

"I don't like it," explained Gerald.

"I take it medicinally—doctor's orders," said Matt. He poured out half a glass of whisky, splashed a little water into it and took a drink of the mixture. "That's better," he added. "I need it, you see. I've got a heart."

"What is the matter with your heart?"

"It's a tired heart. I need a lot of rest. Well, never mind that; let's have a talk. Let's hear what you've been doing. You've been in South Africa."

"Yes," said Gerald. "Then, when I came home, I stayed with Bess in London."

"She's an actress, isn't she? Seems to have made a success of it."

"Yes, she's a tremendous success."

"I was in Rhodesia, growing tobacco, but things were beginning to get a bit uncomfortable, so I thought it was time to get out."

"Did you sell out, Matt?"

"Nothing to sell. I was an overseer on a big estate—it suited me better. I like to move about. If I get sick of one place, I just pack up and move on somewhere else. I was in Australia before that. Ever been to Sidney?"

"No," said Gerald.

Matt began to describe Sidney, but he had not the gift of relating his adventures in an interesting manner, so Gerald did not listen very carefully—and to tell the truth he was getting a little worried about the rapid disappearance of the whisky.

". . . so I told the boss exactly what I thought of him," declared Matt with a chuckle. "Then I packed my traps and got out. I went to Rhodesia—I told you that, didn't I?"

"Yes," said Gerald. He added anxiously, "I say, Matt! you've had enough."

"Don't worry," replied Matt cheerfully. "I know what I'm doing all right . . . no, don't move the bottle! I need a pick-me-up after a long day. You won't have to carry me to bed."

"I couldn't," said Gerald. "You must weigh fifteen stone at least."

"Eighteen," replied Matt, reaching for the bottle.

"I wouldn't if I were you," Gerald told him.

"But you're not me," declared Matt. "You're different. You don't need it. The doc-doctor didden tell you that a little whisky, last thing at night, would do you good."

"But you've had a lot—too much, Matt! I'll put it away now. I'll put it back in the cupboard."

"No, you won't! You'll sit down, ol' chap. I'll tell you something that'll make you laugh. I was in Rhodesia growing tob-tobacco, but I decided to clear out."

"I know. You told me that."

"Yes, but I didden tell you the joke."

"What joke?"

"A pal who was goin' to Jo'burg offered me a lift."

"Why did you want to go to Jo'burg?"

"I didden—not specially—but I'd never seen the place. I tol' you before I like seein' places—an' here was Fraser, with a big car, goin' to Jo'burg, so I took the chance, see?"

Gerald nodded. Matt was a drifter. Matt would go anywhere if he got the offer of a free ride in "a big car." He would have gone with his friend to Timbuctoo or to Capetown. . . .

"Listen," said Matt, chuckling. "Listen an' I'll tell you the joke. P'raps it'll surprise you—or p'raps it won't s'prise you. . . . What was I sayin'?"

"You were going to tell me a joke."

"Yes. Here's the joke. When I got to Jo'burg you were—talk of the town."

127

"I was?" asked Gerald in dismay.

"You were—talk of the town. They all wanted to know if I was a relation of Burleigh-Brown who had done a bunk from Koolbokie with a pocketful of diamonds." Matt lay back in his chair and roared with laughter.

Gerald was speechless. So it had come! It had caught up with him! It had become distorted and had gained size on the way like a snowball! He had put it behind him. He had thought he was clear of it, but it had been there all the time, pursuing him.

He swallowed the lump in his throat and said, "It isn't true."

"P'raps not," agreed Matt, pouring out the last of the whisky with an unsteady hand and tossing it off neat. "P'raps not—really true—all of it. Things get exag-exagger-ated. Makes a better shtory . . . but there's no shmoke without fire . . . no shmoke. Jo'burg full of shmoke . . . all the pubs . . . full of shmoke 'bout Burleigh-Brown. Don' worry . . . I'm not a clype. Know what that meansh? Meansh tell-tale. Dirty trick tell talesh out of sh-sh-cool. Sh-cool. Can't shay it. I mush be a bit drunk. Bad whishky. Cheap whishky . . . poison . . . thatsh what it ish. I don' feel well——"

Matt maundered on for a minute or two about Burleigh-Brown and the pocketful of diamonds and then passed out completely.

Gerald was not surprised. Most men would have been "under the table" long ago. Matt was not literally under the table, he was sprawled across the table—but it didn't make much difference to the problem. Gerald was standing looking at the enormous bulk of his cousin and wondering what to do when the door opened and Man appeared.

"Goodness, I thought you'd gone to bed!" exclaimed Gerald.

"I thought you might need me," said Man. "It happened when he was here before—several times."

"I tried to prevent him, but I couldn't."

"Nobody could have prevented him—not without violence," replied Man calmly. "It's an illness, same as any other illness, so it's no good getting annoyed."

"I'm not annoyed. I was just wondering what on earth to do. We can't possibly get him upstairs to bed."

"No," agreed Man. "He's too heavy. My room is next the pantry, so we can put him in my bed—that's what I did before. It was a job, I can tell you, but it will be easier if you'll give me a hand. You look pretty strong, Mr. Gerald."

They were both pretty strong, but it was all they could do to drag the unconscious Matt through the pantry into Man's room and get him into bed. He was so limp that Gerald was worried about him, but Man seemed unconcerned.

"He'll be better in the morning," said Man. "I'll get him upstairs in the morning. You get to bed yourself, Mr. Gerald. You look all in."

Gerald felt all in, but there was something he had to do tonight—he wouldn't be able to sleep until he had done it—and as it was only eleven o'clock, it was not too late.

"I must telephone to—to someone," he said.

"Telephone now?" asked Man in surprise.

"Yes, it's important."

"The telephone is in my pantry," said Man. "I'll shut the door so nobody will hear what you say—except the girl in the exchange, of course. It will be a thrill for her—a call at this hour!"

"It isn't private," Gerald told him.

The girl in the exchange was not thrilled; she was cross and sleepy, but after some delay Gerald got through to Sir Walter MacCallum's house at Bearsden and immediately a voice said, "Walter MacCallum speaking."

"This is Gerald Burleigh-Brown, sir. I'm sorry to ring you so late, but I felt I had to tell you at once that I find I can't accept your offer of a post in MacCallum's ship-yard."

"You have accepted it. You signed the contract."

"I must resign, sir."

"You are obliged to give me two months' notice."

129

"I know, but it will be better if you let me go now, at once."

"Have you heard of another post?"

"No, sir."

"What are you proposing to do?"

"I'm going to—to New Zealand," replied Gerald. It was the first place he could think of—and the farthest away.

"Have you friends in New Zealand?"

"No, sir. I don't know anyone in New Zealand."

"Well, why on earth are you going there?"

Gerald hesitated and then said, "It will be better for you if you let me go now—at once."

"Better for me?" asked Sir Walter incredulously.

"Yes, better for you—and Bess—and everyone. It would have been better if I hadn't come home at all. It was foolish of me to come home. I see that now. I might have known——"

"Nonsense!" exclaimed Sir Walter briskly. "Listen, Gerald! I understand. It's that Koolbokie affair."

"Yes, I'll tell you about it. I'll explain——"

"Not on the phone. Don't say another word. Tomorrow is Sunday. I shall come to Drumburly. You can meet me, can't you? There's a good hotel near the bridge. We'll lunch there and discuss the matter."

"But it's no good discussing the matter."

"Listen!" repeated Sir Walter. "When you were engaged by me yesterday morning, I told you I wanted you 'at my beck and call.' You agreed to that."

"Yes, I know, but it won't be any good. It will be much better——"

"Will you meet me tomorrow at Drumburly?"

"Yes, if you want me to, but——"

"Good. Twelve-thirty at the hotel near the bridge."

"Yes, sir," said Gerald meekly.

Sir Walter immediately rang off, so Gerald put down the receiver. He stood and looked at it for a few moments and then went upstairs to bed.

17. The River

Gerald didn't sleep much. He kept on thinking of what he should say to Sir Walter. He was determined not to take up his post in MacCallum's; it would not be fair. It would be madness. He must make Sir Walter understand—and let him go. He had been so happy about his job; now he was miserable. The future was dark. Would it be any good coming to Cannochbrae and trying to put the place in order, or should he make a clean break and go to New Zealand? The Koolbokie story had followed him here—and Matt might spread it abroad—but it was unlikely that people here in Haines would be interested in it. Perhaps he should just come here and get down to work; it was a man-size job and worth doing.

Gerald turned over restlessly and remembered that it would take "a mint of money." So that seemed pretty hopeless! It had better be New Zealand and a fresh start.

He slept a little towards morning and woke to find that it was a pleasant day. There was no sun—the sky was pale grey all over—but it was dry and the air was bracing. When Gerald went down to breakfast, Uncle Gregor was there alone.

"Matt is not well," said Uncle Gregor.

"I'm sorry about that," declared Gerald. (As a matter of fact Gerald had looked into his cousin's room and had found him in bed, looking and feeling dreadful.)

"He says he has taken a chill," explained Uncle Gregor.

Gerald didn't reply. He was not sure whether Uncle Gregor knew the real cause of his son's malady, but it was better to say nothing.

"You're coming to the kirk with me. It's at eleven-thirty," said Uncle Gregor after a prolonged silence.

"I'm sorry but I can't, Uncle Gregor."

"You said you would!"

"I know, but Sir Walter MacCallum wants me to meet him this morning at Drumburly."

"When did you hear this?"

"Last night after you had gone to bed. I'm sorry about it, but I shall have to go."

"M'h'm," said Uncle Gregor. "Well, you can't offend the man and risk losing the job he's given you, but he might have more consideration than to summon you to meet him on the Sabbath. I told you these business men have no consideration for other people's feelings, didn't I?"

"Sir Walter isn't like that——"

"They're all like that, Gerald."

"I'm getting paid," Gerald explained.

"You mean you're getting a retaining fee?"

"No, I'm getting my salary."

"But I thought you weren't going to MacCallum's till February."

"The arrangement is that I'm to go whenever he wants me. I'm to be 'at his beck and call.'"

"Well, I hope he's giving you a decent wage—or salary—or whatever you call it."

"Quite satisfactory," replied Gerald. He was aware that Uncle Gregor wanted to know how much he was getting, but he saw no reason why he should tell him . . . and anyhow he had decided that he was not going to MacCallum's after all.

Gerald finished his breakfast and went to see Peg. He made certain that Peg had everything necessary: water, air, petrol, oil. Then he washed his hands, changed into his suit and set off over the hills to Drumburly. He was so afraid of being late for his appointment that he was much too early. He drove into the yard of the hotel and parked Peg beside a Bentley. It was a large green car—a magnificent machine—with a Glasgow number.

Gerald was looking at it with interest when a woman came out of the hotel and asked if he were Mr. Burleigh-Brown.

"Sir Walter is expecting you," she explained.

"Do you mean he's here?"

"Yes, he's away down the river for a walk. We know Sir Walter well. He comes for the fishing—very keen he is—but he's too busy to come as often as he would like. I'm Mrs. Simpson," she added.

"Is Sir Walter fishing today?"

"It's Sunday!" exclaimed Mrs. Simpson in horrified tones.

"Oh, yes, of course!" agreed Gerald hastily. He had not realised that Scottish fish are safe from the hook on Sundays.

Gerald locked up Peg and went out. He took the path along the edge of the river. Presently he saw a tall slender figure in tweeds, standing on a grassy knoll. At first he was not sure if it was Sir Walter: he looked different today (it was not only his country clothes, it was his whole demeanour). He was hatless and his dark hair was ruffled by the breeze . . . but it was Sir Walter! He waved cheerfully when he saw Gerald and came to meet him.

"Good man! You're early," he exclaimed. "We'll have time for a walk."

Gerald was full of all he intended to say, but Sir Walter would not listen. "After lunch," he said. "Not now, Gerald. I want to enjoy a breath of fresh air. It's a fine morning, isn't it? My father would have said 'Another braw day snappit up by the Sabbath!' Do you know what that means?"

"No, sir, I'm afraid I don't."

"Well, jokes are never much good when they're explained (and I can see you're not a fisherman which makes it more difficult), but here goes! Today is a perfect fishing day; it's not too bright and there's a nice breeze but, alas, it's the Sabbath!"

"Oh, I see," said Gerald, smiling.

This was a younger Sir Walter, a happy carefree Sir

133

Walter who stood and gazed at the little river. "Look, Gerald!" he said eagerly. "Do you see that pool beside the big rock, just below the fall? There's a trout there. It's the very place for a big one. If I had my rod, I would cast up the river and let the fly drift past his hiding-place . . . but it's Sunday and I haven't my rod," he added with a rueful smile.

"It was good of you to come, sir," said Gerald.

"You needn't be so dashed respectful—not here," said Sir Walter. "It makes me feel a hundred years old. You'll have to do it in the yard, of course."

"Of course," agreed Gerald. "But I'm not coming to MacCallum's. I want to explain——"

"We'll leave the explanations until after lunch. There's a lot to be said and we don't want interruptions. Mrs. Simpson is letting me have her private sitting-room for the afternoon. You're not in a hurry to get back, are you?"

"No, I'm not," replied Gerald emphatically.

Sir Walter looked at him sideways. "Not enjoying your visit to Cannochbrae?"

"No," said Gerald.

"You can tell me the reason later. Meanwhile let's enjoy ourselves."

They walked on together.

"What does the river mean to you—a man who's not a fisherman?" asked Sir Walter.

"It's very pretty. In fact it's delightful. I like its peaty colour, and the way the water curves over the rocks in a glassy green wave, and the little frills of white round the boulders. I like the little whirlpools and the backwaters near the banks. It must be perfectly beautiful in spring. Is that what you mean? Or do you mean professionally, as an engineer?"

"Do you see it as an engineer? That's interesting."

"Water isn't exactly my line, but it's got quite a lot to do with electricity."

"Go on, tell me about it."

"Well, see that bit of boggy ground? It's useless at the moment—which is wasteful. If the farmer asked my advice, I would throw out a stone groyne from this bank. A small one would do the trick. It would divert the current into its proper course. Quite soon that piece of boggy ground would dry off. You could grub up the rushes and sow grass."

"Yes, I see," agreed Sir Walter, gazing at it thoughtfully. "Your little stone jetty—or whatever you call it—would add at least half an acre of good pasture to the farmer's property and, what's more, it would prevent the current from eating away this bank when the river was in spate."

"Yes," said Gerald. He was pleased with his pupil.

"I've learnt something interesting this morning," Sir Walter declared. "I've learnt a new way of looking at my pet river. By the way, it's called the Burly—but it isn't spelt like your name. Did your family originate in this district?"

"I don't really know," Gerald replied. "Uncle Gregor told me that the family has owned Cannochbrae for over a hundred years. That isn't very long, of course, but they might have been somewhere else in the district before that. It would be interesting to find out, but I don't know how to do it."

"Graveyards," suggested Sir Walter. "Church registers. Old ministers who are interested in local families. There's a very old minister at Haines. His name is Kirke. He might be able to tell you."

It was nearly one o'clock by this time, so they walked back to the hotel for lunch.

18. Gerald Is Turned
Inside Out

Gerald had come to the assignation in a confused state of mind, thinking of all he had to say and feeling miserable about it. The walk and the talk had calmed him down and he was able to enjoy his meal, which was surprisingly good for a small country hotel.

They had coffee in Mrs. Simpson's private sitting-room where there were comfortable chairs, a solid table and a good fire. Mrs. Simpson brought in the coffee-tray herself. She stayed for a few minutes chatting to Sir Walter and then said, "You won't be disturbed, Sir Walter. Just ring if you want tea later."

Then she went out, shutting the door firmly behind her.

"She's a grand woman—one of the best," declared Sir Walter. He sat down at the table and added, "Now, Gerald, what has happened to upset you?"

"My cousin Matthew came home on Thursday. He had spent a few days in Jo'burg and done a round of the pubs. He said—he said everyone asked him if he were related to the Burleigh-Brown who had done a bunk from Koolbokie with a pocket full of diamonds."

"What did you say?"

"I said it wasn't true. He said perhaps not—not all of it. Things get exaggerated because it makes a better story, but there's no smoke without fire—and all the pubs were full of smoke about Burleigh-Brown."

It had come out with a rush. Gerald was breathless. He paused and gasped.

"It's nasty, of course. No wonder you were upset. Did he say it as a joke?"

"He was drunk—and he went on drinking neat whisky."

"I see. Did he give you any more information?"

"Not really. He said he wasn't a clype—he said it was a dirty trick to tell tales out of school—so I needn't worry. By that time he was saying the same thing over and over again and eventually he passed out. We had to put him to bed and it wasn't easy. He weighs eighteen stone."

"Poor devil!"

"Yes, he isn't a bad fellow. There's no malice in Matt, but if he takes too much (which apparently he does, quite frequently), the story is bound to come out. That's why I rang you up. You see now, don't you?" said Gerald earnestly. "You must let me go, Walter. You don't want a man with a story like that in MacCallum's. It might come out any day. It has followed me to Haines, it will follow me to Glasgow! Let me go now—and there's no harm done. I shall take the first ship I can get to New Zealand. It's for *your* sake I'm asking you to let me go."

Gerald had worked himself up to such a pitch that he rose and paced the room. "You see, now," he repeated. "You see why I must go. I don't want to bring trouble to you—or Bess—so I must go away before the story leaks out. It doesn't matter where I go. I just said New Zealand because it was the first place that came into my head, but it isn't a bad idea——"

"Gerald, sit down and listen to me," interrupted Sir Walter. "Sit down and drink your coffee. You're making a mountain out of a molehill. It's bad luck that your cousin blew in to Johannesburg while the pubs were buzzing with your name, but by this time they'll have forgotten you and found something else to buzz about."

"The story has followed me to Haines; it will follow me to MacCallum's."

"I think it unlikely," Sir Walter told him. "But if it should

137

happen—if somebody in MacCallum's gets hold of the story and puts it about—it won't affect me, nor MacCallum's either."

"Won't affect you? What do you mean? Will it be pleasant to have a man accused of the meanest kind of theft as one of your employees?"

"It won't affect me to have a man wrongfully accused of theft as one of my employees. I shall take no notice of the rumours. It may be a bit unpleasant for you, I admit, but the unpleasantness will pass. The men will soon realise that the rumours are false. If anybody speaks to me about it, I shall tell them the truth—or as much of the truth as I think fit. You must stand your ground, Gerald. It's a mistake to run away from trouble. The story might catch up with you again; it might follow you to New Zealand and, if it did, you would be amongst strangers."

"I wasn't really running away," said Gerald more quietly. "It wasn't for my own sake I intended to go away. It was to save trouble and embarrassment to you and Bess."

"It won't affect Bess in the very least."

"No," said Gerald thoughtfully. "No, perhaps not."

"I've told you how I intend to deal with the rumour."

"Yes," said Gerald. "Well, if you're quite sure—if you really mean what you say——"

"I always mean what I say," interrupted Sir Walter, smiling. "I should have thought you might know that, by this time. I engaged you to come to MacCallum's and nothing has altered my intention. Now, Gerald, let's talk it over quietly and get to the root of the matter. I want to know exactly what happened at Koolbokie."

"But I thought you knew! I thought Bess had told you!"

"She told me a good deal, but I want to know more. We can scotch the rumour if we can find out the truth."

"How can we?" said Gerald hopelessly. "I was caught with the stones hidden in the lining of my jacket. I don't know who put them there—nor why."

"You want to get at the truth, don't you?"

"Yes, of course!"

"Well, come on then! Let's consider all the possibilities. I've been thinking about it seriously and I've made some notes," added Sir Walter, taking a small loose-leaf notebook out of his pocket and putting it on the table. "Question one: Could it have been an accident that the stones were there? Could you have picked them up when you were at work and put them in your pocket, intending to hand them in at the office? You might have had a hole in your pocket."

"No, that's impossible," Gerald replied. "It was my best jacket. I never wore it except when I was going out. In fact I never wore a jacket at all when I was working—it was too hot. I wore dungarees and not much under them."

"Well, that's out," said Sir Walter, making a note. Then he looked up. "Bess thinks you were framed. Had you an enemy, Gerald?"

"An enemy?"

"Somebody who wanted to get rid of you."

"No—not that I know of. I'm a peaceful sort of chap; I get on well with people. As a matter of fact we were a happy crowd at Koolbokie. Besides . . ."

"Well? Besides what?"

"There wasn't any sense in it. I mean how could anybody know that the stones would be found in my jacket? I could walk in and out of the place as I liked."

Sir Walter nodded, "You were never examined at the entrance."

"No, I was never screened," agreed Gerald. "I was one of the few people who were above suspicion. That's why Angus Proudfoot was so furious with me. That's why he said I was a traitor and had betrayed my trust——"

"I know! I know!" interrupted Sir Walter in soothing tones. "Don't think about that any more. We must talk about the matter quietly if we want to find out the truth. My opinion is that somebody was using you as a carrier."

"A carrier?"

"Yes. It seems the most likely explanation. You could walk in and out of the place as you pleased, so you were an ideal

139

carrier. Somebody hid the stones in your jacket, intending to get them out later."

"Oh, I see what you mean!"

"It's a possibility, isn't it?"

"I suppose so," said Gerald doubtfully. "But who could have done it?"

"That's what we want to find out. We'll take everybody in turn and make a list. Let's start with the man who shared your bungalow; he had the best opportunity, hadn't he?"

"Pat Felstead? Oh, it couldn't have been Pat."

"Why not?"

"Oh, several reasons. For one thing he was my best friend; for another he could have been his own carrier. He could have walked out with the stones in his pocket if he had liked. Sometimes he asked to be screened—it was a joke between him and Stafford. Pat is a cheery sort of chap; he was always having jokes with people. Everyone liked Pat."

"You never asked to be screened?"

"I didn't approve of it," explained Gerald. "You've got to stand on your dignity; you've got to be a little tin god—if you see what I mean. Unless the men respect you, it's impossible to exercise your authority."

"You and Felstead disagreed about that?"

"Not disagreed exactly. We never had an angry word. We just thought differently . . . and another thing," added Gerald, "It was Pat who wanted me to be screened. I wasn't keen on it, but he wanted me to take part in the fun——"

"Did you show your reluctance?" interrupted Sir Walter.

"Yes, I did (it was another point against me), and then I realised that it would be less undignified to agree than to make a fuss."

Sir Walter hesitated. Then he said, "Felstead believed you to be guilty?"

"Yes. That was almost the worst thing about it. We were friends, you see. I thought I could depend on Pat, but he didn't believe a word I said. He just kept on asking me why I had done

140

it. He was terribly distressed. It was Pat who pled with Angus to let me go and say no more about it."

"That was very foolish."

"Foolish?" echoed Gerald in bewilderment.

"Yes, foolish. Innocent men are rarely found guilty. The affair should have been thoroughly sifted at the time. Instead of which it was hushed up and you were dismissed with a stain on your name."

"You don't understand!" cried Gerald. "Diamond thieves get short shrift in Jo'burg. If Angus had handed me over to the police, I'd have been sent to prison. There was absolutely no hope of an acquittal. There I was with the stones hidden in my jacket. They wouldn't have bothered with any further evidence."

"Are you sure of that?"

"Absolutely certain. We all knew that. If it hadn't been for Pat, I would have been sent to prison—probably for years. It was Pat who saved me. It was Pat who persuaded Angus Proudfoot to let me go. At first Angus wouldn't listen, but Pat kept on and on . . . and at last when I had almost given up hope he *made* Angus listen. It was Pat who helped me into the car and told me to drive hell for leather before Angus changed his mind."

"So that's what you did."

"Of course! My only idea was to escape."

Sir Walter was busy making notes. He said, "You went to Capetown and you were in hospital for several weeks. That's right, isn't it?"

"Yes, it was pneumonia. I was off my head, really. It had all happened so suddenly—it was such a shock. When I came out of hospital, I sold my car. I thought of going to America, but I was home-sick. I'd lived in the wilds for so long that I wanted to see the places I knew! I wanted the lights and the people and the rain. It sounds rather mad, but I think I wasn't quite sane. I wanted to find a job in London, but I couldn't."

"What has happened to all your belongings?"

"My things are still there, in my bungalow, I suppose. I just had a suitcase with me."

"Hadn't you better write for your stuff to be sent home?"

"I never thought of it," replied Gerald doubtfully. "I just wanted to get away."

There was silence for a few minutes.

"Well, let's get on," said Sir Walter at last. "I still think you were being used by somebody as a carrier. It must have been somebody who was examined at the gate or he could have made off with the diamonds himself. It must have been somebody who had access to your jacket. It must have been somebody who was going to Johannesburg and intended to meet you there and get hold of your jacket, somehow or other, and remove the diamonds. Can you think of anybody?"

"No, not really."

"What about that German who was giving you lessons? Did he come to your bungalow?"

"Steiner? Yes, he came to the bungalow nearly every evening, but it couldn't have been Steiner."

"Why not?"

"He's a dear fellow: gentle and kindly and—and romantic. He's a tubby little man with tufty hair and spectacles and a bass voice."

Curiously enough this description brought Herr Steiner before Sir Walter's eyes. He could see the little man quite distinctly! He crossed out the name "Steiner," which he had written in his notebook. "What about the woman who cleaned the bungalow?" he enquired.

"No, she was a native woman. She would never have thought of it."

"Somebody might have put her up to it. Bribed her."

"She would never have dared. She was scared of her own shadow, poor little wretch."

"Did you have a doctor in the place?"

"Yes, Wilson—an awfully good fellow."

"Was he screened when he left the mine?"

"No."

"Then it couldn't have been Wilson. What about a dentist?"

"He came once a month." Gerald smiled, rather wanly, and added, "You're thinking of that book by Fleming in which the dentist took diamonds out of his patients' mouths."

"I was," admitted Sir Walter with a smile.

"But that's just a story! Things like that don't happen in real life."

"Why shouldn't they?"

Gerald hesitated. It seemed impossible that something which had happened in a thriller should take place in real life.

"What was the man's name?" asked Sir Walter, pausing, pencil in hand.

"Edmunds . . . but it couldn't have been Edmunds."

"Was he screened on leaving the mine?"

"Yes, it was a hard and fast rule for visitors . . . but I can't believe——"

"He's a possibility, Gerald. We're looking for possibilities."

"He isn't—really. He never came to my bungalow, so he couldn't have done it. He couldn't have got hold of my jacket."

"Did you ever leave your jacket lying about?"

"No, never. It was my best jacket. I kept it in a tin case—an officer's uniform case—in my room."

"Locked up?"

"No. There was something wrong with the lock—besides it wasn't necessary. I mean, I just kept it in the tin case because of the ants. Edmunds couldn't have known where it was—and he couldn't have known I was going to wear it."

"All the same we'll keep him in mind. Now, think hard, Gerald! Who else was there? We've got to find somebody who was screened regularly at the gate—or was liable to be screened."

Gerald mentioned four names. Two of them were deemed "possibilities" and noted by Sir Walter. One of them, Balmain, was mentioned by Gerald as an afterthought. "But it couldn't have been Balmain," added Gerald. "He was on leave at the time."

"Who was he?"

"He was the head cook. He had been in the Navy. As a matter of fact, he was rather a nasty piece of work; nobody liked him."

"Why didn't people like him?"

"He was a trouble-maker (if there was any trouble, Balmain was pretty certain to be at the bottom of it). And he wasn't too clean. I advised Angus Proudfoot to get rid of him before somebody got poisoned."

"Did Balmain know you had put a spoke in his wheel?"

"I don't think so. Besides, as I told you, he wasn't at Koolbokie when my trouble blew up."

Sir Walter was silent for a few moments. Then he said, "But Gerald, we don't know when the stones were put into the lining of your jacket. Could Balmain have done it before he went on leave? Would you have noticed that they were there?"

"Gosh, I never thought of that!" Gerald exclaimed. "No, I don't believe I would have noticed. They were sewn into the hem, where the material was fairly thick. What an extraordinary idea! You mean it might have been a sort of booby-trap?"

"Yes, a booby-trap."

"But it couldn't have been! The man couldn't have known I was going to be screened."

"All the same we'll make a note of Balmain. Now here's another thing. It's very important, Gerald. Were the diamonds valuable? Were they good ones?"

"I don't know. They weren't cut, you see. You can't tell for certain until they're cut . . . and I didn't really see them. I mean I didn't examine them. They were taken out of the lining of my jacket and put on the table in a little heap."

"By whom?"

"Stafford, I think," said Gerald doubtfully. "They were all there, of course: Proudfoot and Pat Felstead and Stafford and Barnes———"

"You didn't mention Stafford and Barnes."

"They're the X-ray men. They're never screened, of course."

"Of course not," agreed Sir Walter. "Listen, Gerald, this

144

is what I'm trying to get at: If the diamonds were valuable, it means that the man who hid them in your jacket was pretty certain of getting them back. Had you arranged to meet anybody in the town?"

"No . . . and I don't think they were very valuable."

"Why not?"

"Well, I can sort of see them now," said Gerald slowly. "A little heap of stones (they look like pebbles before they're cut) lying on Stafford's table. There were five and they were quite small. Yes, I remember thinking they were a poor lot to mean so much. I'd forgotten that," added Gerald apologetically. "I was dazed and—and rather frightened."

"I wish we knew," said Sir Walter, frowning.

"I don't see that it matters."

"It's vitally important. You know a good deal about diamonds, don't you? Is it likely that you would risk losing your job and your reputation for a poor lot? Would any man in your position be such a fool?"

"Oh, I see! You mean the man who put them there didn't know much about stones?"

"No, I didn't mean that at all," replied Sir Walter smiling. "I meant that anybody who considers the matter seriously must realise that you didn't put them there yourself."

19. "Thank You for Everything"

Sir Walter closed his notebook and put it in his pocket. Gerald had been turned inside out—and spring-cleaned. At least that was what he felt! He relaxed and lay back in his chair. It had been a tremendous relief to talk it over like this. The burden which had seemed so heavy had been shared.

"We'll have a cup of tea," said Sir Walter. "Then I shall have to go. You can have something stronger if you like."

"Tea, please," replied Gerald. "I'm not teetotal, but drink doesn't appeal to me. I saw too much of it at Koolbokie. You had to drink with the other fellows and stand your turn (which meant you had to drink too much) or else give it up altogether . . . and last night was horrible."

"Last night has given you a scunner," suggested Sir Walter.

Scunner was a new word to Gerald, but the meaning was obvious.

"Yes. Poor old Matt," said Gerald. "He's an absolute wreck this morning."

"Alcoholics can be cured you know."

"Not unless they want to be cured—and although Matt is big and beefy, there's something soft about him. It takes a hero to do it. I know, because there was a fellow at Koolbokie who conquered the dragon and became a sane, sound member of the community."

"Good for him!" exclaimed Sir Walter.

They went on chatting. Sir Walter said, "Bess rang me up this morning. She was going to have lunch at Bicester with her new friend, the American millionaire. She was pleased about it."

"Oh, yes, of course!" exclaimed Gerald. He had intended to think of Bess today at lunch-time, having lunch with Mr. Harriman, but he had been too taken up with his own affairs and had forgotten all about it.

"She said they were going to look for his cousins," added Sir Walter. "It seemed pretty hopeless to me. What is he like, Gerald?"

"Oh, he's nice! You'd like him. He's quite old, of course, with a wife and a grown-up daughter. He's devoted to them."

"Don't worry; I'm not jealous. It's good for Bess to have friends."

"He's different from her other friends. Americans are different, aren't they?" Gerald hesitated and then continued, "For instance, when they came to the flat and I introduced him, he said that meeting Miss Burleigh informally in her own beautiful home was something he would never forget. He meant it, of course, and it sounded all right coming from him. Bess liked it. But an Englishman couldn't have said it."

Sir Walter smiled. "An Englishman might have felt it and put it in different words: 'I say, Miss Burleigh, it's awfully jolly of you to have us like this,'" announced Sir Walter with an exaggeratedly English accent.

Gerald roared with laughter.

"Is that right?" asked Sir Walter, smiling in sympathy.

"Almost," replied Gerald. "A little old-fashioned, of course. What would a Scotsman say?"

"Ah, that would be telling! If he were a Highlander, he might make a better job of it. The Gaelic is a language that lends itself to pretty speeches. . . . What's the matter with Cannochbrae, apart from Cousin Matt's little foibles? You said you weren't enjoying your visit much."

"The farm is falling to bits."

"Falling to bits?"

"The barns are leaking, the drains are blocked, the doors are sagging on their hinges, the windows are broken and there isn't a piece of sound wood in the place."

"Good heavens!"

"And the worst of it is the old man seems to have made up his mind to leave it to me in his will. I told him I didn't want it, but I don't think it will make any difference. He's an obstinate old man."

"You could sell it."

"He doesn't want it sold."

"You could put it in order and lease it."

"How could I? It would take thousands to put it in order."

"Oh, well, we'll cross that bridge when we come to it," said Sir Walter cheerfully. He added, less cheerfully, "I don't suppose you've had time to make any enquiries yet?"

"Not yet," replied Gerald. "I've only been there one full day—though it seems like a week—and I thought it better to dig myself in before starting to ask questions, but I intend to go and see Mrs. Inglis tomorrow. She was the cook at Cannochbrae before she was married."

"That sounds a good plan," said Sir Walter. "If you find out anything, don't use the telephone. Come and tell me about it. You had better come to Birkhill, not the office. Come and stay for a few nights, Gerald. Then we can have a good talk and decide what to do."

"If I don't find out anything——"

"Come and stay whether you find out anything or not. I shall expect you on Friday. That should give you plenty of time."

They had tea together. It was "afternoon tea," not the solid meal referred to as "tea" by Uncle Gregor. Then they went out to the yard where the two cars were standing side by side.

"Hullo, you've got Grandpa!" exclaimed Sir Walter.

"Yes, but we changed his name. He's Pegasus."

"Much more suitable," said Sir Walter smiling. "Well, I must go. Goodbye, Gerald—and good luck!"

"Goodbye—and thank you, Walter. Thank you for every-thing. I'm terribly grateful to you. I wish I could make a pretty speech like Mr. Harriman, but I can't."

"That's all right," said Sir Walter.

They shook hands with a firm clasp.

Sir Walter got into the Bentley and fastened his safety belt.

Gerald was about to get into Peg when Sir Walter called to him, so he turned and stood at the window of the Bentley.

"Listen, Gerald! You must be careful. Your cousin has got hold of that story, so he may try to get money out of you."

"Well, as a matter of fact I thought I might help him a bit. He was trying to borrow money from his father, but——"

"You mustn't!" interrupted Sir Walter. "It's dangerous. It might lead to blackmail."

"Good heavens, Matt isn't like that! There's no malice in him."

"He may ask you for money in a friendly sort of way, but whatever you do, you mustn't give him a penny. If a man has something he can use against you, it's extremely unwise to give him money—even if you give it for quite a different reason. It may start as a sort of gentle blackmail, but if he finds he can squeeze you, it may go on to the real horrible thing. Apart from that, it would lend conviction to his story. It would be easy for your cousin to say, 'It must be true. He gave me fifty pounds to keep my mouth shut.'"

"Fifty!" exclaimed Gerald. "Goodness, I couldn't afford anything like that! I just thought it might cheer him up if I gave him a fiver. He looked awful, poor wretch."

"Not even a fiver," said Sir Walter firmly.

"You're wrong about him—Matt isn't like that—but I'll take your advice, of course."

"I'll give you something that will do him good. It's a pre-scription for a hangover."

"Are you a doctor?"

Sir Walter smiled. "No, but I got the prescription from a doctor—and it's pretty good. We use it in the yard. Some of our chaps have a blind now and then—especially at Hogmanay—and turn up looking like death. Ferguson keeps a bottle of the stuff in his office at the gate and doles it out when they ask for it."

"They ask for it?"

"Yes. They tell each other about it. Some of the best chaps have an occasional blind. You've just got to accept the fact and do the best you can to help them."

"Do other big works have the stuff on tap?" enquired Gerald.

Sir Walter replied that he didn't know how other works coped with the problem. The "corpse reviver" was his own idea. He had got the prescription from his own doctor for a man who was suffering from the effects of a blind and the mixture had worked marvels. The man had told his pals about it and the news had spread. That was how it had begun.

"It isn't entirely altruistic," added Sir Walter. "You're apt to have accidents if people are under the weather—and we don't like accidents at MacCallum's. Would you like the prescription? You can get it made up here at Drumburly. There's a chemist's shop in the main street."

"But it's Sunday."

"I know, but Sandy MacLean lives over his shop, so you can knock him up. He's a decent fellow and he won't mind."

Gerald accepted the offer. Fortunately the chemist's shop was open, so there was no need to knock up Sandy MacLean.

It was just after six o'clock when Gerald got back to Cannochbrae. He found Man in the kitchen; a savoury smell of bacon and sausages filled the air.

"Hullo, Man! Where is everybody?" asked Gerald.

"Mr. Gregor is down at the steading and Mr. Matt is still in his bed. He's had a bad go this time. He ought to keep off it altogether, but he's not the kind that could, so what's the use of nagging at him?"

"Not much, I suppose," agreed Gerald. He put the bottle on the table and added, "I met a friend in Drumburly and he gave me a prescription for a hangover. Do you think Mr. Matt will take it?"

"I'll see he takes it," declared Man. He removed the cork and smelt the mixture.

"Smells nasty," said Man. "But that's all the better. A bottle that smells nasty is more likely to do him good. I'll go and give him a dose now—this minute—and maybe he'll be all right tomorrow."

20. The Writing Desk

Uncle Gregor and Gerald had tea together. Uncle Gregor was cheerful: one of his sows had farrowed and had produced thirteen piglets, all strong and healthy—"not a runt amongst them." He gave Gerald a detailed account of the happy event (and the air of Cannochbrae was so bracing that Gerald was able to listen and to eat a large helping of sausages and bacon without a qualm).

"Well now," said Uncle Gregor. "That's enough about that. Matt is still in his bed, so it'll be a good opportunity to open that desk. I wasn't wanting to open it with Matt looking on. Where's the key?"

"We thought you might have it."

"We'll see! We'll see! M'h'm! Maybe it's in my strong-box."

Gerald fetched the desk and put it on the table in the sitting-room and Uncle Gregor found several bunches of rusty keys.

Gerald had been through this performance before, of course—he had become tired of it quite soon—but Uncle Gregor sat down and got to work patiently and methodically.

"M'h'm, this is it?" he said at last. "It's a bit rusty but it catches. . . . There we are, Gerald!"

When the desk had been opened and the top half laid back upon its hinges, the box made a sloping writing-surface covered with tooled green leather at the top of which was a well for an inkpot and a tray for pens. Gerald had never seen anything like it before.

"I remember it!" exclaimed Uncle Gregor. "My mother used it for all her letters. She wrote a great many letters, for she had five brothers and sisters in different parts of the world. Letters were letters in those days—no telephones, of course. I wonder what's in it."

Gerald felt inclined to say, "Why not look and see?", but he managed to be patient.

It was several minutes before Uncle Gregor lifted the lid. The box contained bundles of letters rolled up and secured with elastic bands and several small parcels done up in blue tissue paper. Uncle Gregor opened the parcels and spread out the contents on the table.

"Jewellery!" he exclaimed. "It's valuable, Gerald!"

Gerald did not think so. There was a necklace and some rings and brooches. The settings were old-fashioned, ornate and unattractive. Some of the stones were quite good, but on the whole the treasure trove was disappointing. The only thing that appealed to Gerald was a small oval miniature of a boy's head and shoulders; it was framed in gold, studded with pearls.

"I could sell them!" said Uncle Gregor. "They're worth a lot of money."

"Nobody would buy them," Gerald replied. "They're old-fashioned—but they could be broken up, of course. You'd get something for the stones and the gold settings. Listen, Uncle Gregor! Why not get them valued by a good man, and sell them, and use the money for mending some of the barns?"

"I'll think on it, Gerald."

"Don't think on it—do it," said Gerald impatiently.

"Och, Gerald, you're like your father! That's what Robert used to say: 'Don't think on it—do it.' He was always at me to do things . . . but I missed him when he went to London, and I missed wee Bessie."

"What was her mother like?"

"Bessie's mother? She was always ailing, poor woman."

153

"What was the matter with her?"

Uncle Gregor hesitated. Then he said, "We'll not talk about Bessie's mother. Your mother was different altogether: bright and cheery, up and doing! At first she got on well with Maggie. Maggie liked her at first, they had good jokes——"

"Yes, I know," interrupted Gerald. "You told me that before. I knew Mother quite well, of course. I mean it's only three years since she died. Bess doesn't remember her mother at all and she wondered——"

"She wouldn't," said Uncle Gregor. "Bessie was little more than an infant when poor Joan died. Look, Gerald! Do you think Bessie would like this wee coloured photo? It's your father —and Bessie's father of course—when he was a lad."

Gerald accepted the miniature. (It was the best thing in the box and he was sure Bess would like it.) He had a feeling that it was a red herring, but if Uncle Gregor was determined not to speak of "poor Joan," he could do no more about it. He hoped sincerely that Mrs. Inglis would be easier to draw.

"We'd better put these things away safely," said Uncle Gregor, cutting short Gerald's thanks. "We'll not say a word to Matt—mind that, Gerald! He'd get them out of me if he could. He never comes unless he wants money. That's the truth."

Gerald helped to roll up the little parcels and put them back in the desk. The letters, also, were stowed away securely. The letters might have been interesting but as they were written in spidery writing and crossed in the manner of long ago, they would have been extremely difficult to decipher.

"I'll have a go at them when Matt has gone," declared Uncle Gregor. "Come on, Gerald! You can carry the desk up to the attic and we'll hide it."

They hid it behind a pile of dilapidated chairs. Gerald was aware that Uncle Gregor still believed his mother's jewellery to be valuable in spite of what he had said.

21. Mrs. Inglis

It had been Gerald's intention to see Mrs. Inglis on Monday, but her brother, who worked on the farm, informed him that she had gone to Dumfries for a treatment.

"She's got the rheumatics," Macfarlane explained. "So she goes there once a fortnight and she doesn't get home till late."

This was unfortunate as it meant that Gerald had to potter about the farm with Uncle Gregor, and he had seen quite enough of the farm. He wouldn't have minded if he could have done something about it, but there was nothing he could do. He would have built up the gate-post, but the sack of cement (when at last it was found) had been standing beneath a leak in the roof of the barn and had become as hard as a rock.

"Och, never heed, Gerald," said Uncle Gregor. "Maybe I'll get an extra man in the spring . . ."

Gerald felt inclined to say "M'h'm"—but managed to refrain.

Tuesday was wet. It was not the sort of day that an old woman with rheumatism was likely to be out, so Gerald walked to the village in the afternoon and knocked at the door of the cottage which stood beside the Post Office. The door was opened almost at once by a small thin woman with smooth grey hair, who smiled cheerfully and invited him to come in.

"I'm real glad to see you, Mr. Gerald," she declared. "I'd give you tea in the parlour, but the fire's not on (I'd have put a match to it if I'd known you were coming), but there's a nice fire in the kitchen if you're not too grand."

Gerald assured her that he was not grand at all and followed her into her comfortable kitchen. As it was only three o'clock—and he had just had an excellent dinner—he was not ready for another meal, but he was aware that he would have to accept Mrs. Inglis's hospitality if he wanted to get anything out of her.

"What a nice kitchen!" he exclaimed.

"Yes, it's nice," she agreed. "I've got nice furniture. The boys send me things. They're very good to me, Mr. Gerald. Robbie is in a second-hand shop in Glasgow, so he's in the way of picking up bargains." She continued to chat cheerfully as she bustled round, laying a snow-white cloth on the table and setting out plates of scones and a home-made cake.

"Bess asked me to come and see you," said Gerald, when he was able to get a word in edgeways. "She was worried because you didn't write to her."

"I couldn't," she replied, holding out her hands which were distorted with arthritis.

"Oh, dear, that's bad," said Gerald sadly. "You must suffer a great deal of pain, I'm afraid."

"Off and on, Mr. Gerald. More on than off, really. It's not too bad in the daytime. It's bad at night."

"Does it keep you awake?"

"Yes, it does," she admitted. "I don't say much about it unless people ask. People have troubles of their own, so they're not all that interested in other people's troubles."

Gerald was aware that this was true, so he was genuinely sympathetic. He asked if the treatment was helpful. She replied that it might be, if she could have it more often, but it was tiring going to Dumfries and waiting at the hospital and coming back in the cold. "But it might be worse," she added cheerfully. "It might be my eyes. If I lost the use of my eyes, I couldn't read; I couldn't see the hills. I wouldn't be able to see you sitting at my table." She smiled and added, "You were only five when

156

you went away to London, but when I saw you on my doorstep I knew fine it was you."

This didn't surprise Gerald. Visitors to Haines were not very plentiful—and, of course, she must have heard from her brother that he was staying at Cannochbrae. All the same it was a friendly thing to say; he decided that he liked Mrs. Inglis.

"Miss Bess is wonderful, isn't she?" continued Mrs. Inglis. "There was a long bit in the papers about her acting in that play. Have you seen the play, Mr. Gerald?"

"Yes, several times. It's a good play, some of it is very amusing and there are good songs in it, but it wouldn't be worth seeing without Bess. She looks beautiful and she's so natural that it doesn't seem like acting."

"I'm not surprised. She was always singing and dancing; she was like a sunbeam in the house. There was something about her," declared Mrs. Inglis, pausing, and looking thoughtful. "There was something about her that made you feel she was extra special . . . but you know that better than me! Here am I, havering, when you could be telling me about her!"

"What do you want to know?"

"Has she got a nice house?" enquired Mrs. Inglis eagerly.

"She has a lovely flat, beautifully furnished. It's in London, of course. I've been staying with her there."

"That's nice. You were always friends when you were children; you were always running after her like a little shadow. Take a scone, Mr. Gerald. They're my own baking. And maybe you'd pour out the tea: it's not easy for me with my hands."

Gerald accepted the scone—which fortunately was as light as a feather—and poured out the tea—which unfortunately was black and tasted of tannin.

"You knew Bess's mother, didn't you?" he asked.

"I was the cook at Cannochbrae for years," replied Mrs. Inglis. "I went there when Mr. Gregor got married and I stayed on till I got married myself, so I knew them all. I was very fond of the first Mrs. Robert Burleigh-Brown, and though there was a lot of cooking, I used to help her when I could find the

157

time. She liked chatting to me; she said I was a comfort to her. Well, I did my best."

"She was delicate, wasn't she?"

"Yes, poor soul! And she was sometimes very miserable. Mr. Robert (your father, Mr. Gerald) was kind to her in his own way, but he didn't understand her. He was always trying to cheer her up. He'd come in from the fields and find her in one of her miserable moods and he'd tell her to 'brace up.' He'd try to make her come out for a walk—or to see the lambs. He'd tell her it was a lovely sunny day and it would do her good to come out."

"But if she was ill——" began Gerald in surprise. "I mean she couldn't go out if she was ill! Could she?"

"It wasn't her body that was ill, it was her mind. That's what he didn't understand. She couldn't help it, Mr. Gerald— she couldn't, really. It wasn't her fault," said Mrs. Inglis earnestly. "It was in the family, you see. Her mother was the same, only worse, and poor Miss Anna! It's an illness, you know. People can't help it. That's what Mr. Robert didn't understand."

Gerald was speechless with dismay . . . and Mrs. Inglis, misunderstanding his silence, continued to assure him that "she couldn't help it" and to give him details of poor Mrs. Robert Burleigh-Brown's condition of mind and of all she said and did "when she took one of her miserable moods."

"But, Mrs. Inglis," said Gerald at last, "she had a lot to bear. Perhaps it was just that she wanted a child so badly. She had two miscarriages—that was enough to make any woman unhappy."

"She hadn't really, Mr. Gerald."

"What do you mean?"

"That was just the story that was given out. Mr. Robert didn't want people to know the truth, so he told me I was to say it—and I *did* say it. I did, really! It wasn't me that said she was off her head . . . but it got about. (Things get about in a wee place like Haines.) I told him it wasn't me, but he didn't believe me. He was vexed at me about it. He was never the same to me after that."

Gerald was stunned with horror: Mrs. Inglis's revelation was frightful; it was worse than his direst fears! He had hoped to be able to comfort Bess, to tell her that her mother had been absolutely normal—just like other women—and that the blighting of her hopes had made her sad. He had hoped to go back to Glasgow with good news for Walter! What was he to do now? He would have to tell Walter, of course; it would be unfair not to tell Walter! What would Walter feel about it?

It was such a dreadful blow that Gerald almost fainted. The kitchen was warm; it became hazy; the table began to rock before his eyes.

"Are you feeling well enough?" asked his hostess in alarm.

He managed to say he was all right and to pull himself together. All he wanted was to get away, to leave the cottage and to breathe the open air—but he couldn't. He wished with all his heart that he had never come to Haines and stirred up the mud, but he must go on with it now. It was too late to draw back.

There had been a short silence. Gerald felt it had lasted too long, so he broke it by saying the first thing that came into his head: "But she had a child, hadn't she, Mrs. Inglis?"

"Yes," agreed Mrs. Inglis. "Yes, she had a child. You see there were times when she was better—almost like other people —she wasn't miserable all the time. When she found she was going to have a child, she was so excited that she was up in the clouds. (That was her, all over. She was either up in the clouds or down in the dumps.) She was up in the clouds at the idea of having a baby; she never ceased talking about it. She wanted a wee daughter; it was to be called Elizabeth. I got patterns for her and she made little jackets and I helped her to trim the old cot which Mrs. Gregor had had for Matt. Everything was pink—for a girl. She was so happy and excited that I was worried to death."

"Why were you worried?"

"She was delicate, Mr. Gerald. She was a poor thing. I wondered if the baby would arrive safely and what would happen if it didn't . . . and I wondered if the baby would be all right. I know about babies," explained Mrs. Inglis. "I'd have liked to be a nurse, but I hadn't the money to take my training. All the same I used to do what I could. The neighbours used to send for me if there was trouble in the house. Often and often I helped the district nurse to deliver babies—so I know about them."

"Yes, I see," said Gerald. He added, "I'm sure you must have been a great help to Mrs. Burleigh-Brown."

His hostess was silent. She was gazing at the half-eaten scone upon her plate and frowning.

"Go on, Mrs. Inglis," he said encouragingly. "The baby arrived all right, didn't it?"

"Yes," said Mrs. Inglis in reluctant tones.

"So you needn't have worried."

"No," said Mrs. Inglis.

"Somebody told me that Bess was born in a Glasgow hospital during an air-raid. That's right, isn't it?"

Mrs. Inglis nodded.

The woman had closed up like an oyster.

"Tell me about it," suggested Gerald.

"There's little to tell."

Gerald looked at her—and wondered. There was something here that he didn't understand and he had no idea how to get to the bottom of it. At last he said, "Mrs. Burleigh-Brown was taken ill suddenly, wasn't she? Did they send her to Glasgow in an ambulance?"

"No. Doctor said the train was better. Miss Anna was here and went with her, but she was ill and frightened—and Miss Anna wasn't much use."

"You could have taken care of her much better," suggested Gerald.

"Yes, I could—and that's the truth!" exclaimed Mrs.

160

Inglis defiantly. "She wanted me to go with her, but Mr. Robert wouldn't let me. She clung to my hand when they were taking her away! She said, 'Oh, Jean, will my baby be all right?' She knew it was a risk—a premature baby! I told her she would have the best doctor at the hospital and they would look after the baby and put it in an incubator . . . but, oh dear! I wondered if I'd ever see her again. I never slept a wink all night, thinking about her," added Mrs. Inglis tearfully.

"It was dangerous, wasn't it? Especially dangerous for a woman who was nervous and delicate?"

"Yes, it was dangerous. That's why I was so upset. I could scarcely believe it when Mr. Robert told me that Miss Anna had telephoned to say the baby had arrived safely—and that it was a girl. That was all I was told. Mr. Robert might have told me more, but he was annoyed at me and I didn't like to ask. So then I said to Mrs. Gregor could I have a night off and go to Glasgow to see my cousin at Maryhill and she said I could—and that's what I did. I stayed the night with my cousin and went to the hospital the next afternoon. I was worried about Mrs. Burleigh-Brown and I was worried about the baby. I know about babies, so I thought it would be a poor, weak, miserable wee mite of course."

"But it wasn't," said Gerald.

"How do you know?" cried Mrs. Inglis in dismay.

Gerald might have replied that she had told him herself—certainly she had inferred it—but he remained silent, hoping she would say more.

"Oh, you're too clever!" she exclaimed angrily. "I've kept the secret all these years and you've wormed it out of me in half an hour! You're too clever, that's what you are! Besides I might have been mistaken—it was just my own idea! I couldn't be certain, could I?"

Gerald was not half as clever as Mrs. Inglis imagined; he was completely baffled. "But you know about babies, don't you?" he suggested, clutching at the only available straw.

"Yes, I know about babies," she agreed taking out her

handkerchief and drying her eyes. "I said so to the nurse. A young girl she was—not properly experienced."

"What did she say?"

"She didn't know anything," replied Mrs. Inglis scornfully. "She was young and stupid. She wasn't fit to look after a kitten—far less a baby! So then I said wasn't there anybody who could tell me what I wanted to know and she said I could ask Sister if I liked."

"The Sister in charge of the ward?"

"Yes, but I couldn't because the Sister was off duty and I couldn't wait. I had to get my train. I had just gone to Glasgow for the one night to stay with my cousin at Maryhill and to see Mrs. Burleigh-Brown."

"Was she looking very ill?" asked Gerald, feeling his way cautiously through the entanglement.

"Not as bad as I expected. In fact she was wonderful—considering. She'd had a bad time, and she'd been frightened at the air-raid, but she'd got what she wanted. It gave me a lump in my throat when I saw her with the child in her arms, cuddling it and crooning over it and rubbing her cheek against its hair. She kept on saying, 'Oh, Jean, isn't she lovely? My very own darling little daughter! Oh, Jean, how happy I am!'"

Mrs. Inglis gave a little sob and continued, "I was happy too. I was fond of Mrs. Burleigh-Brown—and sorry for her—and I'd been worried, like I told you. It was only afterwards when I took the baby in my arms and had a chance to look at it properly and feel the weight of it that I was so surprised. It was only then that I realised . . ."

Mrs. Inglis burst into tears.

"You realised that the child couldn't be hers," Gerald suggested. It was difficult to hide his excitement.

"Yes, that was it," agreed Mrs. Inglis, controlling herself with difficulty. "That's what I said, isn't it? If I hadn't known about babies, I mightn't have noticed. It was the weight I noticed first. It must have been well over seven pounds—and it was a beautiful child, as pretty as a doll! I couldn't believe it! I couldn't believe my eyes! Then I looked at its dear wee hands and I saw that the nails were pairfect."

Gerald's ignorance of babies was profound, so the fact that the infant's nails were 'pairfect' meant nothing to him. However, he hid his bewilderment and nodded.

"The nails were pairfect," repeated Mrs. Inglis significantly. "That shows you, doesn't it?"

"Yes," agreed Gerald. He added, "You didn't say anything to Mrs. Burleigh-Brown, I suppose?"

"How could I? She was so happy. She was as happy as a queen! If I'd as much as hinted what I thought, she'd have been demented. I just couldn't do it, Mr. Gerald . . . but I spoke to another nurse as I was coming away; she was in charge of the nursery where the babies were kept at night. They were all there together in little cots so that they wouldn't disturb their mothers if they cried. I asked if they ever got muddled up and she was furious at me. She said that they were labelled with a piece of plaster and their mother's names written on it—and she showed me, so it was true."

"There was an air-raid, wasn't there? Perhaps that was how it happened."

"That's what I thought," agreed Mrs. Inglis. "I thought about it all the way home in the train—anything could happen in an air-raid! And I wondered what I ought to do. Maybe I should have spoken to Mr. Robert Burleigh-Brown, but to tell the truth, I was afraid to open my mouth. He was vexed at me already. Dear knows what he would have said to me if I'd told him about the baby!" Mrs. Inglis hesitated and then added, "Besides, the more I thought about it the more I wondered."

"You mean you weren't absolutely certain?"

"Sometimes I was and sometimes I wasn't."

Gerald could sympathise. He, too, had suffered from the state of indecision which comes from "wondering." He had lain awake night after night wondering about that horrible affair at Koolbokie.

At this very moment he was in a dilemma. His thoughts

were chaotic; he wanted to go away and think quietly about what Mrs. Inglis had told him, but he realised that he must obtain all the information he possibly could before he left the cottage. It was his only chance! When he had gone, Mrs. Inglis would regret her confidences; probably she would be angry with him; certainly she would never speak of the matter again. Unfortunately his mind was in such a turmoil that he didn't know what to ask. He was obliged to sit still and eat his scone, which nearly choked him, and to drink his tea which was now tepid and extremely nasty.

He said at last, "It was a pity you didn't see the Sister who was in charge of the ward. She might have told you——"

"I couldn't wait. I told you that, Mr. Gerald!"

"I know. I don't suppose you remember her name?"

"It was the same as mine; that's why I remember. I thought she might be a distant cousin. I meant to ask her."

"Sister Inglis?"

"No, Macfarlane. It was nearly thirty years ago—long before I was married. It was the first air-raid they had in Glasgow, not the bad one when the docks were hit. Oh, dear! I don't know how you managed to worm it out of me. It was just talking about Miss Bess; I was excited and didn't think what I was saying."

Gerald did not reply. He had no idea how he had "wormed it out of her."

"You won't tell, will you?" she added anxiously. "It would be dreadful if she ever got to hear of it."

"Who?" asked Gerald.

"Miss Bess, of course! It would ruin her whole life! She wouldn't know who she was. What would you feel if you didn't know who you were?"

"I don't think I'd mind very much."

"You wouldn't mind? Well, I would! I'm proud of being a Macfarlane. I don't know what I'd do if somebody told me I was the child of an unknown woman—why, she mightn't even have been married! There were girls in that hospital having

164

babies without knowing who the father was! I'm surprised at you, Mr. Gerald. Really, I am!"

He was a little surprised at himself (he had spoken without thinking); he wondered if he should explain further. He almost asked Mrs. Inglis if she would rather be the child of a woman who had insanity in her family or of a woman who might, or might not, have been married; but he hesitated to put the question; he had no idea what her reaction would be. Better to leave it, thought Gerald.

He said, "Don't worry, Mrs. Inglis. I'm very discreet— and I can assure you I would never do anything to hurt Bess. I love her dearly. You know that, don't you?" He rose as he spoke and thanked his hostess for her hospitality.

"But you haven't finished your tea!" she exclaimed. "You've scarcely eaten anything! Would you not take a slice of cake? It's got three eggs in it—and real butter."

"I'm afraid I must go," he replied, trying to sound regretful. "I promised Uncle Gregor I wouldn't be late."

"Well, you can take a slice with you and eat it on the way," said Mrs. Inglis.

Gerald was obliged to agree (he couldn't escape without it), so he waited while Mrs. Inglis cut a large slice of cake and put it in a paper bag. Then she followed him to the door and said goodbye.

He was turning away when she called him back and asked him to give her kind regards to Miss Bess. "I've got two boys," she explained. "But I'd have liked fine to have a wee daughter."

"Like Bess?"

"Just like Bess."

"I'll give her your love, Mrs. Inglis."

"Well, you could! She was a dear wee girlie; I've always loved her. There's one thing certain, Mr. Gerald: she'd never have been such a healthy, bonny, happy child if she hadn't got muddled up."

Gerald couldn't help smiling. Mrs. Inglis was very "muddled up," but her meaning was perfectly clear.

22. Gerald's Dilemma

The rain had stopped and the sky was blue, so Gerald walked through the village and took a steep stony path up the hill. He had told Mrs. Inglis that he had promised not to be late —and it was true—but there was plenty of time before Uncle Gregor's tea for him to have a good think. Gerald walked some distance and then sat down on a stone; some people could walk and think, but Gerald's thoughts moved better when he was sitting still . . . and he had a lot to think about.

The piece of cake was still in his pocket. He couldn't eat it, for he was full of Mrs. Inglis's scones and before very long he would have to partake of tea with Uncle Gregor, so he crumbled it and threw it to the birds. Then he gave his whole attention to the problem. What should he do?

Could Mrs. Inglis have been mistaken? She had said she knew about babies . . . but in spite of that she was not absolutely certain of her ground. She had said herself that the more she thought about it the more she wondered! How was Gerald to find out the truth without disclosing the secret? Nobody must know the secret except Walter and Bess.

Oh, joy! thought Gerald. Oh, joy! It will make them happy. He discovered that he, himself, believed the story. Yes, he believed it. Could the beautiful radiant Bess be the child of "a poor thing"? It was impossible. All that nonsense about Ophelia was just . . . just nonsense! It was the sympathetic

166

temperament of an artist. Bess and Walter could marry and have children and live happily ever after! Oh, joy!

Gerald was "up in the clouds"!

Then he came down with a bump. . . . But just supposing it wasn't true?

I can't risk it, thought Gerald. I can't go to Walter with a vague story of an old woman who was shown a baby and was surprised at its appearance. I must make absolutely certain before I say a word about it.

Gerald held his head in his hands. How was he to find out? How could he get to the root of the matter? The root lay deeply buried in that hospital; it had been buried for nearly thirty years! There was only one person who could help him; it was the Sister who had been in charge of the ward. Her name was the same as Mrs. Inglis's—she was Sister Macfarlane, of course. Yes, but it was thirty years ago, so she might be dead. She would certainly be much too old to work in a busy hospital! All the same she was the only clue . . . so he must go to Glasgow and do his best to find her.

This was Tuesday. His week's visit to Cannochbrae would not be completed until Friday, but he couldn't wait—he was full of impatience. He rose and ran back to the farm.

Uncle Gregor and Matt were just sitting down to the evening meal when Gerald arrived, breathless with haste and excitement.

"Hullo!" said Uncle Gregor. "You seem in a hurry, lad."

"I didn't want to be late," explained Gerald.

Matt looked up and said, "There was a phone call for you, coz. It was your boss. You're to ring him after ten. I promised to give you the message."

"Oh, thank you! I wonder what he wants."

"Inconsiderate," growled Uncle Gregor. "The man never leaves you in peace. I told you he would be inconsiderate, Gerald. 'Ring him up after ten'! You ought to be in your bed by ten! When does he go to his bed? 'Early to bed and early to rise makes a man healthy wealthy and wise.'"

"He's wealthy," said Matt with a short laugh.

"He's wise," said Gerald staunchly.

"He's inconsiderate," said Uncle Gregor.

"Not really, Uncle Gregor. I told you that I'm not starting work until February, but I'm being paid my salary on condition that I'm available when he needs me."

"That sounds a bit of all right," declared Matt. "Perhaps I could get a job at MacCallum's. You could put in a word for me, couldn't you, coz?"

Gerald did not reply.

It had been Gerald's intention to find some excuse for cutting short his visit to Cannochbrae, but he decided not to. It would be much better to ring up his boss as requested. (Then he could tell Uncle Gregor that he had been summoned to Glasgow on business). He helped himself from a dish of curry and rice which was on the sideboard and sat down to eat it. He was glad to see that Matt looked better and was enjoying his food.

"It will be fine tomorrow," said Uncle Gregor. "We'll go to the market in Dumfries, Gerald. I want a boar—and it'll interest you to see the beasts."

"Yes, if I can," Gerald replied. "Sir Walter may want me in Glasgow. I shall have to wait and see what he says."

"That man!" growled Uncle Gregor.

23. Cousin Matt Says Goodbye!

Gerald made an early start next morning. Fortunately he was able to say with absolute truth that he was wanted in Glasgow to translate a letter from Hamburg and Uncle Gregor had taken the news quite meekly. In fact he had been so impressed with his nephew's ability to "talk German" that he had merely said; "Och well, it can't be helped, but you'll come back another time, Gerald. You'll always be welcome at Cannochbrae and if you're going to be working in Glasgow, it's not very far to come."

In spite of his carelessness and his growls there was much to be said for Uncle Gregor. The old man had courage and was as straight as a die in body and mind. These were virtues which Gerald admired; he decided that when he came to Glasgow, he must make a point of visiting Cannochbrae now and then.

Gerald had been unable to say goodbye to Matt (who had not appeared at breakfast) but, as he was not very fond of his cousin, Gerald did not care. He ran Peg out of the barn and started off. However, when he reached the gate, with its tumble-down gate-post, Matt stepped out from behind a bush and held up his hand.

"Just wanted to say goodbye," explained Matt. "It was decent of you to get that bottle for me. I'd like the prescription in case I get another chill."

Gerald smiled. "I wouldn't risk another chill if I were

169

you and anyhow I haven't got the prescription. The chemist in Drumburly made it up."

"I suppose I could get it from him?"

"Don't drink poison—that's my advice. Cut it out altogether, old boy."

Gerald wanted to drive on and leave it at that, but Cousin Matt had placed a large hand firmly on the edge of the open window. "Listen," he said. "You needn't worry about that funny story I told you the other night. I won't blab. I'm not the chap to put a spoke in your wheel. I like you, coz."

"I told you the story was untrue."

"I know, I know! We'll say no more about it. Are you going to Glasgow today?"

"Yes."

"You're lucky to get that job. If you see an opening for me in MacCallum's, you can drop me a line. I might take it on for a bit."

Gerald hesitated, wondering what to say.

"It would be quite easy for you," Matt pointed out. "You're pretty thick with the boss—lunching with him and all that."

"He wanted to see me on business."

"This place gets me down. Nothing to do."

"You could mend that gate-post," suggested Gerald.

"Yes, it ought to be done. Trouble is I'm not supposed to do heavy work—doctor's orders—bad for the old ticker," explained Matt, putting his hand on his heart.

"Oh, I see. Well, I'm off Matt. Goodbye and good luck!"

"Same to you, coz . . .," but he didn't move. "You have all the luck," he added. "I mean getting that job without a reference. You didn't have a reference, did you?"

Again Gerald hesitated. He didn't like telling lies.

"I suppose you're getting a good screw," suggested Matt.

"I've told you already that I'm quite satisfied with what I'm getting."

"Well, in that case—I mean if you're getting a good screw —you might lend me a tenner. I'll pay you back, of course."

170

"A tenner? No, I couldn't."

"Well, a fiver."

Gerald was sorry for Matt—really very sorry for the wretched creature—and he could have spared a fiver. If it hadn't been for Walter's warning, he would have taken the note out of his wallet and handed it over there and then . . . but Walter had talked of blackmail! Was this what he had meant by "gentle blackmail"?

"No, Matt, I'm afraid I can't," said Gerald.

Matt had noticed the moment of hesitation. "Come on, be a sport!" he said persuasively. "I'm on the rocks—absolutely. It took my last bob to get here, but it's no use. The old man's a skin-flint. You'd think he'd be pleased to see his one and only, wouldn't you? He's a skinflint—that's what he is! If you can't produce a fiver, a couple of quid would do. You could manage that, couldn't you?"

"Sorry, Matt. Nothing doing."

"Oh, well, I shan't blab. We're cousins, aren't we?"

This should have reassured Gerald, but it did not. There was a sly look in the small watery eyes and the large hand remained on the edge of the open window.

Matt added thoughtfully, "It was funny you didn't get a reference from Koolbokie, wasn't it?"

"Matt," said Gerald. "I've told you that the story you heard in Jo'burg isn't true, so if you put it about, I shall have you up for—for defamation of character." Gerald had intended to say "libel" and then it had occurred to him that libel was something that was written, so he had used the other term instead. It sounded fearsome in his own ears and obviously it impressed Matt . . . for Matt started in surprise—or dismay—and his grasp on the window was loosened.

Gerald let in the clutch and drove off, leaving Cousin Matt standing in the road with his mouth open!

All this had wasted time . . . but was it wasted? Gerald thought not. He chuckled to himself when he remembered Matt's face and decided that it had been worth it. Besides, it was easy enough to make up time. When he reached Drumburly and got onto the main road, he gave Peg his head and Peg responded like a race-horse.

Sir Walter had said that the letter from Hamburg had just arrived and he wanted Gerald to come on Friday to answer it. This was Wednesday, of course, so Gerald had two days in which to pursue his enquiries. He had decided not to say a word to Walter until he had found out all he could. He would put up at the hotel where he had stayed before, and do his best to find Sister Macfarlane. If only she wasn't dead! If only he could find her! If only he could persuade her to talk!

Gerald sighed. He had been given a task and he wanted to finish it neatly; he wanted to go to Walter with the story complete. That was how Walter did things.

The traffic in the Glasgow streets was worse than ever, so Gerald made for the garage which Dickenson had recommended and left Peg there in safety. Then he asked a policeman the way to the hospital and boarded a convenient bus. When he saw the size of the hospital and the streams of people going in and coming out, his heart sank into his shoes and he almost turned away. How could he possibly find out anything about Sister Macfarlane, who had been here thirty years ago? However he had to try.

The desk marked ENQUIRIES was in the hall, so he waited patiently in the queue—and made his enquiry.

"Miss Bond may know. She's the secretary," said the girl. "If you wait a minute, I'll find out if she can see you."

Gerald sat down on a bench in the hall and waited. People came and went. A woman with a child sat down beside him. A man on crutches hobbled past. Men in white coats passed up and down wheeling trolleys. Nurses in uniform ran up the flights of stairs and disappeared from view. Every now and then the big doors were opened and stretchers with motionless bodies wrapped in blankets were carried in and taken up in the lift.

It was a busy scene, but there was no confusion; all these people were full of purpose; they knew where they were going and were making for their objectives, not hastily, but without hesitation.

172

Gerald waited and waited. He had begun to wonder whether the girl at the desk had forgotten all about him when she came to fetch him.

"Miss Bond will see you now—but she's very busy."

"It won't take long," said Gerald. It wouldn't take long for Miss Bond to tell him his quest was hopeless and to show him the door!

Miss Bond's office was at the end of the corridor. It was a good-sized room lined with cupboards and furnished with desks and wooden chairs. Miss Bond, herself, was a middle-aged woman with large spectacles and greying hair.

"I'm sorry to bother you when you're so busy," said Gerald politely. "The fact is I'm very anxious to get in touch with Sister Macfarlane. She was in charge of the—the part of the hospital where babies were born."

"The Maternity Wing," said Miss Bond crisply.

"Yes, she was here for years, but it's a long time ago, so she may have retired—or gone somewhere else—or she may be dead. It sounds pretty hopeless, I'm afraid."

Miss Bond rose, opened a cupboard, took out a large green book and, moistening a finger, flicked over the pages.

"Macfarlane, Alice? Macfarlane, Christine? Macfarlane, Janet?" she enquired.

"I don't know," said Gerald helplessly. "She was here during the war."

"Macfarlane, Mary," said Miss Bond. "Sister in charge of the Maternity Wing from 1936 to 1954. Is that her?"

"Yes," said Gerald breathlessly.

"She has retired of course. Do you want her address?"

"Yes, please."

Miss Bond wrote the address on a card and gave it to him. "It's Knightswood," she said. "You'll get a bus at Charing Cross. Goodbye."

"Oh, thank you! Thank you very much. Goodbye, Miss Bond."

Miss Bond had said goodbye; she did not repeat the valediction. Already she had seized an enormous account book and was totting up figures. It was obvious that the admirable woman wasted neither time nor words.

Gerald backed out and shut the door quietly. He felt quite dazed. It had been so easy! Almost too easy. He had expected this obstacle to be Becher's Brook and it had turned out to be a three-foot hurdle.

Now for Sister Macfarlane! Perhaps she was Becher's Brook? Well, never mind! He was going straight for the next obstacle, however large it might be. It was half-past-two by this time (Gerald had breakfasted early and had had no lunch), but he was too excited to think of lunch. He was not a jockey now, he was a bloodhound on the trail.

24. Miss Macfarlane

During his stay in Glasgow, Gerald had acquired the habit of consulting policemen; he had found Glasgow policemen extremely kind and helpful—all except the one who had been cross with Peg—so he got hold of the first one he saw and received clear instructions about the bus to Knightswood via the Great Western Road. Another policeman, at Knightswood, directed Gerald to Sister Macfarlane's abode, which was in an avenue of semi-detached little houses each of which had a small patch of garden. Rather a pleasant place to live, thought Gerald, who disliked noisy streets and traffic. Indeed, it crossed his mind that when he came to Glasgow, he might do worse than live here himself.

Sister Macfarlane's house was empty and shut up. There was no answer when he rang the bell, nor were there any signs of life when he walked round and peered in at the windows. A boy, who was cutting the hedge in the next-door garden, stopped work and remarked, "She's away."

"'Away from home?" asked Gerald in dismay.

"Aye."

"When will she be back?"

"Ah couldn't say."

"Where has she gone?"

"It's the croolty."

"Did you say 'the croolty'?"

175

"Aye. She's gey keen on the croolty."

"Is it a place?"

"Naw, it's a mon. Did ye niver hear tell o' the croolty mon, mister?"

"Never," replied Gerald.

"He's nosey," said the boy. Then he spat on his hands and continued his work industriously.

Gerald waited for a minute or two, wondering what to do. He was baffled. Sister Macfarlane was an elderly spinster—and doubtless extremely respectable—so he could scarcely believe that she had gone away with a man. He looked up and down the road, but there was nobody in sight. Should he call at one of the near-by houses and ask for information or should he have another try at the boy? He decided to try the boy, so he called to him and displayed half-a-crown.

"Listen," said Gerald. "I want to speak to Sister Macfarlane. It's important. Can you tell me in plain language where she has gone and when she's likely to be home?"

"She'll be back for her tea, maist likely."

"Today?"

"Aye. That's right, mister."

"When does she have tea?"

"Och, about four. She'll be back any minit now," replied the boy, holding out his hand.

"Are you sure?" asked Gerald doubtfully.

"That's her," replied the boy, pointing.

Gerald turned and saw a tall, gaunt, elderly woman coming along the road. He was annoyed—he wondered whether the boy had bamboozled him on purpose—but it didn't matter.

The half-crown changed hands and the boy returned to his clipping.

Sister Macfarlane was coming home for her tea. She was carrying a collecting tin and a tray of gaily-coloured little flags. She was walking very slowly, but hastened her steps when she saw the young man standing at the gate.

"Are you looking for me?" she enquired anxiously. "It's not Mrs. Thomson, is it?"

"I'm looking for Sister Macfarlane."

She nodded. "Yes, but I've retired, so I just call myself 'Miss.'"

"But you still do a little nursing?" suggested Gerald. He was sure she did. Once a nurse, always a nurse!

"Oh, I can still fill in gaps . . . but I hope it's not Mrs. Thomson?"

"No."

"Thank goodness for that! I hope it's not tonight you want me?"

"You're tired of course."

"I'm dead beat. There's nothing more tiring than walking up and down the streets and standing on doorsteps ringing the bells and waiting and getting no reply . . . or being told to come back later because Mrs. A is out . . . or Mrs. B has visitors and can't be disturbed . . . or Mrs. C has no change and won't have any change until her husband comes home from work. I really couldn't take on night-duty."

"It isn't that. I just want to talk to you for a few minutes." Gerald glanced at the flags and the collecting tin and added, "I see you're interested in children."

"I love them," replied Miss Macfarlane. "Especially babies, of course."

Gerald took out his wallet and was about to insert a ten-shilling note in the slit.

"Not there," said Miss Macfarlane. "I keep the notes separate because they get torn. Thank you very much."

"It's a good object."

"Yes," she agreed. "The Royal Scottish Society for the Prevention of Cruelty to Children does good work. The inspectors are wonderful. They go about making enquiries about children who are neglected or ill-treated. You wouldn't think anybody could be cruel to a child, would you? But a great many very sad cases are discovered. That's why I like to collect for the Society. It's something I can do to help."

They were still standing at the gate.

"You had better come in if you want to talk to me," added

177

Miss Macfarlane. "My feet are killing me and I want my tea. Perhaps you'd like a cup, Mr.—er—er . . . ?"

"George Black," said Gerald. He had decided that he must be very careful until he saw what the woman was like. It wasn't his secret. Nobody must know—except Walter and Bess.

"You'd like a cup, wouldn't you, Mr. Black?" asked Miss Macfarlane, taking out her latch-key and opening the door.

"There's nothing I'd like better," replied Gerald.

Miss Macfarlane showed him into her little sitting-room, and switched on the electric fire. "I shall be ten minutes," she said. "I left everything ready before I went out—I knew I'd be tired—and I have a quick-boiling kettle."

"I see you know how to look after yourself," said Gerald smiling.

"I have to," she replied. "There's nobody else to look after me."

While she was away, Gerald made a tour of the room and looked at the photographs. He wanted to know about Miss Macfarlane and decide upon his manner of approach. Already he was aware that she was a sensible, practical woman with a warm heart—especially warm for babies—so it did not surprise him to discover that most of the photographs were of babies, all except one, which was on the small table beside her chair. This was the photograph of a young man in officer's uniform and was signed "Yours ever, Teddy." Somehow or other Gerald was quite sure that Teddy had been a casualty in the war.

There was a framed print hanging on the wall over the chimney-piece. It was by Alma Tadema and depicted a beautiful young girl and a handsome young man sitting upon a garden-seat . . . so Miss Macfarlane was romantic and sentimental.

Gerald felt sorry for Miss Macfarlane. It was sad that she had lost Teddy and had nobody to look after her—sadder still that she had spent the best years of her life looking after other women's babies! She would have liked babies of her own.

The ten minutes had almost passed, so Gerald sat down and waited for his hostess to return. He had not long to wait before the door opened and she came in with the tea-tray. She had taken off her coat and hat and was wearing bedroom slippers. Gerald helped to arrange the table, found a footstool and placed it beneath her feet. The small attentions were well received.

"I'm dreadfully tired," admitted Miss Macfarlane. "I shouldn't have taken it on, really. The collecting, I mean. I'm getting too old. I always say I'm never going to do it again, but it's difficult to find collectors—and it's so important."

"Yes, of course," agreed Gerald. He was hungry, so he was disappointed to discover that Miss Macfarlane's idea of afternoon tea consisted of a plate of thin bread and butter and three chocolate biscuits. He could have done with some of Mrs. Inglis's scones and a slice of her home-made cake. Yesterday he had been stuffed with food that he didn't want (so full that he had scattered his cake for the birds!). Today he was practically starving! It was one of life's little ironies. However, it couldn't be helped.

"Miss Macfarlane," said Gerald earnestly. "I want to tell you a story. It's a true story about a beautiful girl and a very fine man. They're deeply in love with each other and I want them to be married. I'm quite sure they would be happy."

"Why don't they get married?" asked Miss Macfarlane, looking at him in surprise.

"The girl refuses to marry him. She's afraid of marriage because she has discovered that there's insanity in her family."

"But that's dreadful! Isn't he willing to take the risk? Doesn't he love her enough? It might be all right, you know."

"He loves her enough. He's quite willing to take the risk—if there is a risk. He says that if she's afraid of having children of her own, they could adopt a child; but she loves him too much to risk spoiling his life and making him unhappy."

"Oh, dear, how terribly sad! You're the man, of course."

"No, I'm—I'm just somebody who wants them to be happy."

"Is that true, Mr. Black?"

"Yes," replied Gerald. He added, "Miss Macfarlane, I

179

think—I hope very much that you'll be able to help me to make them happy."

"I can help you?" she exclaimed in amazement. "What on earth can I do about it? I don't even know them! I've never heard of them in my life!"

"You can tell me something I want to know—at least I hope you can."

She was silent, looking at him in some alarm.

"I'm not mad," said Gerald. "I'll explain everything and then you'll understand. You were the Sister in charge of the Maternity Wing of a big hospital, weren't you?"

"Yes, I was there for eighteen years."

"A great many babies were born while you were there."

"Hundreds."

Gerald nodded. "Yes, of course. You couldn't possibly remember them all . . . but you may, possibly, remember an air-raid. It wasn't the big air-raid when the docks were badly damaged; it was before that at the beginning of the war."

"Oh!" exclaimed Miss Macfarlane. Her face had become quite pale.

"It wasn't a terribly bad air-raid," Gerald continued. "But it was serious enough to alarm the patients."

"They were always frightened—and no wonder!"

"No wonder," agreed Gerald. He added, "I see you remember about it."

"How could I forget? It was the first raid. We didn't know what was going to happen!"

"Dreadful for you!" said Gerald sympathetically.

"Yes."

"I expect there was a good deal of—of confusion?"

"Yes. Yes, there was."

Gerald drank some tea. It was China tea, very weak, and it tasted of hay, but it gave him time to think. "Miss Macfarlane," he said. "There were two women in the hospital at the time. I mean in your part of the hospital———"

"Two? There were dozens!"

"Yes, quite likely. I'm just interested in two," said Gerald patiently. "Let's call them Mrs. A and Mrs. B. They both had baby girls. Mrs. B was delicate and—and rather excitable. She was rushed into hospital suddenly and her baby was born too soon, but she came through the ordeal and recovered. Did their babies get mixed up, Miss Macfarlane?"

"What?" cried Miss Macfarlane. "What did you say?"

"I just wondered——" began Gerald. "I mean, you said there was a good deal of confusion."

She gazed at him in dismay. "Who are you?" she asked in trembling tones. "You don't look like a policeman."

"A policeman? Good heavens, I'm not a policeman! I'm just quite an ordinary sort of chap who wants his friends to be happy. I told you about them, didn't I?"

"Yes, but I don't understand. That raid was nearly thirty years ago, so what has it got to do with your friends?"

Gerald hesitated. Then he said, "I'll explain later, but first I'd like to hear your story. There is a story, isn't there?"

She nodded.

"Please tell me, Miss Macfarlane," said Gerald persuasively.

She hid her face in her hands and was silent.

Gerald waited. At last he said, "You haven't forgotten about it, have you?"

"No, I haven't forgotten," she replied. She had calmed herself by this time and continued, "It's a funny thing, really. At first I worried about it a lot. Then I was so busy in the hospital that I didn't think about it any more . . . but since I retired I've had more time to think. I suppose it's true that when people get older, they remember things that happened long ago. At least that's what I've found. Just lately it has begun to—to worry me again. So I'll tell you. It will be a relief to my mind. If I'm sent to prison, I shall just have to bear it."

She sighed heavily and continued, "It was a frightful night—simply frightful! It was pandemonium. The patients were in hysterics; if one starts it sets them all off. The nurses had lost their heads and were useless. It was the first raid, you see, and we didn't know what was going to happen. Later, we had much worse raids, but everybody got used to them and behaved splendidly."

"The babies were born in the middle of the confusion," suggested Gerald.

"No, they weren't. They were born the day before. I don't know who told you that they were born during the raid— but it isn't true."

"I thought Mrs. B——"

"Mrs. Burleigh-Brown," interrupted Miss Macfarlane. "I shall never forget her name. She was carried into the ward in a state of collapse. She was almost pulseless. I could tell you the details of her condition, but unless you're a doctor it wouldn't be much good."

"I'm not a doctor."

"Oh, well! Doctor Thomson was very skillful, so we managed to pull her through. She came out of the anaesthetic just as the raid was starting. The sirens were wailing like lost souls, so she knew what was happening and the first thing she said was 'Is my baby all right? Where's my baby? Sister, where's my baby? I want it here, beside me, so that we'll both be killed together.' She clutched my apron and wouldn't let go . . . and cried for her baby. She cried and cried. She was in such a state that I didn't dare tell her the truth—I thought she would go completely off her head—I thought I had better wait until she was stronger."

"The baby was dead?"

"No, it wasn't, but it was a seven-month child and very feeble. I had it in an incubator, but I knew it couldn't live more than a few hours—and it didn't. It just faded away like a flower, poor little mite."

Gerald said, "What about the other woman? We called her Mrs. A."

"She was Miss A."

"Oh, I see."

"Her case was very different. We had no trouble with her, so I don't remember her name. It's the difficult cases that one remembers."

"Yes, of course."

"The child was a strong healthy little girl—a lovely baby —but her mother wouldn't look at her. Wouldn't have anything to do with her! When I tried to show the girl her baby, she hid her face in the pillow and said, 'Take it away! It has ruined my life. I wish it was dead.'

"It was wicked," declared Miss Macfarlane. "It made me terribly angry. It made me boil with rage." She hesitated and then added, "I had a mother who was crying for her baby . . . and a mother who wished her baby was dead."

"So you changed them."

"Yes. I must have been mad, of course. I changed the labels. It's nearly thirty years ago, but I remember it all as if it were last week. I can see myself doing it. The bombs were falling—not very near, but you could hear them in the distance— thump-thump—and the guns were roaring—and the nurses were running about like a lot of scared hens. Nothing seemed to matter, if you see what I mean? I expected the hospital to be blown up at any minute. So I changed them. I took Miss A's baby to Mrs. Burleigh-Brown and put it beside her in her bed. She stopped crying at once—she was blissfully happy—she was up in the skies with joy. There, that's the truth. Will I be put in prison?"

"Put in prison? No, of course not! You ought to get a medal—you ought to get half-a-dozen medals!" cried Gerald incoherently. He was so excited that he couldn't sit still; he got up and walked about the room. "You're wonderful," he declared. "You're a marvellous woman! You're simply splendid!"

She looked up at him in astonishment . . . and Gerald stooped and kissed her wet cheek. He did it quite involuntarily, without thinking.

Fortunately Miss Macfarlane took the salute in the right spirit. She smiled at him through her tears. "Is that my medal?" she asked.

"Yes, and here's the bar," said Gerald, kissing her again.

"What will happen to me? I mean seriously."

"Nothing," replied Gerald. "Nothing bad. You did the

right thing. It was terribly brave of you. Besides, nobody will be told the secret except the girl in my story and the man who wants to marry her. It will make them both happy; you're glad about that, aren't you?"

"I don't understand."

"I'll tell you," said Gerald. "I'll tell you all about it, but before I start, just tell me this—if you can. What was Miss A like?"

"What was she like?"

"Yes. I mean she wasn't a—woman off the street or—anything?" enquired Gerald anxiously.

"Oh, no, she wasn't like that," replied Miss Macfarlane. "If she had been that sort, she wouldn't have minded about the baby. She was a nice-looking girl. They tried to find out the man's name—they always do, you know—but she wouldn't open her lips."

"What about her parents?"

"She was dumb about them too. It was only afterwards when they told her the baby had died that she mentioned her mother. She said, 'Well, it isn't any good to pretend I'm sorry. Mother is the only one who'll be sorry. She wanted a grandchild.' Then she said, 'This has taught me a lesson. I've been through hell.'

"I daresay it was true," added Miss Macfarlane thoughtfully. "She looked a respectable girl. I mean she looked as if her parents were in good circumstances. She spoke nicely and her clothes were good. She had a nice clear skin and red hair. I should say she was a country girl, probably a farmer's daughter. That was my impression. Why do you want to know?"

Gerald sat down and explained the matter—or as much of the matter as was necessary. He had decided that he must be very discreet. It was not his secret and the people concerned were too well known for their names to be disclosed. Sir Walter was referred to as "Mr. MacClure" and Bess as "Alice Burleigh-Brown." It had to be Burleigh-Brown, but that couldn't be helped.

"It's wonderful," said Miss Macfarlane when he had

finished. "I never thought of the future, you know. I told you that, didn't I? I expected a bomb to fall on the hospital and the whole place to be blown to bits. Do you think I could see her?"

"Who?"

"Alice, of course. She was such a lovely baby—and you said she was a beautiful girl."

"No, I'm afraid not," replied Gerald. "No, really. It wouldn't be possible. She lives in the south of England."

"Perhaps I could have a photograph of her?"

Alas, this also was impossible. The face of Elizabeth Burleigh was too well known.

Miss Macfarlane smiled rather sadly. "You don't trust me, do you? But you needn't worry. I can assure you that Alice's secret is perfectly safe. I've been silent for thirty years and I shall continue to be silent, not only for her sake but for my own. Do you think I want anybody to know about my moment of madness? That's what it was—a moment of madness! However, it seems to have turned out all right in the end."

"Marvellously right," declared Gerald. He hesitated and then, because she was still looking sad, he added, "Don't you think you were meant to—to do what you did? Don't you think, perhaps, that in all the confusion God spoke to your heart?"

"God?"

"Yes," said Gerald bravely. "Yes, I think you were inspired. Goodbye and thank you very very much." He went away quickly before his hostess could rise from her chair.

25. "Where Have You Dropped From?"

Gerald was so excited that he felt he must see Walter at once, so he decided to go to Birkhill. It was nearly six o'clock by this time and Walter might be home.

Gerald caught a bus at the corner (Glasgow buses were extremely convenient) and, dismounting from it at Bearsden, started to walk up the hill. When he was halfway up, he heard a car coming behind him. It was a large green Bentley—Walter's car! Gerald shouted and waved; the car passed him and stopped. Gerald ran after it, opened the door and got in.

"Gerald!" exclaimed Sir Walter. "Where on earth have you dropped from? I wasn't expecting you till Friday."

"I had to see you!" cried Gerald breathlessly. "I must speak to you! I've found out everything. Can we go straight to your study so that I can tell you the whole story? Otherwise I shall burst!"

"We shall," said Sir Walter firmly. "Mother is having a party, but we can slink in by the side-door. That's the plan! Are you staying the night?"

"No. At least I didn't mean to. I left my suitcase at the hotel . . . or did I leave it in Peg? I can't remember. Such a lot has happened. I meant to get everything tied up neatly before I saw you and I didn't know how long it would take. I thought the hospital would be a snag, but Miss Bond put me on to Miss Macfarlane straight off. Then, when I had seen Miss Macfarlane, I had to get hold of you at once."

"Who is Miss Macfarlane? I thought it was Mrs. Inglis that you were going to see?"

"Oh, that was yesterday. It was she who told me about Miss Macfarlane. Luckily she remembered her name because it was the same as her own. She thought they might be cousins."

Sir Walter gave it up. He said, "Did you leave Cannochbrae this morning?"

"Yes, I meant to leave earlier, but Matt delayed me, so I went straight to the hospital and saw Miss Bond . . . but I'm telling you this all wrong! It will be much better to tell you what happened from the very beginning."

Sir Walter agreed. All this excited talk about Miss Bond and Miss Macfarlane was getting them nowhere. He said, "Did you have any lunch?"

"No, I don't think so," said Gerald. "No, I didn't! I was on the trail, you see . . . and I didn't have much tea either. I suppose that's why I'm so hungry."

By this time they had arrived at Birkhill. Sir Walter drove round to the garage, took Gerald into his study by the side-door and left him there while he went to make some necessary arrangements.

Gerald sat down and endeavoured to calm himself and straighten out his story. It was important to tell it in the right way . . . in fact it was *assential*! Gerald did not anticipate any trouble (he did not believe that Walter would be disturbed by the news that Bess had been born out of wedlock), but all the same he intended to be tactful about it. He must lead up to it carefully . . . and the best way to lead up to it was to describe the disappointments and the thrills and excitements of the chase. Therefore he must take Walter through the whole story from beginning to end. He would begin with Uncle Gregor's reluctance to speak of Bess's mother: "She was always ailing, poor woman. We'll not talk of her, Gerald. Your mother was different altogether." Then he would go on to Mrs. Inglis—

187

and the awful shock she had given him. His enquiries at the hospital could be told in a few words, but he must give a full and detailed account of his interview with Miss Macfarlane.

Gerald had just finished getting his story into shape when Sir Walter returned, followed by Frost bearing a tray of coffee and sandwiches.

"It's all fixed up," said Sir Walter. "Frost knows we don't want to be disturbed, so he'll be as silent as the grave."

"Yes, sir," said Frost, smiling. "But I'd better warn Mrs. Donaldson that Mr. Burleigh-Brown will be staying here. She'll want to get his room ready . . . and what about his suitcase?"

"Oh, yes, of course!" agreed the baronet. "Where did you leave it, Gerald? Mackenzie can fetch it for you."

"Where did I?" said Gerald vaguely. "Oh, yes, I remember! I left it in Peg. I went straight from the garage to the hospital. It's the garage which belongs to Dickenson's brother-in-law. I can't remember the name."

Frost nodded. "It's McBride's, sir. Mackenzie knows it —but I'd better ring up and tell them he's coming. He'll want the key of the car, won't he? And perhaps there'll be something to pay."

"Of course," agreed Sir Walter. "You think of everything, Frost. Just carry on and do what's necessary."

Gerald handed over the key. Frost went out and shut the door quietly but firmly behind him.

That's service! thought Gerald. Walter knows his people —knows the way to treat them—knows it instinctively because he loves them! I shall have a lot to learn when I come to MacCallum's, but the way to talk to the chaps is the most important of all.

"What are you thinking about, Gerald?" asked his host. "Pull in your chair and get some food inside you before you begin your story. I want to hear it in detail."

"That's what I intended," replied Gerald, doing as he was told.

"I'm hungry too," said Sir Walter. "I had to go to the Tail of the Bank this morning—and got a very poor meal.

Dinner will be late because of Mother's party. Oh, by the way, Bess has sent your evening clothes. I told her you were coming here to stay for a few nights and she thought you might want to change. You needn't unless you would rather."

"I'd much rather."

After that the sandwiches and the coffee disappeared rapidly and in silence . . . but the silence was not complete. In the distance a very curious sound became audible.

Long, long ago, Gerald had seen an enormous swarm of bees revolving on its own axis and moving slowly across the garden at Beckenham. The buzzing noise was incredibly loud. Gerald had followed the bees and had watched them settling on the branch of a tree—a huge brown buzzing palpitating mass! He had run to tell Mother, of course, and Mother had rung up the police and two men with veils over their hats, carrying a large basket, had come to deal with the matter. Gerald had watched them making smoke with a queer sort of tin can, he had seen the bees drop off the branch into the basket. It had been thrilling!

"Do you keep bees, Walter?" enquired Gerald.

"Bees?" asked Sir Walter in surprise.

"Listen!"

"Oh, that! No, that's not bees. It's Mother's guests talking their heads off. I'm glad I'm not there."

Between them they finished the sandwiches—Gerald had the lion's share and three cups of coffee, so he felt a great deal better—then they moved to the comfortable chairs beside the fire and Gerald began his tale.

At first there was some hesitation in his words and manner, but he was fortunate in his audience, so he soon got into his stride and told his story, as he had intended, from the beginning to the end. "That's all," he said at last. "I just told poor old Miss Macfarlane not to worry any more about what she had done. I told her the inspiration had come from God. I really think so, Walter."

Sir Walter nodded. "Yes, I think so too. I'd like to do something for her. What can I do?"

"You can't give her money. She wouldn't like it."

"Well, what? I'd like to give her the moon and the stars!"

"You can't do that, either," replied Gerald, smiling.

"I could go and see her and ask her what she would like. Would a small car be any use to her?"

"Walter, you can't go and see her!"

"Why not?"

"It wouldn't do. You're too well known. It would give away the whole show!" declared Gerald. "We've got to be terribly careful because of Bess."

"You're right," agreed Sir Walter. "But all the same I'd like to give her something. I can never repay her for——"

"You can never repay her, so don't try," said Gerald earnestly. "It would upset her if you were to offer her anything valuable . . . but wait! I know what you can do. You can send her a donation for the Society for the Prevention of Cruelty to Children—and of course she'd like a piece of wedding-cake."

"Gerald, are you serious?"

"Perfectly serious. I've seen her and you haven't. She'll put the wedding-cake under her pillow and——"

"I can write to her, I suppose," said Walter with a sigh.

"Yes, you can write and tell her you're going to marry the girl you love . . . but don't forget she's Alice and you're William MacClure. Silly names! But I had to think quickly."

"You've been extremely clever about the whole thing! You've done wonders! I can't begin to tell you how grateful I am!"

"Anyone could have done it," mumbled Gerald.

"Nobody but you could have done it. Would Mrs. Inglis have confided in a stranger? Of course not! She chatted to you in an uninhibited way because you gained her confidence. You seized the clue—the only clue—and followed it up. Peter Wimsey couldn't have done better."

Gerald had hoped for a pat on the back, but this was far beyond his deserts—and he said so.

"Not at all," declared Sir Walter. "And don't worry, Gerald. I shall do exactly as you say."

"It's because of Bess. It's especially important if you're going to marry Bess and bring her to live in Glasgow."

"I'll marry Bess tomorrow if she'll have me. You know that, don't you?"

"It will be all right," said Gerald confidently. "I'm sure it will. The only reason she refused to marry you was that horrible fear—and she needn't worry about that any more. The cloud in her sky has blown away."

They were still discussing the matter when there was a curious little tap on the door: Tap-tap, tap, tap-tap.

"Come in, Alastair!" shouted Sir Walter.

A small boy opened the door, slipped in and shut it behind him.

"Is it all right?" he enquired anxiously. "Frost said you weren't to be disturbed, but I've got to go to bed and I wanted to say goodnight. You knew it was me, didn't you, Dad?"

"Alastair and I have a private signal," explained Sir Walter. "He taps and if I'm busy I don't answer."

"But you did answer," Alastair pointed out.

"Yes, it's all right; we've finished our business. You can come in and talk to us. I want to introduce you to Mr. Burleigh-Brown."

The boy walked forward and held out his hand. "How do you do?" he said gravely.

Gerald was unused to children, so he was surprised at the smallness of the hand; he was even more surprised at the firmness of its grip.

"Mr. Burleigh-Brown is coming to MacCallum's," Sir Walter said.

"Oh, good!" said Alastair. "What are you going to do, Mr. Burleigh-Brown?"

Gerald was wondering what to say when Sir Walter answered the question. "He's an electrical engineer, so he'll be helping with the electrical equipment of the new ship . . . and he can speak German, so he can translate letters and talk to the Hamburg people."

"Oh, I see," said Alastair, nodding. "That'll be very useful. He'll be doing two jobs."

"Yes," agreed Sir Walter.

"He'll be able to translate the German letter you got yesterday, won't he?"

"Yes, that's one of the reasons why he has come."

Alastair perched himself comfortably upon the arm of his father's chair. He said, "I haven't seen Mr. Burleigh-Brown before, but I'll be seeing him quite often. He'll be working with Mr. Carr, of course."

"Yes," agreed Sir Walter.

Gerald looked at them, sitting there together. He could not help smiling, for the two faces, side by side, were so alike that it was quite ridiculous. MacCallum and Son, thought Gerald (and apparently MacCallum junior was well up in the business already—practically a partner).

Gerald was aware that MacCallum junior spent his Saturday morning in the ship-yard, so he mentioned the fact.

"Oh, yes, I go with Dad whenever I can," replied Alastair. "I've always gone with Dad—ever since I was quite a little boy. It's super. There's so many interesting things to see. Besides I'm learning a lot. Last Saturday Mr. Carr showed me his plans for the electricity in the new ship. I forgot to tell you that, Dad."

"Mr. Carr showed you the plans?"

"Yes, and he explained them, too." Alastair turned to Gerald and added, "Mr. Carr is rather cross sometimes. It's because of Jessie."

"Alastair, what do you mean? Who is Jessie?" exclaimed Sir Walter in horrified tones.

"He said I wasn't to tell you about Jessie," replied Alastair.

There was a short but somewhat uncomfortable silence.

Neither of the two men could make up his mind whether to enquire further or to change the subject.

"What shall I do, Dad?" asked Alastair confidingly. "I'd like to tell you, of course, but Mr. Carr said, 'Don't tell the boss about Jessie,' and I said I wouldn't."

"In that case you can't tell me," replied Sir Walter seriously. "You must never break your word, Alastair."

"That's what I thought," nodded Alastair. "But Mr. Carr didn't say 'Don't tell anybody'—so I wondered if it would be all right to tell Mr. Burleigh-Brown?"

"I think it would be admissible."

"Ad-miss-ible? Does that mean it would be all right?"

"Yes."

"Good!" said Alastair, nodding. (It was an exact replica of his father's favourite exclamation and nod.)

"When are you going to tell me?" asked Gerald, hiding a smile.

"You can come up and see me in bed. That's the plan. I'd better go now or Miss Young will be after me, but you won't forget, will you?"

"No, I won't forget."

"And you'll come later, won't you, Dad?"

"I always come, don't I?" asked Sir Walter. He gave his son a gentle push and added, "Cut along now. I'll see you later."

"Alligator!" exclaimed Alastair—and went.

"That's *most* extraordinary," said Sir Walter. "You don't know Carr, or you'd realise how amazing it is. I told you he was dour, didn't I, Gerald? I can scarcely believe he would show Alastair his precious plans—and explain them to him. He keeps them locked up in his office."

"And what about Jessie?"

"That's queer, too. I'd like to know more about the woman, but I think I advised Alastair rightly. Don't you agree?"

Gerald looked at him to see if he were joking, but he was as serious as a judge.

"It's important, you know," continued Sir Walter. "It's essential that a child should learn what's right and what's wrong at a very early age. I must say I should like to know Carr's secret, but I couldn't advise Alastair to break his word. Alastair trusts me . . . and he has no mother."

Gerald had lost all inclination to smile. He replied, "Of course you're right, Walter! Perhaps you will advise me whether it would be admissible for me to pass on the information."

Sir Walter smiled, not very happily, and replied, "You're old enough to judge for yourself. Carr is a queer creature. He lost his wife some years ago and since then his temper— never very good—has disimproved. Just lately I've felt that he has something on his mind. It's this secret, I suppose. I wish he hadn't told Alastair. . . ."

26. "It's About Jessie"

When Gerald went up to his room to change for dinner, he found that his suitcase had come and had been unpacked. Furthermore the parcel from Bess containing his evening garments had been opened and its contents laid out on the bed. He changed quickly and was ready for dinner when he went to see Alastair.

Alastair was wearing blue-and-white striped pyjamas; he had had his bath; his hair had been thoroughly brushed; and he was sitting up in bed reading a very old, well-worn copy of the *Boys' Own Christmas Annual.*

"That looks an interesting book," said Gerald.

"Oh, it's super," declared Alastair. "It belonged to Dad when he was a boy. The stories are thrilling: all about pirates and Red Indians and ship-wrecks and lion-hunting in the desert. Much better than the stories you get now. Space stories are silly. Just fairy-tales."

Gerald had a quick look through the large volume, which was illustrated with hair-raising pictures, and realised that it was indeed a treasure.

"Sit here, Mr. Burleigh-Brown," added Alastair, moving his legs to make room for his visitor. "I'll have to tell you quietly because Dad's room is next door. It's about Jessie."

Gerald nodded and sat down.

"It's about Jessie," repeated Alastair. "Mr. Carr told

me about her. She's his little girl—and she's the same age as me—but she can't walk."

The small face, which was Walter's face in miniature, was so full of distress and horror that Gerald was quite alarmed.

"Can't walk? How dreadful!" he exclaimed.

"Her legs are paral—paral——"

"Paralysed?"

"Yes, she has a wheel-chair to go about in. Mr. Carr takes her out for a little turn in the evening when he gets home—if she's well enough. Sometimes she isn't well enough. She likes going to the park on Sundays and seeing the other children running about. I wouldn't like that," said Alastair in a very small voice. "I wouldn't—like to see—other children—running about—if I was her."

There was silence. Gerald was trying to find something comforting to say—but he couldn't.

"He showed me her photo," continued Alastair. "She looked all right, really. She was sitting on an ordinary chair and her legs *looked* all right, but she can't walk."

"Alastair, why is it a secret? Why doesn't he want Dad to know?"

"I asked him that and he said he didn't want a lot of 'soft sawder.' You see Dad takes care of people that are ill. Dad would be sorry. He would send her things. Mr. Carr doesn't want people to send her things. He can buy things for her himself. I can understand—sort of," added Alastair thoughtfully.

Gerald understood too—sort of.

"I thought I would tell you," said Alastair. "I just thought —perhaps—you wouldn't mind so much if Mr. Carr is cross. He's very cross sometimes."

"I shan't mind nearly so much. In fact I shan't mind at all," declared Gerald.

"Good!" said Alastair, nodding.

It *was* good. It was very good indeed. Gerald seized the small brown hand, which was so much firmer and stronger than it looked, and shook it warmly. "Thank you," he said. "Thank you very much, Alastair. It will be a great help to me."

"Will it, really?"

"Yes, really."

"Good," said Alastair, smiling.

The conversation was over, but there was just one more thing that Gerald had to know. He said, "Do you think Mr. Carr has had a really good doctor to see Jessie?"

"Five," replied Alastair. "He even took her to London to see the cleverest doctor he could find, but it was no good at all. It just made her ill and miserable. So he promised he wouldn't take her to any more doctors. He promised. That's another reason why he doesn't want Dad to know. See?"

Gerald saw. He realised that Walter must not be told. Walter was so benevolent that it would be impossible for him to sit back and do nothing about Jessie. Walter was a little too benevolent and patriarchal.

At this moment there was a tap on the door and the benevolent patriarch looked in to ask if the conference was over.

"Yes, you can come in now," said Alastair. "I've told Mr. Burleigh-Brown all about it and he said it would be a great help to him."

"Do you want me to read you a story?"

"Yes, of course! You always do! Could we have the one about Jairus's daughter?"

Gerald left them alone. He came away feeling very thoughtful.

Walter was sitting on Alastair's bed reading the story of Jairus's daughter from Canon Phillips's translation of the Gospels . . . and Alastair was lying back on his pillow looking quite peaceful and contented. The small hand was clasped firmly in the big one. All was well with MacCallum and Son.

"Are you going to tell me the secret, Gerald?" asked Sir Walter, smiling.

Dinner was over, with its usual excellent fare and vacuous chit-chat; the two men were sitting in the study. Sir Walter was lighting his pipe and Gerald was eating an apple. The scene was the same as it had been last Thursday night, but the atmosphere was different. They had been strangers, now they were friends.

"No, Walter. I can't tell you the secret," replied Gerald.

"What!" exclaimed Sir Walter in dismay. "Do you mean it's serious? Good heavens! It's a woman, I suppose? Carr must have gone completely off the rails! How dare he speak to Alastair about his sordid affairs—and forbid him to tell me? I could see the boy was upset. He's only a child—much too young and innocent to be burdened with secrets! What's to be done? I shall have to think about this. I shall have to speak to Carr—but no, I can't do that. It would never do to let Carr think Alastair had broken his word. This is awful! Oh, it's beyond everything! Carr tells my son about his private affairs and the boy tells you—and you'll find it 'a great help'——"

"Walter, listen!" Gerald had said it before—twice—but this time he almost shouted the words.

Sir Walter had risen and was pacing the room. He paused in his stride. "Don't you see? Don't you understand?" he asked more quietly. "The boy is my responsibility. I can't let it pass. I can't have people upsetting my son and——"

"Sit down," said Gerald. "Sit down and let me think."

Sir Walter hesitated and then sat down. There was a short silence.

"It isn't a 'sordid affair,' " said Gerald at last. "I had made up my mind not to tell you, but now that I see you're so upset about it——"

"Wouldn't you be upset?" interrupted Sir Walter.

"Yes, perhaps. At any rate I see your point of view."

"Are you going to tell me?"

Gerald nodded. "Yes, I'll tell you . . . but only on condition that you promise to take no action. You must do nothing and say nothing. In fact you must behave as if you didn't know about it."

"Behave as if I didn't know about it?"

"Yes. I realise that you will be making your promise in the dark. I can't help that."

"Gerald, is it really so important?"

"It's tremendously important to me. It's important because of my relationship with Alastair—and with Mr. Carr. I'm coming here to work, Walter. I want to be successful in my new post. I shall be of no use to you unless I can get on well with Mr. Carr."

Sir Walter hesitated.

"What about it?" asked Gerald. "Are you willing to promise in the dark? It's really a question of whether or not you can trust me."

"Trust you!" echoed Sir Walter. "Gerald, you know perfectly well I trust you. Would I have told you about Bess's mother if I hadn't trusted you?"

"Well, you must give me your promise."

"Otherwise you won't tell me?"

"No," said Gerald.

Sir Walter hesitated, but not for long. "Very well," he said. "I promise that I shall take no action. I shall behave as if you hadn't told me." He added, half jokingly, "Will that do or do you want me to swear on oath?"

"Walter MacCallum's word is good enough," replied Gerald gravely. He was silent for a moment. Here was another story that must be told carefully if it was to make the right impression upon the hearer. It should be told, as Alastair had told it, in simple childish words. He said, "Jairus's daughter was twelve years old, wasn't she? Carr's daughter is the same age as Alastair. She's eight and a half . . . but she can't walk."

When he had told everything that he knew of the matter, Gerald looked up and saw his friend gazing at the fire.

"Silly fellow!" said Sir Walter tenderly. "Silly, silly fellow! Why doesn't he want sympathy?"

"Because that's the way he's made."

"Yes, that's the way he's made. Well, you've tied me up properly. I can't do anything to help. I can't raise his salary; I can't even be more lenient with his bad humours, can I?"

"No," said Gerald firmly.

Sir Walter sighed. "Perhaps I'm a bit too interfering, Gerald. What do you think?"

"Some people like benevolence, others don't."

"Benevolence!" said Sir Walter with a rueful smile.

"They can't accept it graciously. That's the trouble."

There was another silence.

Gerald broke it. He said, "Have I been making a mountain out of a molehill? It seems important to me, but I daresay——"

"It seems very important to me," interrupted his friend.

They smiled at each other.

"Well, so much for Carr and his troubles," said Sir Walter. "What are your plans, Gerald? Are you going back to Haines?"

"No. I had some unpleasantness with Cousin Matt before I came away."

"You said he had delayed you?"

"Yes, it was funny, Walter! It was just as you thought; he tried on a little 'gentle blackmail.'"

Sir Walter chuckled. "Tell me about it."

"I was just leaving when he came and spoke to me. He was standing beside the car looking in at the open window. He burbled on for a bit . . . then he said I needn't worry, he wasn't the chap to blab. Then he said that if I was getting a good screw, I might lend him a tenner. I said I couldn't. Then he suggested a fiver."

"I hope you refused!"

"Yes, I refused. I was sorry for him. I'd have given it to him if you hadn't warned me, but I remembered what you had said. He was a bit disappointed. He grumbled on about the way his father treated him and complained that he had spent his last shilling on his fare and was absolutely on the rocks. Then he said, 'Oh, well, I shan't blab; we're cousins, aren't we?' . . . but there was a nasty look in his eyes. I didn't like it much. Finally he said it was funny that I hadn't got a reference from Koolbokie. I liked that even less! So I took the bull by the horns and said, 'Matt, I've told you that the story you heard in Jo'burg isn't true, so if you put it about, I shall have you up for defamation of character.' With that I drove on and left him standing in the road—gaping!"

"Oh, rich!" exclaimed Sir Walter laughing. "Oh, well done, Gerald! I wish I could have seen his face!"

Gerald joined in the laughter. "Walter, I've just discovered something," he declared. "It's most amazing—it really is! I've just discovered that I don't care whether he blabs or not. Matt can come to Glasgow and spread his story all over the shipyard if he likes—I don't care a damn!"

Sir Walter was laughing so heartily that he was speechless.

When Sir Walter had recovered, he wiped his eyes and said, "Well, you're not going to Haines. That's settled. Do you intend to go back to London? If so, will you take a passenger? I can't go tomorrow—I've got a Board Meeting—and on Friday I shall have to go down to the yard and make some arrangements with Ferguson—but we could weigh anchor on Saturday morning if that would suit you."

"Yes, of course! That will be grand. Bess has plenty of room for both of us. You can have your own room, Walter."

"My own room?"

"It is yours, isn't it?"

Sir Walter smiled and replied, "It is—in a way. Bess prepared it for me when she rented the flat, but I've only used it once, when she had the doctor's wife staying with her, so we were thoroughly chaperoned."

"I shouldn't have thought Bess would mind about that."

"She didn't—but I did. I intend to marry Bess. I've always intended to marry her. See what I mean? It's different for you, of course, because you're her brother."

Gerald was silent.

Sir Walter glanced at his guest and was astonished to see that all of a sudden his face had become pale and haggard. He looked like a man who has received a mortal wound. "Gerald, what's the matter?" exclaimed Sir Walter in alarm.

"But—but I'm not her brother."

"What? Oh, of course! I hadn't realised . . ."

"Neither had I!"

It was a difficult moment. Sir Walter didn't know what to

201

say. His thoughts flew to Bess. Bess would be distressed—he knew that only too well. He had heard a great deal about Flick. He had heard too much. If he had not been an extremely patient man and tenderly in love with Bess, he would have been sick and tired of Flick before he had ever seen him . . . and when Flick had vanished without trace, he had heard about Flick almost daily: "Oh Walter, what can have happened? He has always written to me once a fortnight—long newsy letters—and I haven't heard for six weeks! Where can he have gone? What can he be doing? Why has he gone away from Koolbokie without leaving his address? Oh, Walter, you're so clever! Can't you find him for me?" . . . and so on and so forth.

One day when Sir Walter had gone to London and was having tea with Bess in her drawing-room, he had said, half in fun, "Flick, Flick, Flick . . . " and immediately she had repented: "Oh, darling, I'm sorry! I know I'm being a bore. But you see he's my little brother and I've got nobody else belonging to me—nobody else that matters!—and he was such a dear little boy, so plump and cuddly. He used to run after me on his little fat legs crying, 'Beth, wait for me! Beth, I want you.' He used to snuggle up to me and say, 'Beth, I love you more than all the world.' He was ill, once—very ill—and they wakened me in the night because he was feverish and restless, so I sat beside him and held his hand and sang to him—and he went to sleep. Then, when we were older, we were friends. I could always depend on Flick—always. We understood each other; we laughed at each other's jokes. Oh, Walter, where is he? Perhaps something dreadful has happened to him and I shall never see him again! Oh, Walter, can't you find him for me?"

All this, and more, flashed through Walter's mind as he looked at Gerald's face of misery and consternation.

"Look here, Gerald," he said. "I wouldn't worry if I were you. I think you should just—just make up your mind to go on being her brother. I'm sure Bess will just go on being your sister —if you see what I mean."

"Do you think so, really?"

"Yes, I do. There's no need for any change."

"Do you mean you don't mind, Walter?"

"I would rather you went on being her brother, *much* rather," declared Walter emphatically.

"Really? You don't mind if I kiss her—and all that? You don't mind if I sit on her bed and help her to open her letters?"

Walter didn't hesitate. "I would rather there was no change—no change at all—in your relationship with Bess. Anyway, I've no right to object. I don't know why you're asking me."

"You're going to marry her!" exclaimed Gerald in surprise.

"Yes," replied Walter. "Yes, I'm going to marry her—if she'll have me."

27. "He Would Have a Lot to Learn"

On Thursday morning Gerald went down to the ship-yard and was fortunate enough to find Dickenson, who had shown him round before. Dickenson was delighted to repeat the inspection. They had more time, so Gerald was able to see a good deal more—and the more he saw the more impressed he became. MacCallum's was obviously a prosperous and efficient business.

"I shall have a lot to learn," said Gerald to his guide.

Dickenson had been of the opinion that Mr. Burleigh-Brown knew a good deal about ship-building, but today he had realised his mistake. He said comfortingly, "You'll soon get into the way of things. Sir Walter knows everything about the yard, so he'll put you wise. Sir Walter likes a man to be keen, but he doesn't expect miracles. Are you coming soon, Mr. Burleigh-Brown?"

"I'm coming when I'm wanted," Gerald explained. "I shall be working under Mr. Carr. Meantime I'm to be on tap as an interpreter in German."

"Perhaps you'd like a chat with Mr. Carr? That's him over there."

"Yes, just tell him who I am."

The introduction was made, but the chat was not a success. In fact Mr. Carr was so rude and disagreeable that Dicken-son was alarmed. As they walked on together, he said apologetically, "Mr. Carr is a wee bit surly sometimes. It's best to take no notice."

"Don't worry, Dickenson; it doesn't matter," declared his companion cheerfully.

Dickenson was surprised. However, he left it at that.

It was after twelve o'clock when they parted at the gate and Dickenson (having received a friendly hand-shake and more than adequate remuneration for his services) went to the canteen for his dinner. He was greeted with a hail of questions. Everybody wanted to know what the new bloke was like.

"Very pleasant-spoken. He's a friend of the boss. Staying at Birkhill," said Dickenson shortly.

"Friend of the boss? Coming here to throw his weight about?" said a large man with red hair and fists like knotted roots.

"No," replied Dickenson. "He said he would have a lot to learn."

"Where's he come from?"

"London. He's got a fine car with a London number, my brother-in-law says."

"What's he been doing?"

"I don't know."

"Did he not tell you?"

"No."

"That's funny, isn't it?"

"It may be funny, or it may not. All I can say is he knows his own stuff—electrical engineering—but he doesn't know much about ship-building. Master Alastair knows more."

"What did Carr say to him?" asked a crane-driver, who had watched the conversation from afar.

"Just the usual—surly as a bear—but Mr. Burleigh-Brown didn't worry."

"Hide like a rhino," suggested the crane-driver.

"Well, I wouldn't say that. It just ran off him like water off a duck's back. When Carr said, 'You'll need to work when you come here—*if you come here*! We don't want slackers in

MacCallum's,' Mr. Burleigh-Brown just smiled and said he liked work."

"Soft," suggested the red-haired man.

"Well, I wouldn't say that either. He's not the sort I'd care to take liberties with."

"He'll not like working under Carr," said the crane-driver with a short laugh.

There was general agreement: "He'll not last long."

"Carr will soon send him packing."

Dickenson listened and said nothing. He had a feeling that Mr. Burleigh-Brown would be difficult to oust. He was friendly and modest (there was nothing stuck-up about him) and he had a humorous twinkle in his eye, but all the same there was something about him . . . Dickenson couldn't find a word that satisfied him in his own mind for what the "something" was and while he was searching for the word, a very curious idea popped into his head: Maybe it would be Carr who wouldn't last long? Maybe it would be Carr who would be sent packing? Dickenson began to chuckle, but nothing his work-mates could say would induce him to share the joke.

Meanwhile the subject of these arguments and reflections was sitting in a small restaurant in Argyle Street having a good solid satisfying meal with a pint of light ale to wash it down. He had had a strenuous morning and was comfortably tired. He was aware that he would have a great deal to learn at MacCallum's—more than he had expected—but he would stick in and learn it. Perhaps Walter would be able to lend him books about ship-building; he would have plenty of time to study them before February.

As he had walked along the street, looking for somewhere to eat, Gerald had noticed an antique shop and it had occurred to him that if he could get a Rockingham china house it would make an acceptable present for Bess. A wedding present, he hoped. If they were not very expensive, he might get two. Walter and Bess were both amply provided with this world's goods, so it was difficult to know what to give them. Then Gerald thought of Penelope. He hadn't been thinking so much about her lately—not nearly so much—he had been too busy. She, too, would be pleased with a china house. He could give it to her for Christmas.

Gerald paid for his meal and returned to the antique shop. It was not in busy, bustling Argyle Street but just round the corner in a narrow quiet alley. The bell jangled as he opened the door and an elderly man with a hooky nose emerged from the back premises.

"China houses?" he said. "There you are! I've got a whole set of them. You can take your pick."

Gerald took one off the shelf and looked at it; then he put it back. "These are no good to me," he declared. "I want one for a lady who knows about china. She has some Rockingham china houses herself. The real thing."

"Well, you're lucky. They're not easy to get nowadays, but I was at a sale some months ago and picked up three. It was a big place and there was a lot of fine china. I had to pay a fancy price for them. My partner was annoyed. We don't get many people here who know the difference. There they are," he added, putting the three little houses on the counter.

Gerald knew the difference because he had seen the ones in Bess's drawing-room. He examined them carefully, trying his best to look like a connoisseur. One of the houses was a replica of one he had seen on Bess's shelf, the others were different, but all three were of the same delicate workmanship. There was a tall house with three storeys. It had steps up to the front door and chimneys; there was a castle, with turrets, a delightful little model which looked as if it had come out of a fairytale; and there was a cottage with a thatched roof and tiny windows and rambler roses over the porch.

"Yes, these are what I'm looking for, but I can't pay a fancy price for them," said Gerald regretfully. He put the little cottage back on the counter and turned away.

"You can have them for what I paid for them," said their owner, laying a grimy hand on Gerald's sleeve. "There, I can't say fairer, can I?"

207

"You said 'a fancy price.' "

"That was just a manner of speaking. My partner was annoyed, see? If I get what I paid, he won't be able to throw it in my teeth every time he sees them."

Gerald had not the slightest idea what he should pay for the little houses, but after some haggling he bought all three and paid for them with a cheque on Barclay's Bank—but he was not permitted to take them away.

"You can ask at the Bank, can't you?" said Gerald, who wanted them then and there. "I'll wait while you make enquiries if you like."

"I've no time for that," he replied nastily. "If you can't pay for them, you can't have them. I'm letting you have them cheap, as it is. You'd better go to the Bank yourself and come back with the money." He had been turning Gerald's cheque over and over in his dirty hands; now he handed it back.

Gerald was annoyed, not so much by the words as by the manner in which they had been spoken. He said, "Look here, you don't suppose I would walk about Glasgow with all that money in my pocket? You said it was a deal—and now you're backing out of it! Is that the way you do business?"

"We don't do business with cheques, but I'll meet you half-way. I'll keep the cheque and ask at the Bank and you can come back on Saturday for the goods. If the cheque is all right, you can have them. If not you can't."

"I'm leaving Glasgow early on Saturday morning."

"That's what you say!" exclaimed the dealer. "I know nothing about you. I don't know where you're staying——"

"I'm staying with Sir Walter MacCallum," interrupted Gerald. "There, that's his address." He produced Sir Walter's card from his wallet and laid it on the counter.

The card had been Gerald's talisman when he had been at the ship-yard and apparently its magic had not evaporated.

"Oh!" exclaimed the dealer. "Oh, I see! Of course if you're staying with Sir Walter, that's a different matter, sir. If you'll just sit down for a minute, I'll make up the parcel . . . or if you'd rather I can send the parcel to Birkhill."

"I'll take it with me," said Gerald.

"Just as you like, sir," replied the man, producing a box and shavings from beneath the counter. "I just thought it might save you the trouble of carrying the parcel—if I sent it. I hope Sir Walter is well?"

"Perfectly well," said Gerald shortly.

"That's good. He's a very fine gentleman, isn't he, sir? He used to drop in on his way to the ship-yard and have a look round, but we haven't seen him just lately, so I was afraid he might be ill. He's interested in old silver. Perhaps, if it wouldn't be too much trouble, sir, you might mention that I picked up a seventeenth-century salt-cellar. It was at a sale in Leith. I thought of Sir Walter the moment I saw it. I just thought it might interest him and I was intending to drop him a card, but as you're staying with him, sir . . . if it wouldn't be too much trouble."

"I'll tell him."

"Thank you, sir! Thank you very much. Be sure to say it's seventeenth-century, won't you, sir?"

"Yes," said Gerald. The man had been nasty; now he was all smiles and much too obsequious.

"If you'd told me at the beginning that you were a friend of Sir Walter's, it would have saved a lot of trouble, sir. We get a lot of queer people coming in here, so we've got to be careful. You understand, don't you, sir? I wouldn't like Sir Walter to think . . ."

Gerald's parcel was ready now; he picked it up and walked out of the shop.

Friday was the day Sir Walter had appointed for Gerald to translate the letter from Hamburg, so he went straight to the office and got to work. He had expected to polish it off in an hour, instead of which it took him the whole morning. There were a great many technical terms in the letter with which he was unfamiliar. However, with the help of a dictionary, he got it done, typed his translation neatly in duplicate and laid it on Sir Walter's desk. He was just coming away when Sir Walter walked in, followed by his secretary.

"I've finished it, sir," said Gerald. "It took longer than I expected. The technical terms were troublesome, but it will be easier next time. I was very careful to get them right."

"Oh, good!" said Sir Walter. "As a matter of fact I thought you might find it a bit troublesome, so I came in to see how you were getting on. Have you had lunch?"

"No, sir—but it doesn't matter. If you have time, perhaps you'd like to dictate your reply. I could take it down in shorthand and it could be sent off tonight."

"You had better go and have lunch. I'll give my reply to one of the girls."

"I'd rather take it myself, sir."

Sir Walter's eyes twinkled, but he said solemnly, "Very well, Burleigh-Brown. I'll give it to you now."

Fortunately the reply was short and not too difficult, so Gerald acquitted himself creditably. He took it in shorthand, translated it and typed it, and by three o'clock it was ready for Sir Walter's signature.

This was Gerald's first piece of work for MacCallum's. He felt pleased with it; he hoped "the boss" would be pleased.

28. Mrs. Bold

The following morning Gerald and his passenger set off to London. It had been decided that the passenger should drive through Glasgow; he knew his way, was used to traffic and had driven Peg before.

"You can take over at Carlisle," said Sir Walter as he settled himself in the driver's seat and fastened his safety belt. "I like looking at the hills and moors and I can't enjoy them if I'm driving."

Gerald was only too pleased with the arrangement and said so. He added, "Perhaps you'd take over when we get near London. I hate traffic—and so does Peg."

The drive was accomplished without incident. They stopped for a late lunch at Scotch Corner, and took their time over the meal, so it was after seven when they arrived at their destination and Sir Walter suggested that they should dine together at his club.

"When is Bess expecting me?" asked Gerald.

"I said between eight and nine. She won't be there, of course, but Mrs. Bold will be there."

"Mrs. Bold?"

"Matilda Meredith has gone. Didn't you know? She left last week. Dr. Ainslie wanted her for a children's convalescent home. I thought Bess would have told you."

"Bess never writes letters and she doesn't chat to me on

the telephone," replied Gerald, smiling. He added, "Who and what is Mrs. Bold?"

"She's the wife of the hall-porter. It seems a very good arrangement. Bess says she's a nice kind woman with a face like the back of a bus—and five grandchildren."

They both laughed.

Sir Walter continued, "Bess said you would be tired and could go to bed. She will look in and see you when she gets back from the theatre. Oh, and she said you were to leave Pegasus in Leonard's yard."

"Right!" said Gerald, nodding. He was aware that all these instructions had been given to Walter on the telephone —Bess lying in bed and chatting.

It was half-past-eight when he arrived at Molyneux Mansions. He had left the car in Leonard's yard and had walked from there, carrying his suitcase. As he went up in the lift, he felt as if he were coming home after a long absence. Mrs. Bold opened the door and welcomed him warmly. His room was ready; there were two hot-water bottles in his bed and the electric radiator gave out a pleasant glow.

"Miss Burleigh wondered if you'd like something to eat," said Mrs. Bold. "There's bacon and eggs—I could fry them for you in ten minutes—or perhaps a cup of Horlick's? Miss Burleigh likes a cup of Horlick's when she gets home from the theatre."

"No thank you, Mrs. Bold," replied Gerald. "I had a very good dinner with Sir Walter MacCallum at his club."

"Oh, he's a nice gentleman, isn't he? I haven't seen him yet, but Bold knows him quite well. He often comes to see Miss Burleigh. He thinks nothing of flying from Glasgow and having lunch—or tea—and flying back again the same day. Bold was wondering if Miss Burleigh was going to marry him . . . but, there, I'm letting my tongue run away with me! Bold says I talk too much."

Gerald was amused. He said, "You've got five grandchildren, haven't you, Mrs. Bold?"

Her face lighted up. "They're lovely children!" she declared. "They're well-behaved children—no trouble at all. Not like some children nowadays. Nora—that's our daughter-in-law —brings them to see us every other Sunday afternoon. Miss Burleigh said she didn't mind them coming. She said she liked children and we could give them tea in the kitchen. We're living here, you know. We had to give up our little flat because the rent went up and we couldn't afford it. We were wondering what to do when Bold heard that Miss Meredith was leaving and Miss Burleigh was looking for a couple . . . so it was all fixed up. It suits Bold and me to be here. Bold likes being on the spot instead of having to trail backwards and forwards in the tube and I like it too. It's a lovely place to live. Miss Burleigh is so kind, it's a pleasure to work for her . . . but there I go, running on like a bath-tap! It's just that I'm excited, Mr. Burleigh."

Gerald liked Mrs. Bold and, what was more, she was the right sort of person for the volatile Bess. There was no nonsense about Mrs. Bold; she was kindly and sensible, with both feet firmly on the ground. Bess had said she had a face like the back of a bus; Gerald disagreed. She was not as beautiful as Matilda, of course, but it was a pleasant face and her smile, when she spoke of her grandchildren, was good to see.

"I expect you're tired," suggested Mrs. Bold. "Miss Burleigh said you'd be tired. She left some books on the table beside your bed."

"Yes, I've done a lot in the last few days. I'll have a bath and turn in and read until Miss Burleigh comes home."

He was tired. He did not realise how tired until he was lying spread out luxuriously in the ultra-comfortable bed. How peaceful it was! Glasgow had been noisy; the farm, high up in the hills, had not been nearly so peaceful. There had been owls hooting at night and cocks crowing early in the morning. Worst of all there had been that uncomfortable atmosphere—the ill-will between Cousin Matt and his father. Here the only sound was the distant hum of London, which was as soothing as the murmur of the sea.

Gerald did not want to read; he was asleep in a few moments, but his sleep was light, so he awoke when the door opened and Bess came in. She was wearing a dressing-gown, her hair was in a net and her face was innocent of make-up.

She kissed him and exclaimed rapturously, "Oh, Flick, how lovely to have you home! I've missed you dreadfully. I saw Walter for a minute; he came to the theatre. He says you've 'done wonders'—but he wouldn't say more. What have you been doing?"

"Just talking to people," replied Gerald, returning her embrace.

"You've done wonders," repeated Bess. "Walter said so. You must have done more than just talk to people."

"You can ask him about it tomorrow."

"I shall. Walter suggested that we should take Peg and go for a spin in the country. There's a delightful little hotel at Limbourne where we can have lunch. We've been there before several times . . . and there's a beautiful little church, very old, with effigies of Crusaders. The vicar, Mr. Heath, showed us over it one day and told us all about it. You'd like that, wouldn't you, Flick?"

"Not tomorrow, Bess. You and Walter can go."

"Why not tomorrow? You'd enjoy it."

"I'm a bit tired, that's all. I've been buzzing about all over the place. I'd rather stay at home and take Gubby for a walk in the park."

"I want you to come."

"No," said Gerald. "No, really. I'll go with you another day but not tomorrow."

"You've arranged it between you!" Bess exclaimed. "You and Walter have arranged it . . . and I know the reason. Walter is going to try again to persuade me to change my mind. I won't marry him! I won't! I've told you why, haven't I?"

"Keep your hair on," said Gerald in soothing tones. "Walter won't try to persuade you to do anything against your will. He knows your reasons and respects them."

"There's only one reason," said Bess sadly. "It's because I love him too much. Walter deserves a wife who will be a comfort to him—not a care and a worry. He deserves children—I can never have children."

"He knows all that," declared Gerald. Then, to change the subject, Gerald enquired if Bess had seen the Harrimans.

"I've seen *him*, of course. The others have gone home."

"You mean to America?" asked Gerald in dismay.

Bess nodded. "Yes, they had to fly home unexpectedly. I had a delightful letter from Mrs. Harriman, thanking me for my hospitality and saying how sorry they were not to see me before they left. She explained that her sister had been taken ill and would have to undergo a major abdominal operation. That was the reason."

"Oh," said Gerald in disappointed tones.

"Never mind, Flick. I expect they'll come back quite soon. They think nothing of flying backwards and forwards across the ocean."

"Mr. Harriman is still here?"

"Yes, Elmer is still searching for his Audleys."

"Oh, he's 'Elmer,' is he?"

"Yes, Elmer and I are buddies."

"And you're 'Bess,' I suppose?"

"No, I'm Elizabeth. He asked if he might have the privilege of using my beautiful name. Listen, Flick! You remember when he was here he admired my fireplace? Well, he asked if he might have it copied."

"Copied?"

"Yes, he found a young man called Bullen, who is copying my Adam fireplace for him. Bullen came and measured my fireplace and took drawings of it."

"Do you mean he's building it here?" asked Gerald incredulously.

"Yes, Elmer is having it built here, in London, and taking it home with him. Just as I might have a frock made to measure in Paris and bring it home with me in my suitcase. Staggering, isn't it?"

"Yes, but after all, if that's what he wants—and he can pay for it—why shouldn't he?"

"He wanted a real one," explained Bess. "I mean a real Adam fireplace, but he couldn't buy one for love or money so he's making do with a copy. When Bullen has finished the job, I'm to go and see it; then it will be taken to pieces and shipped to America and young Bullen will fly over to assemble it. Elmer has taken a fancy to Bullen and intends to set him up in New York."

"You mean to build fireplaces?"

"Yes. Elmer says when his friends see his fireplace, he guesses they'll all want one the same . . . but *his* will be made of English stone and therefore it will be more like the real thing."

"I suppose it will," said Gerald. "The odd thing is that when you said your fireplace was a copy of an Adam fireplace, he didn't seem to know what you meant, so why——"

"Oh, he hadn't a clue!" interrupted Bess smiling. "But two days later he came to tea with me to have another look at it and he knew more about the Adam brothers than I did."

"He had mugged them up."

Bess nodded. "Yes, he had mugged them up. Elmer likes to know about things."

Gerald was getting a little tired of Elmer and his doings (it was not Elmer Harriman in whom he was particularly interested). He said, "I suppose there isn't a letter for me—or anything?"

"There is a letter, but it isn't from Penelope—if that's what you mean? I didn't forward it because Walter said you weren't too happy at the farm and your plans were a bit uncertain. Oh, dear, I want to know all about everything, but it's getting very late, and you're sleepy, so you must tell me in the morning. I'll fetch your letter now. It's in my desk."

Gerald was not very interested in the letter—it wasn't from Penelope—so when Bess had found it in her untidy desk and returned with it, he was fast asleep. This time he didn't waken at the opening of his door, so she put the letter on the table beside his bed and went away quietly.

29. Angus Proudfoot's Apology

It was eight o'clock the next morning when Gerald opened his eyes. He stretched himself and yawned luxuriously. Then he saw the letter. It bore a South African stamp and was addressed to him in small neat writing—writing that Gerald knew well! What on earth could Angus Proudfoot have written to him about?

Gerald didn't want to open the letter; he didn't want to have anything more to do with Koolbokie. He didn't want to think about it. He had left it behind him—all the disgrace and misery and shame! He was cured now. He had made new friends; he had got a job which would suit him down to the ground. Why should the horrible affair be raked up and all the memories revived?

Gerald would have liked to put the letter in the fire, but he supposed he had better read it. He sighed heavily and tore it open. There were seven closely written pages of it:

Koolbokie Mines.

"Dear Gerald,
This is a difficult letter to write. I would much rather talk to you, but as that is impossible, the letter must be written. I want to apologise to you sincerely for the way you were treated here. I hope you will accept my apology and let byegones be byegones. I must explain exactly what has happened.

217

After you had gone, Felstead came to me and asked if I intended to give him your job. I agreed, of course. He had been working with you for eighteen months, so he knew the ropes and it would have been difficult to get another man at short notice. Then he said he was very lonely and miserable and wanted to be married and might he have your bungalow for himself and his wife? I agreed to this also—he had been going about the place looking like a sick jackdaw. Steiner said he would remove your stuff from the bungalow and store it in his own bungalow, so that was settled. Felstead married that girl in Jo'burg and they moved in.

The next thing that happened was that Steiner came to me and said he was feeling unwell and would like a fortnight's holiday. He looked unwell —I knew he was upset about your trouble—so I told him he could go and I asked him if he knew anyone who would come in his place as an interpreter. He recommended a man called Parker, so that was settled too. Parker seemed a nice fellow. He is a good interpreter (though not as good as Steiner), and I thought we were lucky to get him.

Then I found that Parker was nosing about and asking questions. This annoyed people, so I sent for Parker and asked him what he was up to. He told me in confidence that he was employed by Sir Walter MacCallum to clear your name. I said it was quite impossible to clear your name as you had been caught red-handed with the stones concealed in the lining of your jacket. I added that the affair was over and done with and I had let you go. It was no good raking it up again.

Parker replied that he was being paid for "raking it up" and might he see the stones? I could hardly refuse the request (though I could see no object in it) and it was easy enough to grant, for I had been so upset and fed up with the whole miserable affair that I had not examined the stones, but had just put them in an envelope and sealed it and written your name and the date on the envelope and chucked it into my safe.

Parker and I opened the envelope together. Parker knows a bit about stones, so he examined them with a magnifying glass and said, "It seems to me that these are pretty poor specimens, Mr. Proudfoot. But you know more about it than I do, of course." I looked at them and realised that it was true. There was not a decent stone amongst the lot.

I said, "But that isn't the point. The point is that Burleigh-Brown was trying to get away with them. He was in a position of responsibility; he abused my trust and let me down badly. I was so furious with Burleigh-Brown that I would have called in the police if his friend, Pat Felstead, hadn't taken his part and persuaded me to let him go."

Parker said, "Mr. Proudfoot, does Mr. Burleigh-Brown know anything about diamonds?"

I said you did, of course. I said, "Stones were not his job, but he was interested in them and a good judge of their value."

Parker said would I be willing to give evidence to that effect in a Court of Law? This surprised me—I could not see what he was getting at—but when he repeated his question, I was obliged to reply in the affirmative.

Parker nodded in a satisfied manner. Then he said, "Doesn't it seem strange that a man who knows about diamonds should risk losing his job and his reputation for a handful of pebbles?"

The question gave me a pretty severe jolt. I saw the implication at once! After that I was willing to listen to Parker, so I asked him to sit down and tell me the rest of his story. Parker is clever (he is used to detective work and has done a lot of it for Sir Walter MacCallum). He sat down and said, "I think the best thing for me to do is to show you Sir Walter's letter. Then you can judge for yourself."

Sir Walter's letter was addressed to Parker. It was most impressive. It was an exposition of your case, well reasoned and clearly worded. He pointed out that, as you were never examined at the gate, it would have been quite easy for you to walk out with the five diamonds in your pocket, so why should you have gone to the trouble of unpicking the lining of your jacket and hiding them? He went on to say that in his opinion the value of the stones was important. If they were valuable, someone was using you as a "carrier"; if not, you had been framed. He added that no man in your position (and with your knowledge of gems) would have risked losing his reputation for "a handful of pebbles."

Parker had used these very words, of course, but they impressed me even more from a man like Sir Walter MacCallum. (I realised that the arguments were logical and I felt inclined to kick myself for not having thought of them before.)

I told Parker that Sir Walter's letter had convinced me of your innocence (all the more so because he had offered you a post of responsibility in his Ship-building Yard) and I was willing to write you an apology. Parker replied that that was not enough; the guilty man must be found and exposed and your name cleared—those were his instructions from Sir Walter—so I gave Parker permission to go ahead with his enquiries and do whatever was necessary.

Parker said, "Do you mean that, Mr. Proudfoot? Have I permission to give orders in your name? If so, you had better write it down and sign it." By this time I was so keen to get to the bottom of the matter that I gave him what he wanted.

I heard no more until one morning when Felstead and I were going to Jo'burg in my car. The gate was shut, so I called to Stafford's assistant to come and open it. Then Stafford himself came out of the X-ray department. He was smiling. He said, "Sorry, Mr. Proudfoot, but my orders are that everyone, without exception, is to be screened today before leaving the mine," and he produced the paper I had given to Parker.

I laughed and agreed—it was a good joke—but Felstead refused pointblank. His explanation was that he was often screened for fun, but he wasn't going to submit to the orders of a little wart like Parker. I said the order was from me, not Parker, but he was as obstinate as a mule and his behaviour was so strange that our suspicions were aroused.

Then Parker appeared on the scene. When Felstead saw Parker, he broke away from Stafford, who was holding him, and ran back to his bungalow. Parker ran after him and caught him. Stafford and Barnes ran after him too—and the three of them managed to bring Felstead back. He was kicking and struggling and behaving like a lunatic.

By this time we were furious with him, especially Stafford, who had been kicked in the stomach during the melée, so they held him down by main force and proceeded to examine his clothing. Three stones were found: one in each of his shoes and another in the case of his Kodak. Later a fourth was discovered in his hat which he had chucked away when he made his bolt. They were all good stones, very different from the ones which had been discovered in the lining of your jacket.

Parker was not surprised. He had been making enquiries in Jo'burg and had found out various things about Felstead which had aroused his suspicions. That was why he had set the trap.

By this time Felstead was in a hysterical condition. He broke down under Parker's questioning and contradicted himself flatly: First he said he knew nothing about the stones; then he said that Steiner had come to his bungalow the previous night and had been there alone for more than an hour—so obviously Steiner had put the stones there in order to ruin him. (He had forgotten that Steiner was away on holiday!) He stuck to this story for a bit and declared that it was Steiner who had framed you so that he could get rid of you and steal some of your belongings. Chiefly your Gramophone which he had always coveted.

Then, when he saw *that* story would not do, Felstead admitted his guilt and begged me to forgive him and let him go. He said wildly that I had let you go, so why wouldn't I treat him in the same way? He declared that his wife was seriously ill and he was nearly off his head with worry about her. (Wilson says this is untrue.) Then, finally, when he realised that I had sent for the police and intended to prosecute him, he changed his tune again and said it was a "put-up job" and he had never said he was guilty . . . but as four of us had heard his confession and his plea for forgiveness, this did not do him much good.

To make a long story short the police came and took Felstead into custody. He is now awaiting his trial.

Well, that is the story. It is a wretched affair and has cast a gloom over us all. The outlook is particularly gloomy for me as I am responsible for the conduct of affairs in Koolbokie and I have made a complete hash of them. I see now, of course, that your dismissal was a ghastly mistake. I ought to have sifted the matter and found out what had really happened instead of taking your guilt for granted . . . but Felstead was too clever for me; he misled me completely. I knew he was your friend and if he believed you to be guilty, I took it for granted that it must be true. You remember that when the stones were found in the lining of your jacket, Felstead seemed heartbroken—he was almost weeping—he pled with me to let you go and hush it up. So what was I to think? His behaviour was a remarkably convincing piece of acting. I was properly fooled by the performance!

I am not trying to excuse myself—there is no excuse for my foolishness—I am just trying to tell the truth.

I have written the whole story to the directors in London and have asked for their instructions. I cannot accept the responsibility of dealing with Felstead. It will be for the directors to decide what is to be done with him—and what is to be done with me. I shall not be surprised if I find myself in the street! But before I am sacked for incompetence and mismanagement, I am offering to reinstate you. It is the least I can do and perhaps it will go some way to make up for what you must have suffered. I shall feel less miserable if I can put things right for you.

I realise that you may prefer to accept the post offered to you by Sir Walter MacCallum, but I hope not. It would please everybody at Koolbokie if you decided to come back.

Yours sincerely,
Angus Proudfoot.

When Gerald had read the letter he sat and stared at it. He was astounded. He was astounded not only at the news it contained but even more at his own reaction to the news. Six weeks ago he would have been off his head with joy at the discovery that his name was cleared. Today he didn't care! It was as if he were reading the story of another man—not himself at all! What a fool that man had been to make such a fuss!

Presently Gerald got up, put on his dressing-gown and slippers and went along to Bess's room. She was awake.

"Look," said Gerald. "Here's a letter from Angus Proudfoot. There are seven pages of it. Can you be bothered to read it?"

"I suppose they've discovered the truth. It was Felstead, wasn't it? I knew it was Felstead all the time."

He stood and gazed at her.

"I never liked him," explained Bess. "He was too clever, Flick."

"Too clever?"

"Yes, he's clever in a horrid sort of way. He's a cunning Knave. I never trusted him."

"But, Bess——"

"Cunning," she repeated earnestly. "I told Walter what I thought and he said it was my 'woman's instinct'; but he smiled when he said it, so I don't think he believed me. It was no good saying it to you because you were so certain that Patrick Felstead was your friend."

"I was certain of his friendship."

"Well, never mind. We needn't worry any more. Are you very very happy about it, darling Flick?"

"Oh, I'm quite pleased, of course," said Gerald tepidly. "I mean it's just as well to have it cleared up."

Bess began to laugh—and Gerald joined in. They laughed immoderately.

When they had finished laughing, Gerald said, "It's Walter's doing. He turned me inside out. Then, I suppose, he must have written to that chap, Parker. Walter's marvellous. I shall enjoy working for him. I've got a lot to learn, but I intend to stick in and do my best to be useful to him. Angus wants me to go back to Koolbokie—but I'm not going."

"That's good," said Bess.

224

30. "Is It All Right?"

Sir Walter called for Bess at eleven o'clock on Sunday morning and after a cup of coffee, they walked along to the garage to get Peg.

Gerald watched from the window, then he fetched Gubby and took him to the Park. It seemed a very long morning. Gerald thought about Bess and Walter all the time. He wondered if Walter would tell her at once, or wait until after lunch. He wondered what she would think—and say—and do. He had been sure she would be pleased, but now he was not so sure.

Mrs. Bold gave him a good plain meal and chatted to him and went away. Gerald took the book he had borrowed from Walter and sat down to study the elements of ship-building . . . but it was hopeless! He read a whole page without taking in a single word. Had Walter told her yet?

At four o'clock the front-door bell tinkled. It wasn't Bess (Bess had a latch-key); it was the Bold children. Gerald heard the sound of voices in the hall and Mrs. Bold saying "Hush!" Then there was complete silence except for the patter of feet going along the passage to the kitchen.

At five o'clock Mrs. Bold brought in the tea-tray and arranged it on a table beside the fire. She said, "I hope the children didn't disturb you. They're good little things, but they didn't understand. I've told Nora they must be very quiet coming in and going out, so it'll be all right in future. They can chatter in the kitchen, of course. Will Miss Burleigh be back for tea?"

"I don't know," said Gerald with a sigh.

"Well, just ring if she would like it and I'll make a fresh pot. Stewed tea is bad for the nerves, isn't it?"

"Yes. Yes, thank you, Mrs. Bold. I'll ring if she wants it," said Gerald with another heavier sigh.

Mrs. Bold looked at him, but she said no more.

When she had gone, Gerald had a cup of tea and a biscuit. He was not hungry. He looked out of the window. It was getting dark by this time and it had begun to rain.

Where were they? What were they doing?

Gerald was still peering out of the window when the door opened and Bess came in.

"Oh, Flick!" she exclaimed, taking off her fur coat and throwing it onto a chair. "Oh, Flick darling!"

"Where's Walter?" asked Gerald anxiously.

"He has gone to his club. He thought we might like a little time together. He thought we could talk things over . . . but I don't know what to say!" She sat down on the sofa and burst into tears.

Gerald sat down beside her and took her hand. "Tell me, darling. Is it all right?" he asked.

"Yes," said Bess, mopping her eyes. "It has just—been —rather a shock. I'll be better in a minute. I didn't want to cry until I got home—and I didn't. I don't know why I'm crying. It's silly, isn't it?" She leant her head against his shoulder.

Gerald was still not certain if it was all right, but it was better not to ask. Bess would tell him when she was ready.

"It's a funny sort of feeling," said Bess at last. "I can't quite believe it. I wonder how long it will be before I can believe it properly—in my bones."

"Don't try too hard," Gerald suggested. "Just rest quietly. Would you like some tea?"

"No, I don't want anything. We had a late lunch . . . and then he told me. I was rather stupid about it, Flick. I think—I think it would be easier if I knew something—something more—about my mother."

"I know. But I don't see how——"

"It sounds ungrateful," said Bess. "I ought to be thanking you for all you've done. I'm not ungrateful—just muddled. Walter told me you had done wonders. Nobody else could have done it."

"I was lucky, that's all. One thing led to another. All I want to know is: Are you happy about it—or not?"

She was silent for a few moments. Then she said, "I think I shall be happy about it when I've got used to it. I'm just so awfully muddled, so awfully stupid, Flick. Do you think Walter understands?"

"I'm sure he does. He's a very understanding person."

"Yes," said Bess with a little sigh.

There was a long silence.

"Did you make any plans?" asked Gerald at last.

"No," replied Bess. "Walter didn't want to make plans. He said we should wait until I was feeling better, so I just wondered . . ."

"What do you mean, darling?"

"Do you think he wants to marry me?"

"You know he wants to marry you. He has said so over and over again."

"But that was before . . ."

"He said it before—and he has said it since. He said it on Wednesday: 'I'm going to marry her—if she'll have me!' "

"Did he mean it?"

"Does Walter ever say things he doesn't mean? Oh, Bess, you're just being a goose! You know you're being a goose, don't you?"

"Yes."

"Goose—goose—goose!" said Gerald, squeezing her hand.

"Nice," said Bess dreamily. "Nice Flick and nice Walter. How lucky I am!"

Gerald smiled. It was all right. She just wanted a little time to get used to the idea. He sat and held her hand in silence.

227

31. Letter from America

Bess had gone to bed early, so on Monday morning she wakened earlier than usual and when Gerald went in to help her to open her letters, he found her sitting up in bed and smiling cheerfully. She held out her arms and exclaimed, "Flick, I'm better! I don't know why I was so silly last night."

"You weren't silly!"

"Yes, I was . . . but I've got straightened out while I was asleep. It must have been my subconscious, or something. I'm happy now—terribly happy. I've been talking to Walter on the phone. We often chat to each other in the morning."

Gerald knew this, of course. He kissed her (Walter had said he might) and asked if any plans had been made.

"We're going to be married in April."

"Why wait till April?"

"Because of *Venus*. My contract expires in April—I told you that! It wouldn't be fair to break my contract. Perhaps it's conceited of me, but I can't see how they could get on without me."

Gerald wished he could say they would get on perfectly well without her—but he couldn't.

"No," said Bess with a sigh. "Walter agrees that it wouldn't be right, so we shall have to wait. It's only four months till April. I shall leave the stage, of course. I shall make my exit with a bang! It will be fun to have a proper wedding—a smashing affair, with all the doings!"

"Yes," said Gerald . . . but he said it doubtfully.

He would have liked to see Bess married to Walter much sooner. At the moment Bess was vulnerable. If the story of her birth should leak out, it might be exceedingly unpleasant. Elizabeth Burleigh was NEWS and the story of the two babies changed during an air-raid would be a juicy morsel for the less reputable Sunday papers. Gerald did not see how the story could leak out (neither Mrs. Inglis nor Miss Macfarlane was likely to talk), but all the same he felt apprehensive.

Once Bess was married to Sir Walter MacCallum, she would be safe, in an assured position, so the sooner the better!

"What are you thinking about, Flick?" asked Bess. "Sit down and help me to open the letters. Walter said he would come at eleven and take me out. He wants me to choose a ring. It's terribly exciting, isn't it? Oh, here's a letter from Matilda!"

"What does she say?" enquired Gerald. He was determined not to reveal his thoughts to Bess.

"It's all about the children," replied Bess, scanning the letter hastily. "What they do—and what they say! She seems quite happy. Just at the end she says she hopes I've been to see Aunt Anna."

"She isn't your Aunt Anna."

"Oh, I know! But I shall have to go and see her, all the same. As a matter of fact I shan't dread seeing her now, and I shall be able to chat to her quite cheerfully. That's good, isn't it?"

"Very good," agreed Gerald. He added, "Do you miss Matilda?"

"I do—and I don't," replied Bess thoughtfully. "At first I was annoyed with Dr. Ainslie for interfering; but then I saw that he was right. I'm very fond of Matilda—and I miss my cotton-wool—but I used to worry about her. I used to try to make her go out and see people, or do some shopping or go to the pictures, but she wouldn't budge. Curiously enough it wasn't until she had gone that I discovered how much I had worried about her."

"You felt relieved?"

Bess nodded. "It was rather horrid of me."

"It was natural. Matilda leant on you too heavily; she had

229

nothing else to think about. She'll be quite happy looking after the convalescent children—and you'll be happier with Mrs. Bold."

"Yes," said Bess a little sadly.

"Matilda wouldn't have liked you to be married," Gerald pointed out.

"No," agreed Bess more cheerfully. "She always said that neither she nor I could ever be married—so it's just as well. In four months she will be quite settled and won't mind about it. I wonder if she would like to come to the wedding."

Gerald was sure she would not.

"Perhaps you're right," agreed Bess. "Come on, Flick! We must get the letters opened. There are more than usual this morning."

The letters that came to the flat were all addressed to Miss Elizabeth Burleigh or, occasionally, to Miss Burleigh-Brown, but today Gerald discovered one addressed to himself. It was an airmail letter from America.

"Oh!" he exclaimed in surprise. "Oh, I think this must be from Penelope."

He was about to open it and then decided that he would rather open it in private. He took it to his bedroom and slit the envelope with his nail-file.

The letter gave him rather a shock. He sat down and thought about it—and read it again. He was reading it for the third time when Bess came in.

"I've got one, too," said Bess. "Mine is just a few lines. She says she has written a long one to you. Are you unhappy about it, Flick? I was afraid you might be feeling unhappy."

"I'm a little—surprised," admitted Gerald. "I mean it seems so—so sudden. I had no idea that there was anything like this in the wind."

"You were fond of her, weren't you?"

"I liked her awfully much—I still like her—but it wouldn't have been a success. I knew that from the beginning. She's very sweet—and kind—and clever. If she had been the daughter of a grocer, I would have asked her to marry me. She's the sort of girl——"

"If she were the daughter of a grocer, she wouldn't be Penelope."

"That's true," agreed Gerald with a sigh.

"What does she say? Her letter to me was written in a hurry, she just says she's going to marry Teddy—that's all. Who is Teddy?"

"He's Clem's brother."

"Who is Clem?"

"The man Marion is going to marry. The girls are pleased about that. Penelope says she and Marion have always been like sisters ever since they can remember and now they will really be sisters."

"Sisters-in-law," put in Bess. She added, "Clement and Edward who?"

"It isn't Edward, it's Theodore. Their name is Hogan. Their father has a big business (I don't know what, exactly) and branches all over the States. Clem manages the one in Chicago and Teddy is to be in Boston. That's where they're going to live."

"Boston is wunnerful, I suppose?" suggested Bess. She was annoyed with Penelope.

"Yes," said Gerald. He turned over the letter and added, "Mr. Harriman is giving them a beautiful home as a wedding present; Mrs. Harriman is giving them three weeks in Greece; Mr. Hogan is giving them a Mercedes Benz. The two families have known each other for years and everyone is delighted."

"Money marries money—very suitable!"

"Bess, it *is* suitable!" Gerald declared emphatically. "It is, really, you know. They have been brought up in the same atmosphere—see what I mean? They like the same things; they're both used to luxurious surroundings."

"What else does Penelope say?"

"She wants us—you and me—to fly over for the wedding. It's to be a double wedding in April. Her aunt will give us hospitality."

"We can't," said Bess. "Walter and I are going to be married in April and there will be a great deal to do, so it's quite impossible."

"Oh, I know! We can refuse, of course, but it's nice of them to ask us. They're flying to Europe for their honeymoon, all four of them. After their visit to Greece, Penelope and Teddy are coming to London. Penelope loves London, so she wants Teddy to see it and she wants him to meet me. She's sure we shall like each other—and she wants to introduce him to you."

"I don't want to meet either of them."

"You don't want to meet them? I thought you liked Penelope?"

"Do you want to meet her?"

"Yes, of course!"

"I don't understand you, Flick!"

"No," said Gerald thoughtfully. "As a matter of fact I don't understand myself; but, quite honestly, I wasn't in love with Penelope—not like you and Walter—and obviously Penelope wasn't in love with me. We were friends and we liked each other immensely, but that's different, isn't it? I think I could have been in love with Penelope if I had let myself go, but I knew marriage was out of the question. Can you see Penelope settling down in a small house in Glasgow? No, I thought not! Can you see me accepting a beautiful home from Mr. Harriman? Can you see me globetrotting in Greece? No, Bess," said Gerald, shaking his head. "I'm too independent. I want to stand on my own feet. I want a worthwhile job (and, thanks to Walter, I've got it!) and when I marry, I shall want to buy a house with my own money and support my wife on my own earnings. That's all, really."

"And quite enough too," declared Bess, smiling. "I can see my sympathy has been wasted."

Bess had wasted her sympathy but, all the same, in spite of his reasonableness and admirable common-sense, Gerald thought of Penelope rather too often and every time he thought of her there was a little pang in the region of his heart. Penelope was such a darling. . . .

The next thing to be done was to show Bess the china houses and to decide which was to be despatched to America as a wedding present. Penelope would get hundreds of presents, much more valuable than a china house, but she had liked the china houses and she would value the little house as a token of friendship. Bess examined them and approved of them—and suggested that all three should be sent to America—but eventually, after some persuasion, she accepted the little cottage with the thatched roof to add to her own collection.

Gerald was pleased. It was not much, but it was something to be able to give Bess a little present in return for all her kindness.

This had taken time, so Bess was still floating about in a very becoming pale-green dressing-gown when Walter appeared at eleven o'clock. Bess ran to get ready to go out with him and the two men sat down for a chat.

They had several matters to discuss: first and foremost the wedding. It was to be in London at a fashionable church. Bess wanted to invite "everybody" and make her exit from the stage "with a bang."

Gerald had heard this before. He said, "Walter, I really think it would be wiser for you to have the wedding fairly soon. Just supposing someone got to hear about Bess. It would be very unpleasant, wouldn't it?"

"Is it likely to leak?" asked Walter, frowning.

"Not very likely—but it might."

"Well, don't worry, Gerald. Leave it to me. I'd rather marry Bess tomorrow, quietly, but Bess is giving up so much when she marries me that if she wants 'all the doings' she must have them—and as long as I get Bess I can endure anything." Walter added apprehensively, "I only hope she won't miss the stage—all the fun and the excitement!"

"She won't," Gerald told him. "She loves you dearly— you're exactly the right man for Bess—and she can have children. Bess used to say she would like seven children. That was her ambition."

"Seven?" asked Walter, somewhat startled. "Oh, well, if that's what she wants she can have them. It just means moving to a larger house."

Gerald hid an involuntary smile.

"Talking of houses," continued Walter, "my mother has always wanted to live in Bournemouth (you heard what she said about it, didn't you?). She enjoys her visits to Aunt Mildred, but she couldn't make her home with Aunt Mildred, of course, so I shall have to find her a suitable house with a pleasant garden."

Gerald nodded. He was delighted to hear that Mrs. Micawber (alias Lady MacCallum) was to attain her heart's desire.

Having settled these matters, they proceeded to discuss the Koolbokie Affair (as Walter called it). He had had a letter from Parker, but was interested to read the letter Gerald had received from Angus Proudfoot. . . .

"Well, that's a handsome apology," said Walter, folding up the sheets and putting them back in the envelope. "He couldn't say more, could he? Do you want to go back to Koolbokie?"

"I'd much rather come to MacCallum's."

"Good," said Walter, nodding. "All the same you must be glad to have it all cleared up."

"Yes, of course! And I'm very grateful to you for taking so much trouble over my affairs."

Walter looked at him doubtfully. "What's the matter, Gerald? There's something worrying you, isn't there?"

"Well, yes," Gerald admitted. "I suppose it's stupid of me, but it's rather grim to think Pat Felstead hated me. I thought we were friends. We shared a bungalow for eighteen months and got on exceedingly well. We worked together; we had good jokes; he was decent to me when I was ill . . . and all the time he was hating me like poison."

"You've got it wrong! Felstead liked you. He was fond of you, Gerald."

"What on earth do you mean? He ruined me! He planned to send me to prison!"

"No, no! He wanted you to leave Koolbokie, that's all. I'm sure he was sorry that he was obliged to ruin you, but unfortunately he had to, because you were in his way. It was no part of his plan to send you to prison—dear me, no! He went to a great deal of trouble to prevent it."

"Walter, you're talking nonsense!"

"Felstead is a very clever man," continued Walter. "He made a clever plan, and it was completely successful. All he wanted was your job, your salary, and your bungalow for himself and his wife."

"Walter!"

Walter chuckled. "Just think it over and you'll realise I'm right. The plan was masterly. He brought it off. No suspicion was attached to him. If he had been satisfied with what he had got—and hadn't been greedy—he wouldn't have been caught. That's the trouble with people like Felstead: they're never satisfied. If their plans succeed, they're so pleased with themselves for their cleverness that they go on, and on, and on. Eventually they're caught."

"It sounds mad!"

"Completely selfish people are usually a bit mad—and apt to become more so." Walter hesitated and then added, "It's natural that you should feel a bit upset about Felstead, but you must look at it sensibly. People like Felstead ought to be punished; it's the only way to stop them. If he had got off scot-free this time, he would have been so pleased with his cleverness that the next time somebody stood in his way he might have done something worse."

"Something worse! Good heavens, what an awful idea! You mean—like Smith who—who murdered his wives in the bath?"

"Exactly," nodded Walter. "Felstead will be sent to prison—Parker says so—and we must hope he will learn a lesson and come out a sadder and wiser man."

"I'm sorry for his wife."

"Yes, it's hard on her. I've told Parker to see what we can do for her."

You would! thought Gerald. He was a little ashamed of himself. He knew Lily and had felt sorry for her, but it had never occurred to him to do anything to help her . . . and here was

235

Walter, who had never seen the girl, planning to help her! Walter had the money to do it, of course, but it was not always the wealthy people who were the generous ones.

Perhaps Walter had read his thoughts. He said, "Well, I just feel I ought to do something for her. I mean it was I who put Parker on the job."

There was no time to say more. Bess appeared and said she was ready and they went off together to choose an engagement ring.

32. "He Wasn't My Father"

Walter would have liked to stay on for a few days and enjoy his new-found happiness, but business obliged him to fly home to Glasgow on Monday night. However, he said he would come back on Friday for a long weekend. While he was there, Bess had been too excited to think of anything except Walter, but once he had gone, she settled down to her usual routine and began to think of other matters.

"You never told me what was in the writing-desk," she said.

This was on Wednesday afternoon.

Gerald had hoped she had forgotten about the writing-desk, but now that she had asked he was obliged to tell her.

"It was rather disappointing," he replied. "There was some ugly old-fashioned jewellery and bundles of old letters; we hadn't time to read them, and there was a miniature of Father when he was a boy." Gerald hesitated and then added, "Uncle Gregor thought you might like to have it. I should have given it to you before."

"Don't worry," said Bess. "He wasn't my father—that's why you didn't give it to me—but I was very fond of him, so I'd like to see it."

Gerald went and fetched it.

"Oh, what a beautiful miniature!" she exclaimed. "It's like you, Flick! I remember you looked just like this when you went to Marlborough. The pearls are good too. You must keep it," she added, handing it back.

"It's yours, Bess. Uncle Gregor sent it to you."

"He wouldn't have sent it to me if he had known——"

"Don't be silly. I can't wear it, can I?"

"Well, I'd like to wear it," Bess admitted. "It's a beautiful thing—and miniatures are all the rage—but perhaps I shouldn't."

"Of course you must wear it. Father was devoted to you! He would have liked you to wear it. Besides," said Gerald earnestly, "besides it's good for pearls to be worn. Pearls become sick if you shut them up in the dark."

This common-sense argument seemed to convince Bess and she allowed Gerald to put the ribbon round her neck, but she still looked a little unhappy. "He wasn't my father and you aren't my brother," she said wistfully.

"I shall always be your brother," Gerald declared. "Walter said I was to go on being your brother, so that's all right, isn't it?"

She held out her hand. Gerald took the hand and repeated anxiously, "That's all right, isn't it?"

"Yes, of course, darling Flick. You'll always be my little brother who played with me in the woods at Cannochbrae and I shall always be your big sister who ordered you about and bullied you and told you stories. But it's a funny sort of feeling to have no name."

"You've got a name," Gerald told her. "You've made it for yourself! Your name is in lights over the portico of the theatre; your photograph is in all the papers. People stand in the rain for hours to see Elizabeth Burleigh. What more do you want?"

"I don't know who I am."

"Is it worrying you, Bess?"

"It isn't really worrying me," she replied in thoughtful tones. "I just feel I don't belong to anyone. I'm like a dog that has lost his collar . . . but I suppose I shall get used to it in time."

Gerald was trying to find something comforting to say when the telephone bell rang.

238

"Perhaps it's Walter," said Bess, taking up the receiver.

"I'll go," said Gerald, rising.

"It isn't Walter—sit down," whispered Bess.

So Gerald sat down and listened to the one-sided conversation:

"Oh, hullo, Elmer! . . . Yes, it's Elizabeth. . . . Oh, that's very exciting!. . . . No, I'm afraid I can't tomorrow afternoon; I've got an appointment with the photographer. . . . Well, what about Friday morning? . . . Oh, dear, why have you got to go so soon. . . . Oh, I see! . . . No, I can't put it off, I am afraid I've promised. . . . Do you break your promises, Elmer? . . . No, I thought not! . . . Yes, it's a dreadful bore, but it can't be helped. . . . Yes, I know, but Flick will come. . . . Yes, of course he wants to see it! . . . Yes, he wants to see it terribly much and he can tell me about it."

"What do I want to see terribly much?" asked Gerald apprehensively.

"Elmer's fireplace," replied Bess. "You do, don't you?" she added, making a face at him.

"Yes, I do," said Gerald. This was true; he was quite keen to see what sort of a job had been made of the fireplace.

Mr. Harriman was slightly mollified. It was Elizabeth he wanted, but Elizabeth's brother was "the next best thing." It was fixed that he should call for Elizabeth's brother the following afternoon at half-past-two.

Thursday was a very wet day, but as Mr. Harriman was still in possession of the automobile which he had hired to tour the country with Elizabeth, the expedition was performed in comfort.

Gerald was slightly anxious as to what he should say if the fireplace were not a success, but fortunately he was able to admire it with sincerity and to assure its owner that it was an exact replica of the one in his sister's drawing-room. He congratulated the builder (a good-looking young man with a friendly manner) and asked when the fireplace was to be packed for shipment.

"That's for Mr. Harriman to say," replied young Bullen, smiling. "I intended to start packing it tomorrow, but if Mr. Harriman wants to show it to Miss Burleigh we can easily put it off."

"I'm sure she'd like to see it," said Gerald. "She couldn't come today, but you could arrange another day, couldn't you?"

Mr. Harriman nodded thoughtfully. "Yes, that's what to do. I'll cancel my reservation and stop on for another week. Mrs. Harriman won't be pleased—she wants me home—but I guess she can wait a bit longer."

Having decided this, Mr. Harriman took Gerald to afternoon tea at The Country House Hotel. (Gerald had heard about it from Penelope.) He was interested to see that it was a beautiful manor house standing in a park with an avenue of fine old trees, and to hear that it was run by a retired Colonel and his wife.

"I was fortunate in finding this place," declared Mr. Harriman. "There's a peaceful atmosphere about it. You get the feeling that you're living in the real England; that's what I like. Penelope liked it too. Marion didn't like it. Has Penelope written to you, Gerry?"

"Yes," replied Gerald. He hesitated and then added, "Teddy Hogan is a lucky man."

"That's so," agreed Mr. Harriman. "We've been intimate with the Hogans for twenty years, and Teddy has wanted to marry Penelope since they were at high school together, but Penelope just couldn't make up her mind. I must say I was surprised when they called me up to tell me the news—I never thought she'd take him—but Mrs. Harriman is very pleased. Mrs. Harriman says it's because Penelope hasn't seen Teddy for three months." Mr. Harriman sighed and added, "The man who thinks he can understand women is just kidding himself."

Gerald had never kidded himself that he could understand women. (He thought he could understand Bess, but that was different.) It sounded to him as if Mr. Harriman were not very enthusiastic about his daughter's engagement, so he said sympathetically, "You'll miss her dreadfully, won't you?"

"Sure thing," agreed Mr. Harriman with another sigh.

They had tea together in the drawing-room. There was a lavish spread of thin bread-and-butter, hot buns and cakes, but Gerald did not eat much, for he was aware that Bess would expect him to share the evening meal which she liked before she went to the theatre and which usually consisted of a fish soufflé or an omelet and fruit and coffee. Bess called it "dinner" but it was not nearly as substantial as Uncle Gregor's six-o'clock tea. Fortunately Gerald's inside was adaptable and if he became hungry before bed-time, he was at liberty to raid the larder and make himself a cup of cocoa and a cheese sandwich. He explained this to Mr. Harriman as an excuse for refusing a slice of chocolate cake.

"That's interesting; we eat differently in the States," Mr. Harriman averred. "And we drink too much ice water. That's what gives us stomach ulcers. You don't get ice water here unless you ask for it, and I'm better without it. I've decided to cut down on ice water when I get home."

During tea Gerald told his host that he had a small gift for Penelope: two little Rockingham china houses which he had found in an antique shop in Glasgow.

"That's very, very good of you, Gerry," declared Mr. Harriman. "Penelope will appreciate them, I'm sure. If you have them wrapped up, I'll take them home with me; it will be safer than mailing them." He added thoughtfully, "I'd like to see those little houses before they're packed . . . and I'd like to see Elizabeth and say goodbye."

"You can do that quite easily if you're staying on for another week, can't you?" suggested Gerald. "Why not come in tomorrow morning for a cup of coffee? You could see the little houses and arrange a day for Bess to see your fireplace."

Mr. Harriman smiled and accepted the invitation.

"It's a pity you couldn't find your cousins, sir," said Gerald after a short silence.

"It's disappointing," Mr. Harriman replied. "All the same I enjoyed going around Buckinghamshire with Elizabeth. She was kind enough to give me a great deal of interesting information about the places we visited . . . and I haven't given up hope of finding the Audleys. Maybe I'll take a trip over in the spring, after the wedding, and have another try. I'm not the man to give up a project once I take it in hand. Difficulties are stimulating."

Gerald nodded. Mr. Harriman was friendly and pleasant, but there was latent power beneath the surface. He was like a river, thought Gerald. He would roll on quietly but relentlessly and the more you tried to dam him up the more power would be generated. No doubt this hidden force was the secret of his success in the world of business.

Mr. Harriman and Gerald lingered so long over afternoon tea and had such an interesting talk that Gerald was a little late in getting back to Molyneux Mansions for the evening meal. He had been given a latch-key so he could come and go as he pleased without disturbing Mrs. Bold . . . and the first thing he saw when he went in was Walter MacCallum's hat lying on the hall-table. He looked at it in surprise. Walter had said he would come on Friday and this was Thursday of course!

Gerald was standing looking at the hat when Mrs. Bold emerged from the kitchen premises.

"He's here!" whispered Mrs. Bold. "Oh, what a nice gentleman he is! When I went in to tell Miss Burleigh that the omelet was ready, he was sitting beside her on the sofa holding her hand. Luckily I made a nice big omelet with mushrooms, so they're having it together. That's nice, isn't it?"

"Very nice," agreed Gerald in the same muted tones. He added, "It's a pity to disturb them, so I'll go out for a meal."

"I suppose you wouldn't like to have tea with us, Mr. Burleigh?" suggested Mrs. Bold. "We're just going to have our tea. It's fish and chips. Not the kind that you buy in a paper bag, that taste of oil, but properly fried in deep fat. That's Bold's favourite—and there's plenty for three—so if you could make do with that, we'll be proud to have you."

Gerald accepted the invitation gratefully and followed his hostess into the kitchen. He had not been into the kitchen since the departure of Matilda and the advent of the Bolds. The

Bolds had brought their own furniture and had transformed it into a cosy little sitting-room. There were two comfortable chairs with antimacassars on their backs and a fine array of photographs. The photographs were of Bold junior, his wife, Nora, and their family of course.

When Gerald had admired the photographs and had been told the names and ages of the grandchildren, they sat down to the meal. He had been certain that the Bolds' tea would be much the same as Uncle Gregor's—and he saw at once that this was so—but whereas Man's version of fish and chips had been good, Mrs. Bold's (fried in deep fat) was even more delectable. Gerald's plate was heaped with crisp golden fish and crunchy chips, his cup filled with freshly-made tea; toast and butter and home-made tomato chutney were pressed on him by his host and hostess.

When the first pangs of hunger had been stayed, Gerald encouraged the Bolds to talk about themselves (not that Mrs. Bold needed much encouragement) and he heard about the early days of their marriage, their struggle to make ends meet and to "bring up Tom nicely."

"He's got nice manners," said Mrs. Bold proudly. "That's how he got a job in Bean's—the big furniture-store in the West End. Bean's would never have taken Tom if he hadn't got nice manners. He didn't get much pay at first and we had to help him a bit, but he soon got a rise so we didn't have to help him any more."

"He's head of his department now, Mr. Burleigh," put in Tom's father.

Gerald was interested in the history of Tom Bold, but it would be idle to pretend that he had no thoughts to spare for the couple in the dining-room. He kept on wondering what was happening and why Walter had come to London a day sooner than he had intended. Was it just a sudden whim (but Walter didn't indulge in sudden whims!) or was it something important?

Presently he heard voices in the hall; the front-door was opened . . . and then shut. So Walter had gone!

243

Gerald thanked his host and hostess for their hospitality and went into the drawing-room to find Bess.

"Oh, there you are!" she exclaimed. "Where have you been, Flick? I was wondering why you hadn't come home. Did you have a meal with Elmer? Walter came unexpectedly. He has just gone."

"I saw his hat in the hall, so I had a meal with the Bolds."

"That was very thoughtful of you," said Bess, chuckling. Her cheeks were pink and her eyes were sparkling. "I suppose you're wondering why he came?" she added.

"Wanted to see you," suggested Gerald.

"Well, partly. Partly on important business. We had a chat on the 'phone this morning and I told him what I had told you. I said I felt like a dog that has lost his collar."

"What did he say?"

"Nothing. He just got into a plane and came. I wasn't expecting him, so I was surprised to find him here when I got back from the photographer's studio. He said he had my collar in his pocket and he's putting it on tomorrow."

"What on earth do you mean?"

"We're going to be married."

"Tomorrow?" asked Gerald in astonishment.

Bess nodded.

"But I thought you were going to wait until——"

"So did I!" she interrupted. "I thought we were going to wait until April and be married in a fashionable church with lots of people and music and flowers and white satin and orange blossom and bridesmaids and a party with a wedding-cake and champagne and speeches . . . but Walter says not. Walter says he has had my collar in his pocket for several days (he bought it when he was here on Monday after his talk with you) and the sooner he puts it on the better."

Gerald gave it up. He said, "I'm no good at riddles."

"No, you never were," agreed Bess, laughing. "I always had to tell you the answer. It's a Special Licence, that's what. It cost twenty-five pounds and it permits you to be married at any

244

time and at any place. Walter says it's an offence to allow your dog to go about without a collar. You might be fined."

Gerald was not aware of this, but he was willing to believe her.

"It's all fixed," continued Bess. "I told you about the little church at Limbourne, didn't I? Walter rang up Mr. Heath and explained everything . . . and Mr. Heath agreed to do it at twelve o'clock tomorrow morning. He was quite excited about it. You'll like Mr. Heath, Flick."

"I'm sure I shall," agreed Gerald. He added, a little anxiously: "You aren't disappointed about the fashionable wedding and the wedding-cake and all the doings, are you?"

"No," replied Bess. "No, not really . . . and, anyhow, Flick, you remember what I said to you about the Man I should like to marry? I said I should like someone big and strong and full of integrity; someone older than myself—and much more clever—a Man I should be proud to obey. (I was thinking of Walter, of course, but I never thought I should be able to marry him); so if Walter says it's the right thing to do, we must do it . . . and we're going to do it tomorrow morning at Limbourne. We shan't tell anyone and I needn't break my contract. It will be a dead secret. We shall just have you and Dr. Ainslie as witnesses . . . and the Crusaders, of course." She smiled and added, "Walter says he is going to put a collar round my neck with his name and address on it, so I shan't be a lost dog any more."

"You will be Lady MacCallum," said Gerald with a sigh of relief.

"I shall be Walter's wife," said Bess.

245